Taming the Forest King

Claudia J. Edwards

HEADLINE

ISBN 0-7472-3060-9

Printed and bound in Great Britain by
Collins, Glasgow

HEADLINE BOOK PUBLISHING PLC
Headline House
79 Great Titchfield Street
London W1P 7FN

This book is dedicated to Jon and Ginny, Mike and Sally, Mark, Glenn, Jane, Bob, Pat and Jason, and most of all to Isabel. I am uncommonly fortunate in my friends.

—Claudia J. Edwards

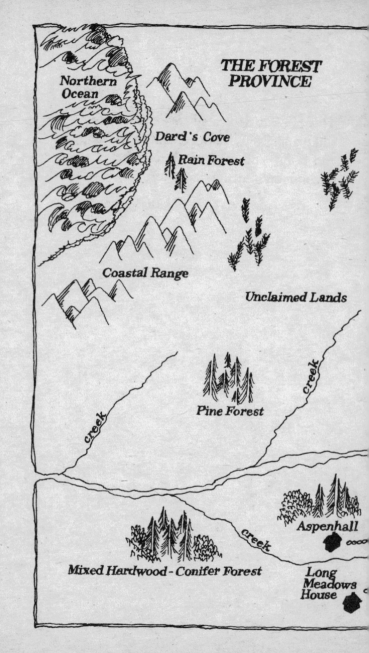

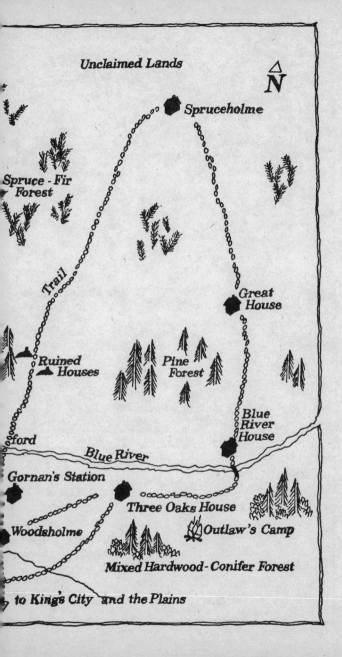

chapter

1

The first arrow hit me right between the breasts. It bounced off my mail shirt and clattered against the pommel of my saddle. By the time I had drawn my saber, Hetwith had booted his horse past me, yelling orders to the company. "Look out, colonel!" he shouted at me, and plunged into the forest from which the arrows were flying.

A glowing, throbbing, greenish globe of magical energy burst out of the forest on the opposite side of the trail. It hummed with half-sentient hunger, and the name it sang was mine. "Tevra, Tevra," it wailed.

I reined my horse sharply and the globe keened with eerie disappointment as it missed me, checked its flight, and came at me again. Arrows rattled into the leaves above my head as I ducked.

I set my boot into my horse's side and he sprang obediently aside. The seething globe of magic blundered past me again. The hair on the nape of my neck crackled with its energy. I wheeled my horse again to put the bole of a huge old pine between me and the ravenous destruction that sought me.

It struck the tree's trunk. The grave old forest giant groaned like a feeling thing as liquid green fire surged up its trunk and out each limb and twig until it sizzled on the ends of the needles. That stately tree in the full growth of its maturity shriveled and blackened and died in a shower of green sparks and popping resin.

Concentrating on the magical attack, I had had no attention to spare for the physical assault. Now I heard, off in the underbrush, a scream of pain and thudding of milling hooves. Hetwith rode back into the trail.

"Did you get them, captain?" I asked.

"No, ma'am," he said. "We marked one but they faded into the deep forest. It seems someone knows we're coming."

"Evidently. They know me, too. That thing was after me personally."

"It isn't going to make our job any easier, ma'am."

I shook my head. The job was not going to be easy in any case. The king himself had summoned me from my regiment to explain to me that this far northern province of his vast kingdom was beset with a galaxy of problems. Famine and plague and the depredations of bandits were only the easiest problems to solve. Years of corrupt and mismanaged government had left a confusion of misappropriated taxes and unfulfilled military drafts. The governor should have applied for help and relief from the king; he had not done so and the problems had multiplied and worsened. The Forest Province was also heavily infested with supernatural predators and parasites and with political disaffection. A grandson of the last Forest King was widely supported by the people as aspirant to the Forest Throne, and was titled the Forest King by many.

The king had given me extraordinary power to deal with the mess. He had made me viceroy, speaking with his authority and answerable only to him; and justiciar, with powers to try and sentence bandits and seditionists on the spot. He had cautioned me to use diplomacy rather than force if possible, and had provided me with one company out of the regiment of Light Cavalry that I had commanded until accepting the mission.

I was proud of being the youngest regimental commander in the Light Cavalry, at thirty-seven, and one of the highest ranking women in that demanding branch of the service. We were not dashing, we of the Light Cavalry; we wore a plain gray uniform, and instead of the massive armored charges of the Heavy Cavalry, we scouted and raided. I had accepted this mission reluctantly, for the regiment was my only home and my only family. I had shaped it from a half-mutinous rabble to a respected fighting outfit, superbly mounted and competently officered. But a soldier obeys.

We continued down the aisles of the forest with caution, but our enemies, whoever they were, made no further attempts at assassination. The lumbering wagon train of relief supplies stirred a golden haze of dust in the morning slant of light. The hundred troopers rode with lances ready. I listened and thought and felt the ambiance of these miles of woodlands to the tips of my fingers. The land welcomed us. Only its human inhabitants resented our coming.

We rode out of a long aisle of the splendid pines into a sundrenched meadow, the largest we had yet seen. Involuntarily, I pulled my horse, Traveler, to a halt even as I heard a gasp from Hetwith and a muted cry of astonishment from Jevan, the accountant His Majesty had sent along to help me get the province's financial affairs into order.

Confronting us across the flower-spangled meadow was a confection of a building perched on a rocky eminence. All white lace and delicate cantilevers, porched, and balconied, it was a froth of a palace with a dozen levels and who-knew-how-many rooms. We could see that it was built of stone, but so delicate was the pierced carving that adorned it that it seemed to be made of the lightest pastry. In this grand wild forest it was incongruous, precarious, as if it had alit there for the moment and would any instant be flitting away.

As a fortress, I realized, the thing was impossible. There were doors and courts everywhere. This palace was completely indefensible. Even my Light Horse could have stormed it in an hour. But it was undeniably charming. Also undeniably expensive. I would need to look no farther, I surmised, to find the destination of much of the misappropriated tax money His Majesty had strictly charged me to find.

"Hetwith," I said quietly.

"Ma'am?"

"The baggage and relief train stays here. Scouts out, the company in parade order but battle alert. Tell off your four most reliable troopers. If we find the governor here, I want him cut out, disarmed, and under arrest before anyone knows what's happening. Right flankers hold the horses, the other three riders secure the palace when I give the signal. Keep casualties to a minimum; we're here to help these people, not to conquer them. But be alert for hostilities."

"Yes, ma'am." He began to give low-voiced instructions to his lieutenants.

"Jenny," I called my striker, the soldier assigned to tend my uniforms and horses. "Bring up Pride."

"He's ready, ma'am."

Traveler was my distance horse, a leggy narrow-chested bay with a loose-limbed trot he could maintain all day and never jar his rider. Pride, a spectacular dapple gray, was my parade horse. He had the bearing of a monarch, the unflappable disposition of a turtle (and about as much speed), a gorgeously arched neck, high-stepping action, and a long flowing tail. I rode him when I wanted to look like a colonel. I had put on my dress uniform that morning to be ready for the arrival, ruefully aware that riding in it would do it no good. But dressed in its somber magnificence and mounted upon Pride, I knew that I looked the part of a viceroy.

Our first reception was by an elfin girl child of six or seven, who was waiting by the arched opening that led to the center courtyard. When I rode through it, she looked up at me with enormous awed eyes and fled. She dashed up the three steps to the entrance, her bare feet making hardly a sound on the creamy marble, and I could hear her shrieking excitedly, "They're here! They're here!"

The double doors were flung wide and a family emerged. There were an indeterminate number of children, all looking like the sentinel, delicate, very fair and dressed in gauzy smocks with embroidered vests. They clustered about the lacy carved balustrade and oohed. Pride, who accepted the homage of any crowd as his right, nodded his regal head at them.

Following the children, who had resolved themselves into four once they settled in place, were a couple who were obviously their parents. The woman was as fair as her offspring, lovely and slender as a girl, with enormous silver-gray eyes and delicate hands. She was dressed in pearls and silver filigree and sky-blue silk. The man was a few shades darker, only a few inches taller than his wife, and dressed much more simply. They came down the steps, arm-in-arm, smiling a welcome. Courtiers and servants and clerks spilled out of the doors after them and massed themselves to either side of the open portal.

"Welcome to Woodsholme, Your Excellency," the man said, his voice as warm as his smile.

I didn't return the smile. This man before me might very well be the very one who had tried to assassinate me, though he certainly had neither the look nor bearing of the thieving villain I had pictured in my mind. I sat still and erect on Pride's broad back, and he, sensing a ceremonial occasion, arched his neck and froze. The smiles were beginning to fade from the couple's faces, when the littlest child dashed forward and pulled on the man's sleeve.

"Will the pretty lady let me pat her beautiful horse, Papa?" she inquired, looking up at him.

"Not now, sweetness," he said, smiling down at her and ruffling her pale hair. "Go back to your sisters."

"Please direct me to Governor Eyvind," I requested coldly.

I hoped the head of this charming family was the palace steward or the gardener's cousin or anyone but the governor. But I let no sign of uncertainty appear on my face.

It was as well. "I'm Governor Eyvind. This is my wife, the Princess Morir-Alsis-Alina. Won't you dismount and come in? You must be tired."

I gestured, the merest flick of my right hand, and the four troopers, who had unobtrusively dismounted and eased their way into position, stepped smoothly forward, separating the governor and his wife. Two of them seized his arms, while one escorted the princess to one side and the other deftly checked him for concealed weapons. He was unarmed.

There was a rattle from the company as three troopers in every rank dismounted and drew their weapons. I took the arrest warrant from the breast of my uniform and opened it as if to read from it, though in fact I knew perfectly well what it said. "Governor Eyvind, by order of the king, I arrest you for misappropriation of royal funds, negligence of your duties, and malfeasance in office. You stand accused of these crimes, and of high treason in that you willfully disobeyed the king, your liege lord and lawful protector; and in that those of his subjects who were placed in your charge and whose well-being is dear to His Majesty's heart, have suffered grievously from your wrongdoing."

Eyvind blanched as pale as the marble behind him and flinched with every new charge. Guilt sat upon him like a visible mantle, and my heart sank. His wife glared at me from between the two troopers who held her; if Eyvind failed to understand that retribution for his misdeeds had arrived, she did not. First one and then another of the children began to cry bewilderedly.

Feeling perfectly wretched, but determined not to show it, I pulled out my viceregal commission and read it pompously aloud. "In the king's name and as viceroy, I relieve you of your governorship and take it unto myself until such time as

6

the present emergency is past and a suitable and trustworthy person may be found to undertake the office." Though I think by that time he was too numbed with shock to comprehend my words.

I repeated the performance with the appointment to the justiciary, and finished off, "As King's Justiciar, I bind you to trial for these crimes and any others which you may be found to have committed. I charge you, in peril of your life, to stand prepared to answer these accusations tomorrow." I stepped off Pride and tossed the reins to Jenny. "Seize the palace," I told Hetwith. "Jevan, find the governor's office and secure his records. See what you can unravel and report to me. You," I turned suddenly to a functionary who was standing mutely by the door, "is there a prison or jail in this palace?"

"No, Your Excellency, but there are some strong rooms that can be locked from the outside," the man gulped.

"Very well. Show these men where they are and assist them to imprison ex-governor Eyvind." I gestured and the troopers bustled past me to secure the palace, but there was no resistance.

A hand caught at my arm and I turned to face the princess. "You can't mean to put my husband on trial," she said.

"Ma'am, I do mean to put your husband on trial. Furthermore, if the evidence indicates that he's guilty, I mean to hang him." I was perhaps colder than I needed to have been with her, but I wasn't at all happy with the prospect myself.

Her face twisted in rage. "Oh, no, you can't," she spat. "I love him. I need him. The children need him."

"Go to your children, ma'am," I said. "Find a friend for your husband, one who will keep his head, and send him to help prepare a defense. Your husband's life depends on it." I shrugged off her hand and turned away, to meet Hetwith coming out of the door.

"Palace secure, ma'am," he reported with a snappy salute. "Eyvind is locked away and under guard."

"Any casualties?"

"No. Not even much muttering. Jevan's in the provincial office, going through the books. There's a meal laid out inside and guest rooms were ready for us. That tall fellow over there is the palace steward, and he's been most helpful."

I glanced in the direction he pointed, but the Forest Folk seemed to run to height and the word "tall" might have fit a dozen men and women grouped around the door. I was accounted tall, especially among Light Cavalry officers, where lack of size is an advantage, but here I would do well to attain medium height. They were also the handsomest folk I remembered seeing; clear-eyed, long-limbed, graceful, with regular features. I found it hard to believe that we had not met with more resistance. By the look of them, these people were neither cowardly nor passive.

"Stay alert, and warn your people," I said in an undertone to Hetwith. "Some of these folk are bound to be loyal to Eyvind."

If the exterior of Woodsholme was elaborate, the interior was opulent, intricate, overwhelming. Colors rioted everywhere. Every wall had a mural, every molding was gilded, every fabric was expensive, every item of furniture was a masterpiece of the craft. In niches and on pedestals were works of art: porcelain vases, carvings in semiprecious minerals, conversation pieces from the far corners of the world. Mobile sculpture hung from brackets and tinkled in the breeze from the open doors. The great hall was enormous. It would have been a vast and echoing cavern, except that the furniture and carpets had been grouped to create smaller, more intimate areas where a few friends might gather and converse.

Long tables had been set up at the far end of the hall, and upon them was a feast. The variety and amount of foods that were laid out there would have done credit to a fashionable hostess in King's City. The rich aromas wafting to us lent credit to the tempting appearance of the foods—until I happened to glance at the servitors standing by. I saw hunger there, long-standing hunger. Many of them were adolescents, fourteen or fifteen, but instead of the overabundant energy natural to the age, I saw pinched cheeks, pale faces with overlarge eyes, lank hair that should have been glossy and vibrant. They moved with the lackadaisical air of those who live on the borderline of starvation. I have seen hunger before; I have been hungry myself. I know its traces. This was not the hunger of a healthy appetite that has missed a meal; this was the hunger of long-standing famine. Suddenly the opulence of the feast seemed obscene.

"Summon the folk of Woodsholme!" I barked at the man whose responsible manner marked him as the steward my captain had found so useful. "All of them, every scullery maid and gardener and groom from the stables." The fellow was clearly startled, but turned to do my bidding. I noticed now that what I had taken for a becoming slenderness in the Forest Folk was gauntness. Many of them had bones that would have given them powerful frames if they had been properly fleshed. "Round them all up," I said to Hetwith. "Get them in here. Don't leave out a grandpa or a grandma or the littlest baby."

He looked at me for an instant. Then he glanced at the servers I had been studying and understanding dawned in his eyes. He grinned. "Yes, ma'am!" he said. "And I'll send for the relief train and the baggage wagons and put the cooks to preparing marching rations for the company, shall I?"

I couldn't help grinning in return. Hetwith understood me far too well. "Oh, very well," I agreed. "Go ahead."

When the amazed populace of Woodsholme had been herded into the great hall—and I saw many that had to be helped along by the troopers who had found them—I curtly ordered them to eat the food that had been laid out. They were first incredulous, then ecstatic. Hungry as they must have been, their manners were good, even those of the dirt-smeared gardeners. If one of the youngsters began to eat too fast or tried to claim more than his or her share, a stern look from an adult soon quelled him. Still, in an incredibly short time the last plate was as slick and shiny as if it had been washed. Perhaps it was fortunate that there was not enough for these poor people to gorge themselves. As it was, each had a full meal but not a heavy one.

The meal finished, I ordered the steward to show me to the Governor's quarters, thinking that it would be as well for me to take up residence there at once. It was important that I leave no doubt in the minds of the Forest Folk that I intended to act as their governor, and I expected there to be convenient offices and other governmental facilities.

I had thought the public rooms of Woodsholme to be expensively decorated. I had been wrong. The private apartments of the governor and his family were furnished with every imaginable luxury. The curtains were sheerest silk gauze, the carpets were imported from the faraway western continent and piled three or four deep, so that I waded laboriously through their lushness. The fitments were of gold and silver. Low couches and armchairs were piled with rare furs and pillows of satin and velvet. The toys that lay abandoned by the little girls were decorated with real gemstones. The governor's bedroom was graced by an enormous curtained bed on a dais; the sheets were silk and the blankets the softest cashmere. The bath, a jungle of rare plants lit by peaked skylights, contained a sunken marble tub big enough to stretch at full length in.

"Get me the steward," I told Jenny, who had followed me up the stairs with my gear. She put it down (and very shoddy my duffle looked, sitting forlornly in the midst of magnificence) and departed upon her errand.

The man came in shortly, and bowed gracefully. "Your

Excellency, the folk of Woodsholme have asked me to express their appreciation for the meal," he said.

"Yes, well, they're welcome. The food should have been theirs in the first place," I said. The opulence with which I was surrounded was as ill-suited to me as golden shoes to old Traveler, and I felt uneasy, as if the rich stuffs might rise up and smother me if I were unwary. The sheer staggering cost of all this was appalling, but even worse was the reflection that the money which had been spent on these expensive gewgaws should have gone for food for the hungry and medicines for the sick. "What's your name?" I asked.

"Garabed, Your Excellency."

"All of this must have cost a very great deal of money, Garabed."

"Yes, although it was acquired slowly over the last two decades."

"Well, I want the gold and silver and most of the carpets and trinkets put somewhere safe. Clear this raffle out of here. This room (we were in the central room of the apartments) will be my office. Is there a desk? Storage cabinets?"

"I'll see to it, Your Excellency. Shall I have the princess's things removed?"

"Her clothes and the children's. Have the valuables that can be readily transported packed up; I'm sending them back to King's City when the relief train goes." I had it in mind to use the money the sales would bring to buy medicines and hire physicians to come. "One more thing, before you go. I shall need a secretary, one of the Forest Folk who is familiar with the province and its customs and will be willing to advise me. Do you know such a person?"

"I will inquire, Your Excellency." He bowed himself out. I gathered up Hetwith and a couple of troopers and set out to explore the palace.

It was quite a walk. I lost track of the number of rooms I saw. The public rooms were uniformly magnificent. The apartments reserved for the Forest Lords—there were several wings of these—were comfortable but not luxurious. The commoners' quarters and work areas were drab and utilitarian. The kitchens were stocked with every imaginable delicacy, but only in amounts sufficient for the governor's family and a few guests; the lesser orders were evidently expected to subsist upon a coarse mush and a little withered fruit.

I found Jevan poring over some dusty ledgers in a cramped, disorderly office. "He's guilty, all right, colonel," he said when I came in. "Look at this." He showed me in the books how much had been collected in taxes, how much had been used for legitimate provincial expenses and how much had been forwarded to King's City. "These records are for several years ago," Jevan told me. "Lately he hasn't even been bothering to keep his records straight. And look at this—a double tax was paid last year, and three years ago. The fellow was collecting the taxes twice and sending a quarter the amount he should have to King's City."

"How did he get away with it?" I asked, amazed.

"The main business of the constabulary seems to have been collecting taxes. Look here, listed under tax collectors. These 'enforcement officers' are probably bully boys—their pay is twice what a tax collector would get back home."

"Good work, Jevan. I'm counting on you to present the case against the governor tomorrow."

He nodded acknowledgment. "The princess was in here a while ago," he said. "I think she was disconcerted to find me here. She tried to order me to alter the evidence."

"Ah. What did she offer you?"

"A fortune—and seemed astounded when I pointed out that it was no longer hers to dispose of." He bent his head back to his work and I left him to it.

When I returned to the governor's quarters I was astounded at the transformation. Most of the furnishings were gone. A polished desk of rare woods sat in the center of a single carpet.

Records in storage cabinets lined one wall. A table stood in front of them, a handsome piece and probably worth more than my salary for the year, but obviously useful for work and staff meetings. The opposite wall was centered with a fireplace. Tall windows were on either side of it, and a couch and several comfortable chairs were grouped intimately before it, where they would catch the sunlight by day and the firelight by night. "Well done, Garabed!" I exclaimed.

The steward bowed silently and indicated the bedroom. The changes there were fewer—the overwhelming bed was still there, but much of the expensive clutter was gone, leaving another arrangement of couches and chairs with only a few furs draped comfortably over them. I would still not be at ease in this room but at least it was tolerable. Jenny clattered about in one of the two large dressing rooms, hanging my pitiful few clothes in presses meant for fifty times their number. The King had insisted that I use viceregal funds to purchase what had seemed to me a lavish wardrobe of ball gowns and other fancy clothes; my mission, he had told me, would include considerable diplomatic responsibility, and I would have to be able to dress appropriately for the elaborate social functions favored by the Forest Lords. But my new clothes failed to fill even one of the presses and my uniforms occupied a corner of another.

The bathroom was almost unchanged. The rare plants were still there, and the scents and soaps and tottering piles of thick towels. So was the enormous marble bathtub, but as it was built into the floor it would have to stay. I must confess to a little shiver of anticipation for my first bath in this luxurious setting.

I changed into a garrison uniform, simpler and more comfortable than the resplendent dress uniform. I did, however, take the precaution of wearing a mail shirt under the tabard, which ordinarily I would have done only with the even simpler and more serviceable campaign uniform. This was still strange territory, and the inhabitants might or might not be hostile. Then I went to check that the company had been properly quartered and the horses cared for.

I might as well have trusted Captain Hetwith. He had commandeered part of the commoners' quarters and moved the men in there, two to a room, each officer with his section. Most of the ousted commoners had had to double up. "I thought the guest quarters might make a good hospital," the captain told me. "They connect to the rest of the palace only through the great hall. The company's quarters are right behind yours and down the back stairs. One loud scream and the whole outfit can be in your bedroom."

"I sincerely hope I won't be screaming very often. The prospect of having the whole company in my bedroom is a bit daunting," I said austerely, but he just grinned. "Where are you billeting?"

"I took over the ... er ... nursery," he said, a glint in his eye defying me to tease him about it. "It must have been the youngest girl's room. I had the furniture changed, of course. It's down the hall that leads out of your office and past your bedroom, the last room at the head of the back stairs. I'll be close to the men and near to you too. I put your striker in the bedroom across the hall from yours and Jevan in the one next to that. Your secretary, when you find one, can have the one right before mine and the two rooms behind yours are empty for now."

"That should be satisfactory. What about sanitary facilities?" The bathroom opened directly out of my bedroom and I wasn't too enthusiastic about all these people tramping across my room in the middle of the night.

"Each of the rooms has its own bathroom. Smaller than yours, but just as fancy."

"Gods! No wonder there are so many folk living here! It must take dozens just to carry the hot water up."

"No such thing. Hot water is piped directly. Just turn a tap

14

and there you are. There must be a boiler around somewhere and pipes through the walls. The King doesn't live so well," Hetwith said, with evident satisfaction. Which was true; the King's Palace was built over a thousand years ago, during the First Civilization, and was nowhere near as comfortable as many of the private homes of the Kingdom.

"What about the horses?" I asked, letting a little severity creep into my tone. The younger officers must be encouraged to keep their minds on business sometimes, though I had to admit that Hetwith had all the dash and flair I myself lacked. He was not a comfortable officer to have under one's command, I must admit, but a most comforting one to lead into battle.

"The horses are a problem. There's nowhere near the necessary amount of stabling. The officers' mounts are in stalls, but the troopers' horses are picketed under guard. There's something funny about that, too, ma'am."

"What's that?" I asked patiently.

"Well, I intended to put the local stable staff on guard, with a couple of troopers to keep an eye on things, and they were terrified at the idea. Seemed to think it was dangerous to be out at night. When I asked why, they gave me a long list of scaries out of old stories that they seemed to think would get them. I'd have laughed, but they seemed really frightened, ma'am."

"The King's report mentioned an infestation of supernaturals. Put our people on guard in pairs. Most supernaturals are extinct, down in the Kingdom, but here—who knows?"

"Yes, ma'am."

We were interrupted then with the announcement that dinner was ready. It was marching rations, served on the elegant porcelain and at the polished tables that had been set up earlier. Marching rations are nutritious and light enough that a trooper can carry ten days' supplies in his or her saddlebags, but they are not exactly tasty. They consist of soup or stew made of flaked dried meat, dried vegetables, and parched grain with a dry, hard, slightly sweetish biscuit. (I have rather a fondness for the biscuits, when dunked in hot tea; I have often been told that there's no accounting for tastes.) A good commander supplements these meals with fresh food whenever possible. Nothing is so destructive of morale as monotonous food.

The bath I took before going to bed was even more delightful than I thought it was going to be. Plenty of hot water, creamy scented soap, privacy—it was wonderful. The vast bed made me feel about six years old. I had to climb up to crawl in, and then I took up only a corner of it. My feet came only halfway to the foot. It was soft, soft, soft—I felt in danger of sinking out of sight and having the mattress close over me forever.

I dismissed these imaginings and stretched out to sleep— tomorrow was going to be a hard day. It was not so easy as that, though. Eyvind was guilty, that was clear enough, and I was going to have to hang him. I loathe executions. It's bad enough taking another human life in the heat of battle, when your opponent has an equal chance to kill you, but it is far worse coldbloodedly to destroy a bound, terrified person in the full sight of a fascinated and horrified crowd. I'd done it before, twice, and on both occasions the victims had been irreclaimable scum, men without whom the earth was a better and cleaner place. Even then I loathed it. But I had never condemned a man, and then carried out the sentence. I didn't rest well, that night.

chapter

2

There was no courtroom at Woodsholme. We set one up in
the Great Hall, which had been cleared of its luxuries. Hetwith
and some of the troopers rigged a judge's bench by balancing
a serving table on some of the crates the relief supplies had
been shipped in and draping it with purple velvet curtains. It
was wobbly, but as long as I was still, it looked impressive.
I sat solemnly in my full dress uniform, appointment to the
justiciary squarely before me in case anyone challenged my
right to be there. No one did.

Jevan laid his facts out in an assured, carrying voice that
filled the hall. Methodically he added one bit of evidence to
another like a mason constructing a brick building. The ed-
ifice was a damning one. Eyvind sat at his table with his
friend, some forest lord who had arrived the previous afternoon. The ex-governor's face was pale, his eyes on the clasped
hands he kept on the table before him. His friend whispered
urgently into his ear without eliciting a response; his wife sat
near him, straining tensely forward.

At last Jevan concluded his presentation. "Your Honor,"
he said, laying aside a last sheaf of papers, "I can think of
no other interpretation of these facts than that the accused is
guilty of all the crimes of which he is charged."

"Thank you, Master Jevan," I said. "Governor Eyvind,

this is your opportunity to refute the facts Jevan has given, offer your own interpretation of events, and give whatever extenuating circumstances and justifications you wish."

Slowly, Eyvind rose, levering himself up with his hands. "I cannot," he said.

"Do you wish your friend to speak for you?" I asked.

"No, Your Honor."

"Do you wish a postponement of the remainder of this trial so that you may prepare a defense?"

"A postponement would be useless."

"I must warn you that although the king's law places the responsibility for proving your guilt upon your accusers, if you choose not to respond to the charges, that in itself may be taken to be the admission of guilt."

"Very well. I'm guilty."

I waited, but he said nothing further. "Have you anything you wish to add?"

He tossed his head with a kind of bitter desperation. "I've admitted my guilt and you'll have my life for it. What more do you want of me?" There was a stir and a mutter among the onlookers.

"Does anyone here have any testimony to add in this case?" I asked the room at large. A stillness fell over the crowd. I waited long enough to be sure that no one was going to respond.

"Eyvind of Woodsholme, I sentence you to be executed by hanging tomorrow at noon in the main court of Woodsholme. All your properties and possessions are confiscated in the king's name, the proceeds to be used for the benefit of the people of the Forest Province. So be it!" I struck the bench with the hilt of my dagger, the words and the blow being the traditional signal that the final decision of the court has been reached.

I rose, and Hetwith materialized at my side to assist me

down from my precarious perch. Four husky troopers escorted the condemned man away.

"Hetwith," I said, "I see several of the Forest Lords here. Send the junior officers with an invitation to each of them to meet with me in my office before they leave."

"Yes, ma'am."

"Circulate among them yourself and see if you can get the sense of their feelings about all this. Let the younger officers know that they're to pick up any information they can by mingling with the families and retinues."

"Already done, ma'am. Also, the troopers have been told to listen more than they talk when they offer the grooms and servants a cup of wine. A detail has been told off to build the gallows. And there's hot tea in your office."

"Hetwith, you're a jewel." He grinned modestly, as if to say he knew it but was too humble to mention it.

I caught Jevan's eye, intending to ask him to send any maps of the province he might have found to my office and to begin drawing up plans to revitalize the economy. Garabed approached me before I could do so.

"Your Excellency," he said, "Will you be wishing to give a ball tomorrow night?"

I was appalled, but kept my face as impassive as I could. "A ball?" I didn't add, 'the same day as hanging a man?'

"Yes, to celebrate your victory."

Just in time, I kept myself from stupidly repeating, 'My victory?' Instead, I gave the steward one of my haughtiest stares. "No, I won't be giving a ball for a few days. I'll inform you."

I turned back to talk to Jevan, to discover that the Princess Alina had pushed between us. She was panting with rage and agitation. "You mustn't hang my husband," she said. "He won't do it again."

"Your Highness," I interrupted coldly, "the enormity of your husband's crimes apparently has not been made clear to you. Nor am I entirely certain of your innocence in the matter. Have you family you can go to?"

The princess stared bewilderedly at me. Obviously she had never in her life been refused her lightest whim. She nodded.

"Then I suggest you do so. Today. Your children shouldn't be exposed to the spectacle of their father being hanged. You may take your clothing and the children's."

Slowly her expression changed as she began to realize that she couldn't set all right just by giving orders and that Eyvind really was going to die. From stunned realization, starkest hatred spread across her face as she looked at me. It was clear that in her mind, I was to blame for all that had happened and all that was to happen. Her husband's guilt was not at issue, only her wish that he not die, and I had thwarted her.

"If you hang my husband," she said at last, evenly, "I'll destroy you." She meant it.

I stood and looked at her calmly, grateful for Hetwith's protective presence at my side. I didn't allow myself to flinch when she took a sudden step toward me, nor sigh in relief when she whirled and pushed her way into the crowd. "Garabed," I said coolly, "see that she has all the help she needs in removing to her family's house or wherever she wishes to go. Gentlemen," I said to Hetwith and Jevan, "we have work to do. Shall we go?"

I walked out of the room with dignity, neither rushing nor dawdling. Hetwith followed at just the proper distance to demonstrate that I was leading, but not so far away as to leave me unprotected. The crowd parted before me as I made my way to the stairs. The faces that I passed were shocked, but I got no sense of rising rebellion. I thought there was even some feeling of relief among the folk.

In my office I sank into the chair at the head of the table. The hours until the execution were going to be tense ones. "As long as you're here, gentlemen, we may as well discuss the situation." I indicated the chairs on either side of me.

"Jevan, will the sale of the transportable valuables, along with whatever is in the Treasury, permit us to cancel or reduce tax collections this year and still operate the government?"

Jevan pursed his lips. He was a serious man, not given to frivolous answers. "I believe it to be possible, ma'am. I'll investigate the matter further. There is a considerable sum in the Treasury. Even Eyvind couldn't contrive to spend the income of an entire province immediately."

"If the people have a little money to spend," I said musingly, "traders from the plains cities will be here with goods to sell. I'll be sure that the news gets to them, and that they know that foodstuffs and medicines would be particularly welcome. What else will it take to put the Forest Province back on a sound economic footing?"

"Something to sell in the south. There is a great deal imported into the province, and only furs, nuts, and lumber exported. What little cash there is here that doesn't go to pay taxes is spent on luxury goods from the richer provinces."

"Very well, look into the matter and give me your recommendations."

"I'll have the estimate of expenses for the year and an exact accounting of resources on hand for you within a week, ma'am," said Jevan.

"Excellent. And send me up any maps of the province you can find. We'll need to plan the distribution of relief supplies and a campaign against the bandits."

"I haven't seen any maps, ma'am, but I'll search more carefully."

"Very well. Hetwith, I particularly want you to be thinking about the bandits. Even finding them in this forest will be difficult."

"I expect it would be easier to let them come to us," Hetwith began. At that point the door to my office was flung open with a bang and a leather-and-fur-clad Forest Lord came striding arrogantly in, his retinue following. "I want to talk to the viceroy," he stated.

Slowly I rose from my place at the head of the table and walked to my desk. I sat down. "I am the viceroy. You may be seated." I looked the man steadily in the eye. He flushed dully under my cool regard.

"I'll stand," he snapped.

I inclined my head one tiny gracious half-inch. "As you wish. State your name and business, please." I had hoped that he would refuse the chair. It left him standing rather like an erring schoolboy before the principal.

He glared at me. "Who do you think you are, marching in here with your immoral soldiers and passing judgment on one of our people?"

I sat there, one eyebrow coolly lifted. There was no point trying to respond. The fellow didn't want to talk to me, he wanted to rant at me. Out of the corner of my eye I saw Hetwith whispering to Jevan, who slipped unobtrusively out the door which led to the hall and to the troopers' quarters. If he followed the instructions Hetwith had doubtless given him, there would very shortly be a reserve force within call. It made me feel a lot better. This Forest Lord was a powerful man not long past his prime, armed and attended by armed men. I was wearing my dress saber, intended for show and not for use; nor was a saber the weapon I would have chosen for a close-quarters brawl.

"We won't tolerate being treated like cattle," fulminated the lord. "You'd better just go on back to the King and tell him we can handle our own problems. We don't need a nanny to wipe our noses here!"

"What problems are those?" I asked quietly.

"What?" he said, confused by the unexpected question.

"What problems do you have that need to be solved?"

He drew himself up and glared at me. "Never mind what problems. Who are you, anyway? Who ever heard of your house? What's your house lord thinking of, to let you go around in that indecent attire, carrying a weapon and pretending to be a soldier?"

"I am Tevra of Willow Crossing, Colonel of Light Cavalry, Viceroy of the King, King's Justiciar. Who are you?" I let my name and titles roll sonorously off my tongue, and I asked the man's identity with the icy courtesy one of the famed King's City hostesses would have accorded an uninvited guest.

The man stopped in mid-bluster. He gave me a startled look. "Do you want to know who I am? Well, I'm Ragnal Menwin, Lord of Three Oaks House." He stopped and waited for me to be properly impressed.

I looked at him with disinterested incomprehension. "And you wished, my lord?"

"I wished to tell you that if you think you can claim Woodsholme, you've sadly mistaken the situation. Custom takes no account of women ousting the current lord. Even if it did, the nobles wouldn't recognize the claim of a southern commoner."

"I see. I'll make a note of your complaint. Was there anything else?"

Baffled, he stared at me. "No," he said reluctantly.

"Then you may be dismissed, my lord. But do feel yourself welcome to bring your concerns to my attention." I rose courteously. He could do nothing else but withdraw, unless he wanted to start a fight. Whatever the common people might feel about the overthrow of Eyvind, the Forest Lords were not pleased, if Ragnal Menwin was typical.

He had hardly stalked out, red-faced and fuming, before another of the Forest Lords sauntered through the door. This one was unarmed and attended only by a nondescript middle-aged man dressed in colorless hunter's leathers, but he was even more arrogant than Ragnal Menwin. He was considerably more dangerous, too; his nature was concealed beneath a layer of sophisticated charm. "I hope Ragnal Menwin hasn't behaved like a barbarian," were his first words to me, as he scanned me up and down like a trader looking over the horseflesh at a country fair. "Permit me to welcome you to Woodsholme, Your Excellency. I am Anlon Carmi, Lord of Long Meadow House."

"Thank you, my lord," I said, returning his appraising stare with a distant glance. "You may be seated."

"Perhaps we could sit by the window," he suggested. "A desk seems so merchantish, don't you think?" Before I could respond, he took my hand, placed it in the crook of his arm, and ushered me ceremoniously to the sofa, where he sat down beside me considerably closer than was comfortable. "We are, I hope, going to be friends," he said breathily, and leaned even closer.

I gritted my teeth and made myself sit still. It would be extremely undignified, I reminded myself, for a colonel to scramble backwards over the arm of the sofa. This Anlon Carmi knew what he was doing; he was clearly a master of prestige games. Best to keep the interview businesslike, I thought. "I would very much appreciate an estimate of the need for relief supplies in your demesnes, my lord. I'm eager to get started with the distribution," I said.

"Your diligence does you great credit, Your Excellency. It seems a shame for such a beautiful and accomplished lady to have to concern herself with mundane matters of relief supplies."

Aha, I thought. You won't put me out of countenance that way, my friend. Aloud I said, "I understand that there has been some disease in the Forest Province. Do you have many cases among your folk?"

"Very few. Allow me to assure you that if you should be frightened, you'll be welcome to seek my protection at Long Meadows. There you'll be safe and," he positively leered, "well cared for."

"Thank you for the invitation, my lord. I'll be visiting

many of the Great Houses in the next few weeks. If Long Meadows isn't on my itinerary, a contingent of my troops will certainly stop there. If you would have the figures I requested, it would expedite relief efforts." I rose to my feet (for once my saber stayed out of my way), and he got up too, still much too close to me. He took my hand again. "Thank you for your visit," I said, restraining myself from yanking my hand out of his grasp.

"I shall be counting the minutes until we meet again," he murmured intimately, staring into my eyes in what he no doubt thought was an irresistibly attractive manner. I let a flicker of amusement cross my face. I'll have to admit that the fellow had class. He must have seen my expression, for he looked fleetingly annoyed, but he kissed my scarred and callused fingers lingeringly before he made a graceful exit.

"Hetwith," I said, "do we have any snakebite powder in the company medical kit?"

"I don't think so. Why, did he bite you?"

"I think that comes next."

"Ah," said Hetwith wisely, "but what comes after that? Shall I check into convenient spots to bury a body?"

"You never know when a nice soft piece of ground may be useful."

chapter

3

Eyvind went to his death with courage and composure. He was pale, and his hands shook as he mounted the gallows steps, but he walked unsupported by his escort and with his head erect. He even marched to the slow beat of the single drum that played him upon his way.

I closed my eyes an instant before the trap was sprung and kept them closed until a thud and a sigh from the onlookers told me the execution was accomplished. I waited, watching the flight of a flock of some cheery small birds until the healer declared Eyvind dead and the body was removed and coffined. Anyone who presumes to act as judge upon another human being shouldn't be too squeamish to attend upon the carrying out of the judgment, but Eyvind had not been an evil man, only one who should never have been given the opportunity for wrongdoing. He would have lived a long, happy, moderately useful life if he had never been made governor—but such speculations as these are useless, and we all have our choices to make and the consequences to face.

I turned to go back into the palace, slowly because I knew that the crowd was watching me curiously and also because my knees were shaking, and found Hetwith there offering me his arm. I took it because I couldn't very well snub my second-in-command in front of the company and the crowd and because I was grateful for the support. I worried, though, as we proceeded across the great hall and up the staircase to my office. It was vitally important for Hetwith and all my officers to have faith in my courage and self-control. They had to think of me as the sort of person who could hang a man with equanimity. If Hetwith thought I needed his support, I had erred seriously, and the error must be retrieved. I forced myself to quit trembling.

"Well," I said briskly when we were inside the office. "Now we can get on with business. Would you ask Jevan and the lieutenants to meet here in an hour? You might send a message to the drivers of the relief train to load up and head out today, too."

"Yes, ma'am," he replied, but he made no move to leave. I sat down and shuffled some of the papers on my desk impatiently.

"Well?" I grouched.

"Pardon me, ma'am," Hetwith said, "but would you mind if I had a little of this brandy?" I looked over at the conference table where he was standing. Sure enough, there was a crystal decanter and a tray of glasses there, although why it was there I didn't know. I hadn't ordered it. "Would you join me in a glass?" Hetwith asked. "I must admit, ma'am, that work like today's is a shock on my nerves." The young rascal. He didn't have any nerves.

Without waiting for a reply, he poured two glasses and brought one to me. I took it, and he tactfully looked away so as not to see my shaking hand. The brandy tasted incredibly nasty—I have no fondness for hard liquor—but it did steady me, and I realized that I must have been very pale as I felt the blood creep back into my cheeks. I thought wryly to myself that I might have spared my efforts to fool Hetwith. I would have to watch him carefully for any tendency to take advantage of my weakness.

He drained his glass and sat it down. "I'll just see about those errands now," he said with a covert glance at me.

Jenny came in from the hall. "When the colonel changes clothes," I heard him whisper to her, "see that she wears her mail shirt." Jenny nodded. He left and I wavered between amusement and exasperation. I had intended to wear my mail shirt, damn it.

"I'll change clothes now," I said to Jenny, loudly enough to be heard at the head of the staircase. "I'll want my mail shirt." It was childish, perhaps, but I didn't want either of them to get the idea that I could be manipulated. On the other hand, I didn't want a dagger between my ribs either.

That afternoon my officers and I planned. Our first necessity was to discover the exact nature and extent of the problems we faced. I dispatched the three senior lieutenants, each with a detachment of ten troopers, to explore and map the province. The few maps we had found were deplorable, none even as good as the sketchy trader's map I had brought from King's City. As they did so, they were to investigate the bandit problem and estimate the severity of the famine and disease. Each was also entrusted with a wagonload of relief supplies with orders to distribute them cautiously.

I intended to visit all the Great Houses—the houses of the Forest Lords. If the three I had met so far were any indication, these haughty, selfish noblemen were going to be our worst impediment to success.

The whole question of how to deal with the Forest Lords was a difficult one. It would be inexcusably stupid to choose another governor from among their number, and yet they would accept a commoner, I was afraid, only under threat of arms. I had to find a competent governor, though, and quickly. I hoped to have matters straightened out and to depart before winter set in, as I knew that traveling would be difficult and uncomfortable after snow fell.

What I really needed was an advisor who understood the

ways and customs of the Forest Folk and would be willing to share this knowledge with me. I was all too aware of the damage that might be done by the most well-meaning actions of an administrator who failed to understand the customs of his charges. Though I inquired for a suitable person from among the palace folk, none offered for the position. I was forced to set out upon my tour without filling it.

It was a wild and beautiful land, this Forest Province. There were fourteen Great Houses to visit, and they were spread out over the length and width of the land, connected by narrow trails. I soon found that one might ride for days through forest and meadows and never hear the sound of a human voice. I chose to ride first to Spruceholme, the farthest of the Great Houses, and then to work my way back. It was so quiet, riding north through the thickening conifers, that sometimes the silence rang in my ears. I had, of course, a more than adequate escort: Hetwith; Corra, a junior lieutenant who showed a lot of promise; and twenty stout troopers, including Jenny, dour and uncomplaining as always. But we were all taciturn. The forest seemed to enforce its own silence upon us.

I had thought to leave Hetwith at Woodsholme to coordinate the relief efforts there. But he objected strenuously to the plan, pointing out that Jevan could do that just as well and that I was not likely to find out much while I was being diplomatic to the various lords. This argument I couldn't disagree with, and besides, I privately thought it might be just as well to keep him under my eye for a while. Hetwith was the most brilliant and original young officer I had ever had under my command, but he did take careful handling.

I remembered well when he had first come to me, transferred to my company from another Light Cavalry regiment by a peevish major who had told me that he was a trouble-maker, unreliable, and disloyal to his superiors. However, since I knew the major to be narrow-minded, thickheaded, and barely competent to eat his dinner without dribbling it onto his uniform, I thanked him politely (being merely a captain myself at the time) and took a bit more interest in the boy than I might otherwise have done. Oh, he was a wild one! Sullen, shy, unruly as a half-broken colt; determined that I and everyone in his new outfit were going to hate him on sight, he was disconcerted to be treated no differently from any other very junior lieutenant.

He was only a year or two younger than I, but had come later into the military than I had. His undisciplined spirit, always impatient of unreasoning restrictions, had made him unpopular with the less imaginative sort of officer, so he had not been promoted as he should have been. But I found him to be responsive to reason.

It took him nearly a year to unbend and allow me to see how really original he was. We were on frontier duty in the deserts south of the River Groan, and by some incredible stupidity at headquarters had been ordered (only one under-strength company!) to besiege and reduce a fortified slave-brokers' city. The place was manned by approximately five times our number of experienced slave raiders from the Republics, and it seemed that they would regard our attack on the place as a very convenient volunteering on the part of eighty or so prime slaves. As I always did when some action was impending, I had summoned my officers and explained our orders to them as well as the odds against us.

"It seems, ladies and gentlemen," I had said, "that in this case a simple frontal assault will be unlikely to be successful. Nor will the usual Light Cavalry tactics of raid and ride apply. What we need is a stratagem. We need a way to get in the gate without their noticing."

From the foot of the table had come a quiet voice. "Slaves can get in without anybody noticing." It was Hetwith, and in the event, half our company walked in through the front gate, either wearing chains or swinging whips. In the small hours of the morning, exactly as the rest of the company rose up out of the desert near the gate, the "guards" simply opened the doors of the slave pens and the gates of the city, and before the slavers were quite awake, they were incarcerated in their own filthy pens.

I gave him the credit he deserved in my report, and he got a commendation. It was far from the last time that one of his plans saved me and my detachment. They were always elegant, they always depended upon split-second timing, and they (nearly) always worked perfectly. We had one small contretemps when I found it necessary to convince him that I was not an appropriate target for his schemes. After that, I always made sure he was included in whatever outfit I was commanding at the time—and I always read anything he asked me to sign from the first capital to the last period, glancing over my shoulder occasionally as I did so.

But he was always moody and difficult. He was as full of self-doubt as he was brilliance, and a reprimand more often sent him into a gloomy fit of drinking and whoring than it changed his behavior. He was completely fearless in the field, but unfortunately he was just as reckless on garrison duty. On several occasions I had volunteered whatever outfit I was commanding at the time for action, just because I knew that Hetwith had controlled his restlessness about as long as he could. It got me an undeserved reputation as quite a fire-eater—but it kept Hetwith out of prison. He, of course, had no idea why mine was the most active company in all the Light Cavalry.

I was never sure just how he felt about me. At first, I know he resented me, as many young male officers resent a female superior. I insisted that he treat me with the respect due my rank, and there were times when I was almost sure that he actually felt some respect for me. At other times, though, I would catch a glimpse of . . . what? Contempt? Anger? Sometimes I thought he was just waiting for me to make that fatal mistake, as the young wolf waits for the pack leader to miss his kill, and then he would show a little flash of solicitude, as he had after the hanging. He was a complex young man. Many times I was forced to console myself with the thought that I didn't really have to understand him, as long as he was willing to obey me.

Most evenings we stayed at log houses, both more comfortable and more useful for collecting information than bivouacking in one of the forest glades. There was plenty of room; the plagues had burned themselves out over the winter, and in many of the houses half or more of the inhabitants had succumbed. We saw few new cases. But the famine was bad. The remaining folk were pathetically eager to accept the food we brought with us. We saw plenty of the nut trees that supplied the principal source of flour for bread, but of course the fall crop was not yet ready to harvest and the last year's crop had gone largely ungathered, what with the ravages of the plague and the fear of bandit attacks. There was also a lot of superstitious fear of the deep woods.

We had been traveling for nearly a week. All that day we had been finding evidence of bandit attacks, including several burnt-out log houses. One had been so recently destroyed that the ruins were still smoking and the folk of the house were still lying where they had been brutally murdered. We buried them and then, grim and downhearted, rode on. We were dirty, and by late afternoon had found no standing house to shelter us for the night. So, when we came to a small meadow through which ran a stream deep enough to bathe in, I ordered a bivouac. I sent Hetwith to ride a scouting circle, but he soon returned. "Colonel, I wish to report that we are completely surrounded by (dramatic pause) trees," was how he put it.

"As long as they aren't hostile," I replied mildly.

"To be honest about it," Hetwith said, handing his horse

over to his striker, "it's a relief to be just among ourselves for a while. It's wearing watching every word you say."

"And having to pry into everyone's misfortunes," I said. "They're proud, these Forest Folk. They don't like having to accept help from outsiders."

Hetwith nodded. "They've got some very strange customs, too. The owner at the house we stayed at last night offered me his daughter. Not for a trade, he said, but as a gift, because he knew she'd have plenty to eat and that I'd protect her."

I looked at him suspiciously. Hetwith had been known to exaggerate before this. But his expression, at least, was serious. "Did you accept?"

"Of course not. I told him I had no house to take her to." Hetwith sighed. "Pretty girl, too. About sixteen and all legs. She didn't seem a bit upset that her daddy was trying to give her away."

"Did he seem to be trying to give her to you for a wife or for a slave?"

"I'm not sure there's much difference here."

"The nobles seem to follow the customs of the rest of the Kingdom."

"But I don't think the common folk do. Has anyone said to you, 'I'd like to present my wife' or anything like that?"

"No, they haven't. It's always, this is So-and-So, woman of Such-and-Such House. But the women don't act like slaves. And the men treat me with respect due a woman of rank."

"To them you're nobility. The same rules don't apply. One of the younger fellows told me that it was a pity they were so short of food or he'd ask his House father to set up a trade for some of our daughters, as he put it. He thought they looked exotic in their uniforms."

While we chatted we had been eating our supper of marching rations. The conversation trailed off into military trivialities as night fell, and the troopers gathered around the oversized campfire and lied about what they were going to do when they got home.

Of course, we followed standard procedure as to the setting of sentries. As Colonel, I didn't take a turn as watch officer, but I usually slept very lightly in bivouac, especially in enemy territory. The sights we had encountered that day made it very clear that this was no friendly land.

It was delightful, though, to stretch out in my blankets, looking up at the stars winking through the swaying needles of the pines, the green living smell of the forest in my nostrils, the soothing sounds of the horses ripping up the lush grass and the chirp of night creatures for a lullaby. So I was rather more relaxed than I ought to have been when Corra grasped my shoulder, the military signal to wake silently. I did, slipping out of my blankets, saber in one hand and boots in the other. My cadet master had had the nasty habit of dumping ice water on you if you weren't out of bed and ready to fight before he could pick up the bucket.

"You'd better come and see this, ma'am," she whispered.

"Is Hetwith up?"

"No, ma'am. Shall I get him?"

"Depends. Are we under attack?"

"I'm not sure. I went to check the sentries and found one dead and the other gone. But the horses are quiet and everything seems all right in the camp."

I listened. The horses had eaten their fill and were resting. A night bird called, and the breeze sighed in the trees. There was no other sound or movement. "Show me," I said.

Quietly Corra led me across the camp to the first sentry post. The sentry was dead, right enough. He was not only dead, but partly eaten. Of the other there was no sign, except for a few grisly scraps and stains. I could only assume that her body was either carried away or completely devoured.

I glanced up at the stars. It would be dawn in another hour; in the meantime, it was as dark as the inside of my left boot.

"Rouse out four troopers," I told Corra. "The rest might as well sleep a bit longer. There doesn't seem to be much we can do until it gets light, but I want the sentries paired up."

Dawn revealed a horrid spectacle. The unfortunate trooper had been gutted and most of the flesh on one shoulder and haunch consumed by something with very sharp teeth. The face was untouched, and the expression was a little startled but not terror-stricken. Whatever had taken him had done it so rapidly that he had had no opportunity to cry out a warning or even feel much pain. The blood-spattered tracks around the body were rather canine, but shaped differently from any dog or wolf track I had ever seen. Almost obscured by the stench of blood and the discarded gut contents was a heavy musky smell.

Neither Hetwith nor I could make a guess as to what it had been that had killed the man. There was a patch of blood-soaked ground where the other sentry had been stationed, but no trail could be followed over the layer of old pine needles. There was no other evidence of a fight. We buried the dead sentry when I was sure that there was no further information to be got from studying the remains, packaged up the few personal belongings of the casualties to send to their next of kin, and rode on.

Even knowing that there was something out there that was capable of killing and eating two fully armed, alert, well-trained sentries in the prime of condition, I still couldn't feel that the forest was gloomy or threatening. It wasn't safe, no, not safe, but now we were warned; and we ourselves were dangerous when we had reason to be.

Some of the troopers were a little apprehensive, but even they soon succumbed to the beauty of the day and of the open forest, mottled with shade and sunlight, fragrant with the scent of the pines and the sun on the black earth. We grieved for our two lost ones, of course, but a soldier becomes resigned to losing friends, and their end had been swift and easy compared to some we had all seen.

We found two more burned-out log houses that day, old enough that wildflowers were growing in the ruins. At mid-afternoon I sent a scouting party ahead, stripped of extra gear and baggage for speed, to see if they could find a house to spend the night in. Corra commanded; the lightest of the troopers rode with her, and they had a glorious gallop, I'm sure. But they rode back in the early dusk to report that there was no sign of human habitation for many miles ahead, not so much as the smoke of a cooking fire.

"We'll have to bivouac again," I said to Hetwith and Corra. "Double sentries, in pairs. Build a fire ring, horses inside. Watch officer on her feet at all times—I'll take a watch. No one is to go anywhere to do anything without an escort. I want this camp alert!"

I felt fairly secure with these precautions. Nevertheless, I took the first watch and managed to stroll about the camp a time or two during the midwatch, when Hetwith was on duty. It was during the last of these walks that I walked across the camp and spoke softly to Hetwith, who was checking one of the eight fires that circled the camp. The ground was clear when I crossed, I know it was. It had been carefully scraped clean to avoid the danger of forest fires. When I turned to go back to my blankets, there was a line of paw prints running diagonally across the camp from the gap between two of the fires. It deviated to skirt a row of sleeping troopers, zigged to avoid the remnants of the cooking fire, and exited between two more of the watch fires.

My sudden complete stillness must have alerted Hetwith. I heard the wheet! of a quickly drawn saber and he was at my side. There was a quickly indrawn breath as he too sighted the prints.

"When you walked over here, were those . . . ?"

"No."

My first concern was for the safety of the sleepers. I checked them quickly, Hetwith guarding my back with drawn saber. They were sleeping comfortably, but, thank goodness, not permanently.

We examined the prints. They were the same elongated canine-like prints we had found beside the dead trooper. "Hetwith," I said softly, "how did that get across this camp, in the full light of the fires, without either one of us seeing it?"

"Ma'am, I don't know. I'd have said it wasn't possible . . . ah!"

I turned to see what had caused that exclamation, drawing my own saber. Another line of prints crossed the first at an acute angle, passed within three feet of my right foot, led into the clear space in front of the cooking area, and stopped. I caught a much stronger whiff of the musky scent I had smelled at the site of the sentry's death. But what had become of the creature that had made the tracks?

"There's nothing there," Hetwith whispered. "Where did it go?"

"Back to back, Hetwith. It must be still in the camp and I want one of us to see it when it goes."

We faced in opposite directions. I'll admit that the feel of his powerful shoulders against mine was comforting. I was facing the spot where the tracks ended. The ground was rather trampled just there, where the troopers had been issued their evening ration, but not so much that anything heavy enough to have made the tracks we had seen wouldn't leave marks.

There was a sudden thud off to my left. We both started and turned that way; it was a horse shifting its dozing position. As we turned back, I caught a flicker of movement out of the corner of my eye, an instantaneous impression of a baleful red eye, a spark of firelight on a gleaming fang, and then whatever it was had gone back the way it came in, so close I felt the wind of its passing. But aside from those two impressions, I saw nothing at all. The creature that made those tracks was virtually invisible!

I'd never been so frightened in all my life. A colonel, however, doesn't have the comforting options of gibbering in fear or even whimpering and trembling, so I straightened myself up, got my weak-kneed body back under my control, and told Hetwith what I had seen.

"I felt it go by, too, but I didn't see any eyes. Gods, what was it?"

"I don't know. All I hope is that there's just one and it doesn't like being seen even a little. Do you know, Hetwith, it has to be supernatural. Natural creatures can hide themselves, or be camouflaged, or even partly transparent, but they can't be invisible."

"No, ma'am, I don't think they can. I wish we had an Exorcist."

"I wish we were back in the barracks at King's City."

Suddenly Hetwith grinned. "No, you don't, ma'am. Deep down, you think this is the most exciting thing that's happened to us for years, and you're already musing over plans to protect us all."

"Hmpf. I'll leave the schemes to you. See that you come up with a good one, soon. Let's go check the sentries."

The sentries were fine, nervous perhaps, but it's good to have nervous sentries. They had all been able to see at least some of what had happened. I warned them to watch for footprints on the ground and keep the fires built up. The rest of Hetwith's watch passed uneventfully enough that when Corra came on duty, I felt that I might go back to bed.

I was just wriggling myself comfortably into my blankets when Hetwith arrived with his and threw them down beside me. "I really don't think I need you to protect me," I said crossly.

"Protect you, hell, ma'am. I'm scared to death. Don't make me spend the night all by myself."

I won't say I didn't feel a whole lot better knowing he was there.

chapter

4

Spruceholme was a surprise to me. I don't know whether I had expected a palace like Woodsholme or one of the ordinary log houses such as we had been guesting in, but the reality was different from either. Oh, it was a log house, like its lesser satellites, but far grander. Its walls were built of huge old pines, six feet and more in diameter. It had more than two hundred rooms, and we could easily have ridden the cavalry drill in its great hall. Where the log houses were simple, almost stark in their furnishing, Spruceholme was comfortable. The inhabitants—the lord and his family, the men and women and children of the House—must have numbered over a hundred when the House was fully inhabited, but now were little more than half that.

Ernin Eaven, Lord of Spruceholme, was a courtly, kindly old gentleman, far closer to my ideal of a nobleman than the brash, arrogant bravos I had met at Woodsholme. We of the Kingdom, where there is no hereditary aristocracy, tend to build up a romanticized image of lords and such, knowing them as we do only from the old tales from the First Civilization. I had been sadly disappointed by my first contact with the real thing, but Ernin Eaven restored my illusions.

He met us in the great hall, where all the residents of Spruceholme met for meals, with his dependents ranged behind him. He greeted us with grave courtesy, showed not the slightest surprise to find that I was the viceroy, and spoke kindly to Corra, who was a little flustered at being presented to a real lord. Then he conducted Hetwith and me to a sitting room on the second floor, having given orders for the comfort of my troopers.

The room was delightful, as were all the rooms at Spruceholme that I saw. It was decorated with a profusion of woven blankets and throws in rich earth colors, a cosy circle of deep, high-backed settles near the fireplace, and embroidered wall hangings depicting forest scenes and animals. The furniture was obviously made here of local woods, lovingly carved and polished by generations of use and care. The vases and bowls were of hand-thrown earthenware, glazed with grays and blues. The walls were so thick that the windows, round ports bored right through the thickest part of the enormous logs and shaded by stately old spruces, let in little light. Even though oil lamps were lit, the room was dim and peaceful.

Ernin Eaven conducted us to the fireplace, where a small fire was burning, for the air was cool. I sank down upon the settle he indicated, and immediately felt as though I had come home to stay. The settle was just exactly constructed to enfold and support a tired body. I wanted to pull off my boots and tuck my feet under me.

"If you're cold," said Ernin Eaven, "pull that blanket over your laps."

"Thank you, my lord, I'm quite comfortable," I said, as Hetwith sank down beside me, an expression of delighted surprise on his face. He immediately relaxed and I think he was half asleep before long; he was leaning heavily on my shoulder, anyway.

"My lord, I'm a stranger to the Forest Province and to your ways, so if I inadvertently offer offense, I apologize in advance, and hope that you'll correct my errors."

Ernin Eaven chuckled. "I believe Your Excellency is quite capable of giving offense or not as you find it necessary. Of course, I'm happy to welcome you to Spruceholme, but I can't help wondering why you chose my little house, so far from Woodsholme, to visit."

"I intend to visit all the Great Houses in time. I was sent by the King to investigate and remedy the disorders he had heard were besetting the Forest Province. I can't do that until I know exactly what the problems are and how they may be solved with the least dislocation to the Forest Folk."

He nodded. "I'm pleased that the King sent a wise and discreet representative. How may I help you?"

"As you know, I brought a considerable amount of relief supplies with me from King's City, and more are coming. If I had some idea of the extent of the famines and the plagues on your demesnes, I could offer you food and medicines enough to at least alleviate hunger and illness."

He hesitated and looked at me shrewdly. "I've always prided myself on caring for my own people. It's part of the obligation of lordship."

"Being a colonel is much the same," I said sympathetically. "You like to feel that your troopers can depend on you."

"Yes, much the same, I suppose. Except that, Spirit be praised, I don't have to send my people into battle and watch them die. I won't deny that we at Spruceholme and its subsidiary houses are hungry and sick and the help you offer will be welcome. I'll give you a count of my folk."

"Thank you, my lord," I said, inwardly sighing in relief. The stickiest problem was safely negotiated. Evidently the stiff pride the two lords at Woodsholme had exhibited was not universal.

"Not at all, Your Excellency. I should be thanking you. Is there any other way I can help you?"

"Well, my lord," I said hesitantly. "The thing I most lack to be able to help, not just your folk but all of the people of the Forest Province, is information. Is there one among your people who would be willing to answer a few questions?"

Ernin Eaven gracefully inclined his head. "Your Excellency, I'm at your service." He settled back in his seat, pulling a robe across his lap. Now that we were sitting still, the air in the room was beginning to feel cool, so I draped a blanket across Hetwith's and mine. The yarn from which it was woven was incredibly soft and luxurious, the dyes subtle and harmonious. Recalling what Jevan had told me about the need for exports, I made a mental note that if these blankets could be produced in any quantity, they would sell very well in King's City and up the river.

We talked for nearly an hour, and Lord Ernin Eaven told me as much as I could absorb about the Forest Province. I learned, for example, that there was no northern border. Knowledge of the trails just petered out twenty or thirty miles farther north, and while there were only a few half-savage tribes of nomadic woodsmen living there, the declining population and the extreme danger of traveling in that direction had precluded expansion.

We also found out what the creatures that had attacked our sentries and walked invisibly through our camp were. They were indeed supernaturals, though fortunately for us not the sapient, deliberately evil kind. They were a distant relative of the weasel or wolverine called "lopers." They were not too difficult to guard against, as they depended upon their magical invisibility to make their attacks effective and could be easily located by sound, scent, and the prints they left. The invisibility spells were short-lived, too, and they could muster the energy to hold themselves unseen only two or three times a week.

It comforted me to know what it was that we faced, but Lord Ernin Eaven warned me that there were many other kinds of supernaturals in the deep forest, some not so easily guarded against as the lopers. We should not, he told me, travel in the forest where there were no log houses in which to take shelter unless we had a wizard with us to protect us against the supernatural. But when I asked him how a wizard could be hired, he said only, "One will come to you when he wishes to."

I also asked him about the bandits. On this subject he was more reticent. "Well," he said, "there are many who turn to banditry from hard necessity, and some who are forced into outlawry by unreasonable laws, and a few who kill and destroy for the love of it. It isn't always easy to tell the difference."

I thought to myself that it was easy enough to tell that whoever had destroyed the log houses was the kind the Forest Province could do without. Ernin Eaven was clearly disturbed by the questions, and I forbore to press him on the subject.

He described a route to the nearest Great House that would allow us to spend the nights at log houses. "They will be pleased to see you," he commented. "Your reputation as a generous guest has preceded you, and while we of the Forest take great pride in not accepting guest gifts from those we offer hospitality, in these times of famine even a Great House is glad to accept an addition to the food supply."

"I'm happy to visit in the houses, whether Great or small," I said. "But I would also like to have the freedom to travel where I want to and to bivouac safely. Can the techniques the wizards use to protect their clients be learned by anyone, or only by a wizard born?"

"It isn't so much a matter of inborn talent as it is that the spells are kept secret and passed from master to apprentice. You could learn them, I'm sure, but it would be difficult or impossible to find a wizard who would teach you. Only the Forest King could command one to do so, or teach you himself—one of his powers is the right to learn and use any spell."

This was the very first time that the Forest King had been

mentioned to me. I tried not to pounce on the opportunity. "The Forest King?" I asked, as casually as I could.

Lord Ernin Eaven laughed. "I'm sure you won't expect me to fail in discretion. You are, after all, the loyal servant of the king who has displaced our royal line."

I smiled. "His Majesty in King's City has no objection to the existence of the Forest King, as long as the gentleman remembers that he has a higher loyalty. But he won't allow sedition. You may tell His Sylvan Majesty that if you see him."

"I will, if I see him, or you may tell him yourself. I don't think he will remain hidden from you for much longer."

Then supper was served in the Great Hall. After the meal, the folk of Spruceholme danced and sang and played sad songs in a minor key for our entertainment, and before long my ever-adaptable troopers were dancing with them. I saw Hetwith dance several times with a lovely fair-haired girl, as tall as he but much lighter. He was laughing and cheerful, obviously as enchanted with her as she was with him. Even I danced one or two of the simpler figures with one of the lord's shy sons, but most of the men were too overcome with awe to ask me to dance. I enjoyed watching my troopers enjoy themselves while I chatted inconsequentially with Lord Ernin Eaven and his gracious wife.

We didn't stay long at Spruceholme. Lord Ernin Eaven was old and easily tired—most of his energy went into his duties as lord of a Great House and the surrounding lands. I left some of the relief supplies we had brought with him, confident that they would be distributed promptly and fairly.

Then, as I turned to step up on Traveler, the old lord said something that destroyed the illusion that I was beginning to understand the Forest Folk. "If you need a home, someday, and a lord to protect you, you're welcome to come to Spruceholme. You liked it here, I think, and our men are the sort of kind and affectionate lovers a lonely woman needs.

I'm sure I speak for my son, who'll be lord here after me."
Behind him, the quiet man I had danced with the night before
nodded shyly. "I'll send my House daughter Ilena to Woodsholme so you needn't feel that you are unbalancing the
numbers. She's rather taken with your young captain and I
won't have any peace unless I send her anyway."

"Thank you, my lord," I said, trying not to gulp in surprise.
"If ever I need a home, I'll remember your offer."

Following the route Lord Ernin Eaven had laid out for us,
we visited three more Great Houses on our way back to
Woodsholme. I found that Ernin Eaven was no exception in
his hospitality, but he was unusual in his open-minded acceptance of the new and different. One lord, Quarmot Ultin
of Blue River House, managed to convince himself that he
had been personally insulted by any Viceroy having been sent
to Forest Province. When I persuaded him that I had been
sent to help, not to dispossess the lords, he decided to take
it amiss that I was a woman. We had a very difficult stay at
Blue River House. It gave me an opportunity to see to what
an extent the folk of one of the Great Houses took their lead
in opinions and behavior from the lord; the people were barely
civil. I left them a fair share of relief supplies, but I saw to
it that each package was delivered by a couple of my troopers.

The other two Great Houses and their lords were neither
as friendly as Ernin Eaven nor as irrationally hostile as Quarmot Ultin. I gained very little new information from either
of them.

Aside from Spruceholme, I most enjoyed staying in the
smaller subsidiary houses, where we passed the nights between Great Houses. The common people were universally
friendly, dignified, gracious hosts. They were open and frank,
unless we strayed onto topics their lords had obviously warned
them not to discuss. I found that the more I saw of them the
more I liked them. I still could not claim to understand their
customs, however. I was coming to the conclusion that Hetwith

had been right and that marriage as a monogamous contract did not exist among the common folk. The women of a house were all from elsewhere, at least those of breeding age, and seemed to belong to the head of the house. At least, he referred to all the children as his, and they all called him "Father." But the other men seemed to regard the children as just as much theirs, and some men and women were obviously paired. It was all very confusing.

As I grew to like and respect the Forest Folk, I was coming to love the Forest. The peace of the long rides between houses, the abundant animal and bird life, even the stillness of the night with its spice of supernatural danger, were at once soothing to my restless soul and stimulating to my spirit. I found that I longed to know every species of tree and wild-flower, to understand the lives of the furred and feathered inhabitants, to wander through the uncharted glades and aisles of stately trees until I encompassed the whole forest and all its life.

In fact, it was just this desire to be alone with the forest that very nearly forced me to send Hetwith back to King's City under arrest and in disgrace. We had stopped to breathe the horses and for a bite of lunch in a tiny meadow by a little splashing waterfall. I had stepped aside to relieve myself. That taken care of, I saw an inviting path, cushioned with fallen needles, lined with flowers and small trees—scrub oaks, perhaps, or locusts; at any rate, their leaves were a bright fresh green—that simply invited a leg-stretching stroll. The houses were twenty-five or thirty miles apart, here in the north, a distance that was a hard day's ride even for light cavalry, and we grew cramped from hours in the saddle. A few steps were all I meant to take, but those revealed a sunny prospect a few steps farther, and beyond that was a dim, mysterious, tangled grotto formed by several fallen trees leaning against each other—and before I knew it I had wandered a bit farther from the others than I should have. Oh, I was in no danger of getting lost; I automatically checked my backtrail every few steps, and could have returned directly to the meadow.

I had crept through the woodsy cave and was gazing down the nave of a sylvan temple whose pillars were the trunks of immense pines, whose roof was a shifting canopy of foliage, and whose holy of holies was a centered grove of graceful walnuts about a tiny welling spring, when there was a crashing in the woods beside me. Yanked abruptly out of my reverie, I reached for my saber as I whirled to face my attacker. It was only Hetwith, and I let my saber slide back into its scabbard as I straightened and tried to steady my pounding heart.

"What do you mean, wandering off like this?" he shouted. His face was red and congested, his eyes staring. "I thought something had gotten you!"

I was completely taken aback. His words and manner were insubordinate; there was no kinder interpretation that could be placed upon them. Captains do not yell at colonels. Nor do they grab them by the upper arms and shake them. Men and women have been hanged for laying violent hands on their superior officers.

"Captain Hetwith!" I snapped, finding my voice. "You've forgotten yourself!"

Hetwith was so angry, I noted with amazement, that he was shaking. "You've gone mad," he said, ignoring my words. "You're acting like a stupid recruit. There are bandits, and lopers, and who knows what out here! You're coming back to the camp." And he actually took my hand and started to drag me.

I jerked free. "Captain Hetwith!" I barked. "At-ten-TION!" Years of discipline overrode his rage and he snapped to. "Are you actually trying to get yourself hanged?" I asked quietly, ominously. "Or do you feel that being cashiered would do?" I stepped closer to him and stared him quellingly in the eye.

"You know better than to behave like this. You know me better than to think that I would tolerate it. You know that you're very close to putting me in a situation in which I'll have no choice but to invoke the full penalties required by regulations. I'm surprised at you."

He must have suddenly realized what he had done, for he began to pale, and grew paler and paler until I really thought he would faint. He drew himself into an even tighter brace. "I beg your pardon, ma'am. I forgot myself. I was frantic when I couldn't find you. I remembered that sentry and all I could think of was that you had been..." he stammered and trailed off, aware that nothing he had said was an acceptable excuse for his behavior. I'm not the sort of disciplinarian that refuses to allow a culprit to offer reasons for his actions, but neither have I ever accepted "I was so upset I didn't know what I was doing," for an excuse, especially from an officer. Part of being an officer is keeping one's head whatever the provocation.

The words "Consider yourself under arrest," were forming themselves in my mouth when I saw a sudden mental picture of Eyvind being lowered into his coffin, his head dangling grotesquely crooked. My throat closed up and I choked. It was not impossible that if I sent Hetwith to King's City, a court-martial might order the death penalty. And it was at least partly my fault that Hetwith had gotten so far out of control; I had allowed him far too much license since we had arrived in the Forest Province. I was lonely here, so far from any companionship of my own rank, and I had almost made a friend of him—but "I was lonely" is no better an excuse than "I was upset." Of course, Hetwith couldn't be allowed to know that I was ready to accept the blame, and he must not be permitted to think that I would tolerate any insubordination.

I had been staring coldly at him while my mind raced, and

he shifted uneasily. "I assure you, ma'am, that I meant no disrespect," he said.

"I'm sure you didn't," I said. "And I'm sure that in the future you'll take care not to appear disrespectful."

"Yes, ma'am," he said so dispiritedly that I wondered if he even realized that I had just saved his neck or at least his career by interpreting events as I had. I marched off through the forest in the direction of the camp, leaving him to follow. I was a little surprised to find that I had come so far; it was definitely stupid, I was chagrined to admit, to wander a good ten minutes' brisk walk in enemy territory.

"Beg pardon, ma'am," came Hetwith's chastened voice from behind me, "but camp is off to your left."

He was right. "Thank you," I said icily, and corrected my course.

chapter
5

At Woodsholme, I checked over and approved Jevan's plans for economic improvements. They were designed to give the common folk a chance to improve their condition by making and selling woodcrafts, fur garments, and such to the rest of the Kingdom, thus enabling them to buy cereal grains from the plains. "I've discovered," he said, "that the diet of the Forest Folk is seriously deficient in starches. The only bread they get is made of ground chestnuts, and that's scarce. The trees aren't cultivated, but grow wild scattered throughout the woods. Often the nut crop of an entire tree may go ungathered. The folk don't like to get too far away from home. They think it's dangerous in the forest."

"They're right, it is."

"I would also recommend the importation of milk and meat animals. Sheep or goats would be good. Although the people are expert hunters, and manage the wild herds of deer and such almost as well as we do our domestic animals, hunting is dangerous and uncertain. They also need some kind of small draft and pack animal; development is hindered by the lack of transport. Those ponies from the Windy Islands might do very well."

"There isn't much feed for livestock."

"That's why I would recommend small animals. Goats, for

example, are browsers, and the ponies can live on just about anything. They do need a source of fiber here, too, and there are breeds of goats from the western continent that give beautiful wool."

"They weave the softest, most beautiful fabric I've ever seen." I told him about the blankets and throws I had seen on my travels.

"I've seen some of those, too, and they are indeed lovely. Unfortunately, the source of fiber is strictly limited. It comes from the dogs. I've watched them combing out the silky undercoat and spinning it into yarn. But only a few dogs can be supported by any one house."

I had seen the dozens of medium-sized, fluffy dogs that lived in each house. I had thought they were pets, for they were affectionately treated. I had seen the girls combing their fur by the hour, while the dogs, tongues lolling, enjoyed the grooming. But I had not realized what a practical reason lay behind their kindness. "It's a shame," I said. "The blankets would have sold well. Go ahead and send for the livestock, but wait a bit before you organize your handicraft guilds. We don't understand these people well enough yet to undertake any major changes in their social order."

In my next trip out of Woodsholme, I traveled to the east, where I found few evidences of bandits but much of supernatural infestation. Lopers were not so much a problem here, for the breathdrinkers kept them out. But breathdrinkers were intelligent and malevolent. They had no qualms about venturing into an inhabited dwelling to seize their prey. They could be defended against with a mirror, for they stunned their victims with a hypnotic spell, and could be caught in their own trap if they could be made to look at their reflection. I kept Jenny in my room with me and made sure all troopers and officers had a partner.

I took Hetwith along as my second-in-command, but was careful to keep him at an appropriate distance. He showed no signs of insubordination; he was almost too punctiliously polite. He was moody, but the hard riding and lack of opportunity prevented the kind of debauch he had often indulged in when reprimanded.

He cheered up when we arrived back at Woodsholme after this second trip to find Ilena, Ernin Eaven's House daughter from Spruceholme, eagerly awaiting his arrival. She was a beautiful girl, charming, too, and Hetwith was flattered by her obvious adoration. I restrained the impulse to warn him about involvement with one of the folk; no doubt his wealthy parents back in King's City would have a fit if they found out, but I was not his mother, thank goodness, and his morals were no concern of mine.

Summer was wearing on and I was beginning to expect the arrival of the second caravan of relief supplies. The famine was easing as the summer fruits began to ripen, and disease, although we still received some reports of infection, was coming under control. The matter of bandits still worried me. I had taken no constructive steps yet toward their suppression. It was proving damnably difficult to identify them; when they weren't out robbing and murdering they looked and acted much like ordinary folk. The lords knew who they were but they were proving to be as proud and recalcitrant as I had feared.

I had intended to visit the nearest of the Great Houses, Aspenhall, the lord of which was a little more cooperative than some. I got along very well with his lady, who had a bright and inquiring mind and loved to lure me into talking of the Kingdom and King's City. They had been the source of the few scraps of information I had been able to gather since leaving Spruceholme.

I took an honor guard of four troopers with me, because the lords believed in pomp—but it turned out to be a good thing. As we rode down a gentle declivity along a winding trail, a dark form rose suddenly out of a stand of brush and fired a crossbow at me. The range was only a few yards; the only thing that saved me was that I was wearing my mail shirt under my tabard. Traveler shied, startled by the sudden movement; I heard a thrashing in the brush, a sudden shout, and the incident was over, the would-be assassin vanishing into the depths of the forest. He or she left behind one of my troopers, Maret, with a thrown dagger in his chest. The wound bled profusely when I removed the knife and the man was coughing up flecks of blood, so I ordered a hasty return to Woodsholme.

Woodsholme's herb doctor treated the injury, expressed concern that the lung might have been nicked, and told me that she didn't think Maret was in danger but that she would stay with him just in case. The healers of the Forest Folk had a marvelous medicine for the prevention of infection in wounds, made from a golden liquor produced by bread mold. It was dripped onto spider webs and pressed on a fresh injury. I intended to send a description and a sample of it to the Royal College of Healers when I sent my next report to King's City.

I gave Maret an affectionate pat. "Don't think for a minute that we can get along without you," I said with pretended severity. "You're under orders to get well quickly. I'll be back to visit tomorrow, and I'll expect you to be better by then." He grinned weakly up at me, and I left.

I was considerably bloodied and dirtied by the incident, and upset, too. I had warned the King that I might be the victim of assassination attempts, but I hadn't really believed it myself. I knew I was helping the Forest Folk and I guess I expected them to be grateful, not resentful. I should have known better. I headed wearily for my luxurious bathroom, intending to have a good hot soak and think things over.

I had my saber draped over my arm as I walked into my bedroom, and was unfastening one of the waist hooks of my tabard, when I stopped short, halted by a scrambling on my bed. I had a confused impression of a tangle of naked limbs, of Ilena's long pale hair, of Hetwith's back and brawny buttocks between long slender legs and his horrified face staring over his shoulder; then I backed out and slammed the door.

I was so angry I nearly drew my saber and slaughtered them both. I nearly raged and shouted and called for the company to come and haul them away and lock them up. I leaned against the wall beside the door and breathed through my clenched teeth until the redness subsided and I could see again. Then I walked to my desk, threw my saber down on it and sat down. I wanted to humiliate Hetwith. I wanted to murder him. A dozen fantastic revengeful schemes roiled around my mind.

But stop, I told myself. A colonel never loses her temper, and she certainly doesn't decide to destroy one of the service's most promising young officers on the basis of a tantrum. After all, I had overlooked a far more serious transgression than this not so long before, when I had let Hetwith's insubordination pass. Making love to your sweetheart on the Colonel's own bed, while perhaps not in the best of taste, wasn't against regulations. I didn't understand why I had reacted so violently. I had a right to be annoyed, certainly; I was tired and upset and I wanted my bath, but I had no right to be outraged. I had never required celibacy of any of my young officers.

By the time Hetwith, fully dressed and neatly combed, arrived before me and braced, I had myself under control again, though in the aftermath of my violent emotion, I felt a little sick to my stomach. "Not on my bed, Hetwith," I said, without looking up. "Dismiss."

He hesitated. "Ma'am..."

I had no wish to listen to his lame apologies. To let him go on about it would be to prolong an incident best forgotten immediately. Besides, I found that his mere presence exacerbated my sickness into active nausea. "Dismiss!" I said firmly.

He turned smartly and marched out. He had no choice.

The next morning I called a meeting of Jevan and all the officers who were in Woodsholme at the time. I told them about the assassination attempt. "There must be considerable resentment among the Forest Folk. Whether it's directed at me personally or at any of us is not yet clear. I want you all to take every precaution. Mail shirts are the uniform of the day, and no officer is to go anywhere without a guard. The troopers are to buddy up, too."

Corra said shyly, "Will you stay here at Woodsholme, ma'am, where we can protect you?"

That should have been Hetwith's question, I thought, but he was silent and downhearted. I couldn't think why. He had no way of knowing how angry I'd been, and I hadn't even indicated disapproval of his recreational activities, except for a polite request to change their location. I felt simultaneously smug that I had handled a sticky situation so well and disgusted at Hetwith's childish behavior. "Certainly not," I answered Corra. "I have too much to do to lurk around here. I will, however, be careful."

I felt restless. Over the next few days, I began a major effort to discover and eradicate the bandits. I gave out the news that I was sending a shipment of plunder to King's City, contriving that the gossip should be spread by a seemingly drunken trooper. It was a ruse that Hetwith and I had used before. Hetwith's keen intelligence planned the ruse carefully, and it worked very well. The troopers stealing quietly through the forest parallel to the track arrived at the scene of the holdup just as those concealed in the wagons threw back their coverings. The reinforcements coming along behind, mounted on the company's swiftest horses, arrived in time to prevent the still-living bandits from bolting into the forest.

We were able to trace them back to their house, which we

found to be crammed with loot. There were some badly abused prisoners whom we freed and treated as well as we could, though I feared that some of them would never recover their wits. I convened court on the spot, tried the bandits, and hanged the scum before sundown.

I found that I could hardly stand to have Hetwith around me. I gave him as many detached assignments as I could, reasoning that it was just as well to give him a chance to overcome his embarrassment. Besides, as the old saying says, rank does have its privileges, though I've found that those who quote that saw oftenest are usually the ones who do the least to deserve the privileges. I assured myself, though, that it was better for Hetwith to be kept away from me until this disgust of him had had a chance to wear off.

Garabed, the steward of Woodsholme, came to me one day when I was in my office, wrestling with the mountains of paperwork that I had discovered went with the job of governing. Hetwith could have been a great help with that; surprisingly, considering his usual energy, he was very good with administrative details and actually seemed to enjoy making things run smoothly, but I had sent him off to investigate rumors of another bandit house over to the west.

"If I may make a suggestion, Your Excellency, it might be a very good idea to hold a ball. Governor Eyvind would have held two or three by now, and none of the lords will feel free to do so until the season has been opened at Woodsholme."

"Oh," I said. "I didn't realize there was a season for that sort of thing."

"Any sort of celebration that involves travel is usually held in the summer before the nut crop ripens. The trails are almost impassible once snow falls."

"I see. Very well, Garabed. What's involved in holding a ball?"

"My staff and I can take care of the food, the musicians, and so on. You'll be expected to open the ball by dancing with the highest ranking lord there, and to dance with every lord present at least once."

"If someone will point the highest ranking gentleman out to me, I believe I can handle that."

"It will be unnecessary to point out the highest ranking lord, Your Excellency. He'll present himself at the appropriate time, as will the others. May I ask if you'd like the dressmakers to make you a ball gown?"

I remembered the neglected dresses His Majesty had caused to have made for me. "I brought some with me from King's City," I said doubtfully, "but I have no idea whether they'll be in fashion here."

"What Your Excellency chooses to wear will set the fashion."

"Oh. Well, I'll wear one of those, then. Is there anything else I should know?"

"Perhaps Your Excellency would employ a lady's maid to dress your hair and apply your cosmetics."

I ran my fingers through the hair I kept cut short for convenience and comfort on campaign. "I don't have much hair to dress, but I'm willing to let a maid try. Do you know of one?"

"I've asked a very well-trained girl to apply for the position, if she suits Your Excellency."

Position, was it? Obviously Garabed thought me hopelessly unfashionable and intended to do something about it. Well, I could hardly wear my uniform to a ball. "Very well, Garabed," I said. "Send her along when she gets here and I'll talk to her. When shall we hold the ball?"

"I think two weeks would give invitations time enough to arrive at all the Great Houses and the lords to make arrangements to come."

I had had no idea that preparations for a ball could stir up a household so much. The entire two weeks was a complete chaos. I left with fifteen troopers on about the third day and went bandit hunting. I didn't have much luck. The bandits were becoming scarcer and warier; Hetwith had been making substantial inroads among them with a variety of clever schemes that tricked them into revealing themselves. I did, however, discover and wipe out a nest of night stalkers, the foul little subhuman cannibals that prey on the old and the very young, so the expedition was well worth while.

I returned the day before the ball, to find Woodsholme transformed. The great hall was to be the site of the revelries, and it was decorated and illuminated. I found that I would be expected to give an intimate supper for twenty-five or thirty of the most important guests, and that my office had been cleared out and made into an elegant formal dining room. Even Jevan had been routed out of his offices to make "conversation rooms," where small groups could retire from the excitement and noise of the ball proper to drink a cup of tea or a glass of wine and chat with their friends. I felt annoyed, aggravated, and apprehensive.

Hetwith was in Woodsholme, having just returned from his mission, and he sought me out. "I would like to report, ma'am," he said, standing at stiff attention, "that the bandit house was completely uninhabited. Shall I take a contingent out and search farther east?"

I gave him a hunted look. He had tracked me down in one of my dressing rooms, where Jenny and my new lady's maid were trying to get me to decide on such things as shoes and jewelry and which dress I was going to wear. Well, really they were telling me these things, but they were trying their valiant best to make it seem as if I were making the decisions. "Certainly not. I have to have an escort for this wretched ball." He made a sudden movement, swiftly restrained. "Now, Hetwith, it won't be so bad. It's only for one evening," I added sympathetically.

He got a peculiar expression on his face. "I'd be honored

to escort you to the ball, ma'am," he said. "Er—aren't you looking forward to it?"

I sighed. "Hetwith, do you remember the time we had to get over that river before sundown to rendezvous with the King's forces? And we just had a bobtail company? And the Republican army was coming up fast in our rear and about twice our number of heavy cavalry was blocking the way across the river? And the only thing to do was charge them and hope we took them by surprise?"

"Yes, ma'am, I remember. Why?"

"I'd rather be back there."

He grinned, the first time I'd seen him smile for weeks. "Ma'am, the ball will be a tremendous success and you'll be just beautiful, no matter which one of these you decide to wear. Umm—May I suggest the wine-red one?"

That was the one Jenny and the maid had been trying to convince me that I had decided to wear, but I had my doubts. Of all those daringly cut dresses, it was the most daring— and it was such an intense color that I had no hope of going unnoticed. "That's easy for you to say," I said bitterly. "You'll be wearing your dress uniform. Oh, all right, all right. If it falls off I'll post all three of you to the Seaward Islets and you can hold your breath every high tide."

He grinned again, gave a jaunty salute, and left. I caught myself grinning too; it was a tremendous relief to be on an easier basis with Hetwith, I found to my surprise. I had halfway expected him to enact a martyr's role at having to escort his commanding officer to the ball, and actually I wouldn't have blamed him much. He enjoyed the flirting and banter and dancing that went on at these social functions, which I regarded as a rather severe punishment for all the sins I had ever committed or was ever likely to commit. Being obliged to squire me about would hamper his enjoyment severely.

Dressed in that preposterous costume, draped in jewels

(garnets in gold settings), subtly painted and powdered, scented and curled, I felt awkward and strange. I had last worn a dress nearly twenty years ago, and I had been another person then. I had never worn so splendid a garment, and I had never even imagined one that would make me look so ... well, wanton. No, not exactly that, but ... disreputable? No, but different, anyway.

"Captain Hetwith's here, ma'am. It's time for you to go and greet your guests," Jenny said.

I walked carefully in my delicate slippers into the formal dining room, to find Hetwith looking absolutely magnificent; shaved, combed, his dress uniform of somber gray and black with silver accouterments suiting him perfectly. I had never really thought of him as handsome; appearance was not one of the qualities I took into consideration about a young officer, male or female, but I had to admit, dressed up, with a humorous sparkle in his eye and a cheerful smile on his lips, that I could see why the young girls flocked around him.

He turned as I entered, and came forward, offering his arm. "Ma'am," he said, "may I say that you look delicious? No impertinence intended."

"Thank you," I said doubtfully. It was a peculiar kind of compliment to be giving your colonel. "I'd rather you said I looked well-covered."

"Ma'am, I try to be truthful whenever possible." He gave me a slow appreciative smile that I ought to have cashiered him for on the spot.

I thought it wise to change the subject; I had an uneasy feeling that I was getting the worst of this conversation. "You look very handsome yourself tonight. What a pity!"

"Pity, ma'am?" He took my hand and placed it in the crook of his arm.

"Yes, that you're stuck escorting the colonel, when that whole ballroom will shortly be full of women yearning to make your acquaintance."

"Ma'am," he said earnestly, not looking at me, "I consider it an honor and a privilege to escort the colonel." That was a very proper thing to say. I gave him mental points for tact.

"Look," he said. Several large mirrors had been placed on the walls to reflect the candles and flowers and to make the room seem larger; he was indicating one of them. There we stood, my hand on his arm. Black and silver, wine-red and gold. We were almost of a height, but I was wearing those wispy slippers and he had on exquisitely polished black boots; that made him just exactly the perfect amount taller than I. Both of us dark-haired, but his eyes were darker than mine, and flashed with the same fire a spirited stallion shows in the pride of his youth and sex. I couldn't help gasping with surprise.

"We look . . . magnificent!" I blurted.

He chuckled. "Yes, don't we, though. Shall we go and give the Forest Folk a treat?"

Once out of sight of the mirror, though, my courage began to drain away. I felt ludicrously exposed. As we walked through the door and to the head of the stairs, I lagged farther and farther behind Hetwith, until he was almost pulling me along. "Hetwith," I said, "I can't do it. I'm going to go put my uniform on."

"No, ma'am, you aren't. You're coming down the stairs, smiling." He turned and looked me straight in the eye. "You can do it. Remember the mirror."

Thus encouraged, I managed to get halfway down the stairs. Suddenly Hetwith whispered in my ear, "Remember Colonel Otwin and the pig?"

I laughed. I couldn't help it. Colonel Otwin had been our regimental commander when I earned my majority. He had been very handsome, and convinced that any woman would consider it a treat to grace his bed. He had been decidedly miffed when I refused his advances and had threatened to block my promotion unless, as he put it, I learned to be a little more accommodating. Hetwith had heard about it, and come up with a plan, and the upshot of the whole thing was that the handsome colonel found himself making impassioned love to an unappreciative and very muddy sow. He had been grateful enough for our silence...

When we entered the great hall, I was still laughing. The guests looked around, and there was a gratifying rustle of whispers. Hetwith and I moved among the groups of people, greeting them, introducing ourselves, learning their names and Houses. I heard Hetwith repeating the names and Houses under his breath, and knew that at the appropriate times he would be able to remind me. I was beginning to relax a little— at least the dress hadn't fallen off yet, I reminded myself, and there were only four more hours to go—when I heard the orchestra begin the opening promenade. At the end of that would be the first dance, and I, according to Garabed, would be expected to dance with the highest ranking guest here. I looked around a little wildly, wondering who that might be.

"Steady," said Hetwith. "What's wrong?"

"Who's the highest ranking guest? I'm supposed to open the ball with him."

"I imagine this must be him coming now."

I turned, and Hetwith obligingly swung with me. The guests, colorful in their formal costumes, were drawing aside to form a bowing and curtseying aisle. Every eye in the enormous room was drawn to the tall figure that came walking with enormous stately dignity down the open space that was created before me. A murmur of astonishment ran around the room.

I was no less astonished. Standing before me, smiling a little, was the most incredibly sexually attractive man I had ever seen. It was not his looks, although he was handsome enough, nor his figure, though he was tall, broad-shouldered, narrow-hipped and clean-limbed. Nor was it the gleaming golden hair that formed an unruly halo about his head, nor the appealing boyishness that lingered around his lips, nor his eyes, that precise shade between gray and blue that can freeze you to your bones or warm you to an intimate conflagration in a second. It was the sheer charisma of the man, the utter self-confidence in combination with a gentle sensuousness.

"You're gaping," hissed Hetwith out of the side of his mouth. I hastily took a breath and stilled my trembling.

Garabed appeared beside me. "Your Majesty," he said, his voice ringing with pride, "allow me to present Colonel Tevra, Viceroy of the King. Your Excellency, may I make known to you His Majesty Dard, the Forest King."

"Your Excellency." The Forest King looked into my eyes and smiled, softly, intimately. Almost, almost, I sank into a curtsey, the same curtsey I would have offered my own king, so great was the impact of the man's personality. "You won't be recognizing Dard's claim to royal blood," the king had said to me.

"Your Highness, it's indeed a pleasure to meet a representative of the former royal line," I said.

He caught the implication of that right enough. A shadow passed across his eyes. He'd hoped to trick me into acknowledging his claim to the Forest Throne. But he wasn't dismayed. "May I have the honor of opening the ball with you, Colonel?" he said. If I was going to use the lesser of his titles, he would use the lesser of mine.

"With my escort's permission, I would consider it a privilege," I said, turning to Hetwith, who had been ignored so far. It was plain to see that he did not feel the impact of Dard's charm. The muscles along his jaw were knotted and bunched. "May I present Captain Hetwith, commander of the detached company of the Ninety-Third Light Cavalry and my second-in-command? Hetwith, this is Prince Dard."

Much to my relief, Dard turned the full power of his charisma on Hetwith. I had been feeling about like a flower under the full force of a driving rain. Dard's manner altered subtly. Without any perceptible changes, the sexuality was gone, replaced with a cheerful fellowship, a rueful invitation to share a comradely closeness. "Captain Hetwith, I realize that it's grossly unfair to ask you to surrender Colonel Tevra to me even for the space of a dance. But you have her companionship in your work, and the rest of us must be content with a few short moments. With your permission?"

"Certainly, Your Highness," said Hetwith, with icy civility.

The orchestra was playing the introductory notes to a dance that was done in pairs, a slow, graceful, swinging thing that involved a near embrace. Oh, gods, I thought, he's going to put his arms around me. I'd hoped for one of the romping fast dances; the only personal contact in those was at arm's length when the man swung his partner around in a circle. But it was too late; the music was beginning. He held out his hand to me, and I put mine into it; he pulled me gently into his arms, and we were off.

I'm not a good dancer. I've never had much opportunity to practice. The only way I can be sure of keeping time is to look into my partner's eyes and hope that he's a good strong leader. Dard was, I guess. From the moment I looked into his eyes, I was lost. That manifest sexuality was back, doubled now that I was actually touching him. A palpable sensation tingled through my body from the places where his arms circled my body and from my hands resting on his shoulders. I was drowning in the blue-gray sea of his eyes, and I knew that I was smiling dreamily at him. For the first few steps of the dance, I managed to keep a few inches between our bodies, but as we swung about the floor, we drew together until almost the whole length of our bodies was in contact. Whether he gently drew me closer or whether I, drawn by his irresistible magnetism, swayed against him, I couldn't say. I did know that his body felt warm and natural and exciting against mine. He smelled faintly of almonds and sunshine.

As we danced, his eyes darkened to a smoky gray. I reminded myself that colonels simply do not behave like lovestruck teenagers, that what I felt was probably mere physical attraction (mere?!), that he was a stranger and was no doubt doing this to me deliberately from some dark seditious plot and that he probably felt nothing at all, but looking into those darkening passionate eyes, I couldn't believe any of it.

Then the music was ending, and we were parting, without having spoken a word. I looked around me as if I were returning from some primeval voyage. The guests had drawn back around the perimeter of the room; we were standing together in the very center, alone, the focus of every eye. An awed whisper came from somewhere in the crowd, "Beautiful!" And then they began to applaud. And went on applauding. I could feel a blush rising to suffuse my face.

Dard turned to me, smiling ruefully. "They recognize the significance of that dance," he said, below the clapping. "I wonder that you aren't a queen already, or the cause of wars and revolutions. I've never met anyone like you." He caught my two hands and raised them to his lips, kissing them; and I trembled.

chapter

6

I didn't dance again with Dard. I dared not. I danced with every lord there, and I saw Dard dancing with all the ladies, as etiquette no doubt required him to do. I danced once again with Ernin Eaven's shy heir.

Hetwith was acting strangely. He was at my elbow every minute I was off the dance floor, not seeking a partner himself until I was safe in the keeping of one of the lords, and he was there when my partner walked me off the floor. The intervals between the dances were long, by forest custom, to allow the dancers time to rest and chat, and during these intermissions he tucked my arm into his and strolled about the floor with me. When I slipped upstairs to visit the bathroom, he came with me and waited outside the door. When I finally decided I had better sit down, he steered me into a quiet corner of one of the conversation rooms. I suspected that the place was designed for a little quiet kissing and tickling; there was only room enough for two, and others in the room could only see into the place by walking right around it.

"All right, Hetwith. What is it?" I said quietly.

He started guiltily. "What is what, ma'am?"

"Why are you following me around like this? Do you expect another assassination attempt?"

"I don't want you to worry. I've never seen you having such a good time."

"I'm not having a good time. I loathe these social functions." Then I paused. I realized with a bit of a shock that I was lying—I had been enjoying myself, some of the time, anyway. When I danced with Dard, and Ernin Eaven's heir, and when I was strolling around with Hetwith, knowing how well we looked together. "But that's beside the point. I want to know why you're sticking so close to me."

Uncharacteristically, Hetwith dropped his gaze. "I'm concerned about Dard, ma'am. He's trying to cast some kind of a spell on you."

"A spell! Nonsense. What gives you that idea?"

Hetwith positively squirmed. "When he was talking to you, and when you were dancing with him, you looked..." he hesitated and bit his lip. "I don't mean to be insubordinate, ma'am, nor to intrude where I'm not wanted."

"I'm giving you a direct order to report any observations you may have made, about me or anything germane to this discussion."

He took the point. Having been given a direct order to speak, nothing he might say could be interpreted as insubordination. "Very well, ma'am. You looked enchanted. You had a kind of radiance around you—I've never seen you look like that. And he had it too. Like no one else in the room even existed, and you and he were dancing together all alone. And I saw his lips move as if he were saying something, when he was holding you so close, but there was no sound. He's a wizard, you know. He might know spells that could entrap you. And he's Princess Morir-Alcis-Alina's brother, Eyvind's brother-in-law. He's the pretender to the Forest Throne—you saw how he and Garabed tried to trick you into acknowledging him."

For a moment, rage swelled within me. How dared Hetwith! Did he think no man in the entire world could find me attractive for my own sake? It was fine for him to sport with his inamorata not only behind my back but on my own bed, but let me so much as enjoy a dance with an attractive man and he came sneaking around with his foul lies . . . He glanced up, and must have seen my face, for misery washed over his, and he turned defeatedly away.

I held myself very still for a moment. Hetwith had not lied, he had reported the facts as he had seen them. He had obviously seen much more clearly than I had; I was letting an instant's casual attraction override my better judgment. I knew Hetwith was no liar, nor any petty sneak, either. His was a keen intelligence, and I myself had encouraged him to develop his powers of observation and analysis.

Furthermore, looked at objectively, he might well be right. I knew my own limitations. I was no beauty, never had been even when I was young. Dard was surpassingly attractive. He could have had almost any woman he wanted. Why would he choose a battle-scarred old soldier, unless he had some reason? I felt suddenly foolish, painted and bejeweled like an aging whore.

"Hetwith," I said, "I believe you're right. Thank you. If he was casting a spell on me, I've thrown it off now. But warn me if you see me glowing again." I rose and he rose with me, looking anxiously into my face. I tried to smile reassuringly, but I'm afraid it drooped a little. "The ball's nearly over. I don't really want . . . I've danced with all the lords. I'm sorry to keep spoiling your fun, but would you please dance this last dance with me?"

"Ma'am," he said gravely, "I'd be honored to dance with you. I've been looking forward to it all evening." A gallant liar is the best sort of liar.

So I danced the last dance of the ball with Hetwith, very correctly and at a proper distance for a captain dragooned into dancing with his colonel, and smiled at him and made light conversation, feeling old and wretched.

At supper after the ball, Hetwith sat at the foot of the table, and Dard, as the ranking guest, was placed at my right hand. "I had hoped to have another dance with you," he said, smiling at me, and even knowing what I did I felt a surge of desire.

"And I had hoped to have another dance with you, Your Highness," I said, as indeed I had until Hetwith had pointed out to me what was happening.

"I'm glad you danced with your young captain, though," Dard said casually. "He was positively seething with jealousy. I don't think he took his eyes off me all evening."

I could hardly explain that it was not jealousy but suspicion that had kept Hetwith's attention on Dard. "He would, of course, be interested in your activities. We had hardly hoped to have you attend the ball."

"Why not?"

The question disconcerted me a little (as well as the fact that he was looking into my eyes again, and his were darkening. I gave my soup my full attention.) "We thought that perhaps you might bear us hard feelings over the death of your brother-in-law."

"My sister does. I think she really believes that you hanged him only to spite her. But I would have been a king. I was brought up to understand justice, and to respect the law. I know that you hanged Eyvind, very much against your own inclination, because under the law there was nothing else you could do."

Startled, I looked at him again. He was leaning toward me, and his eyes were lighter, very serious. Justice was obviously important to him, and he was giving it his full attention. "I'm glad that you understand that," I said. "I hope you understand that I'll always do my duty. I would, for example, hang any man who rebelled against the king, no matter what my personal feelings toward him might be."

He understood me. "You're loyal as well as just and cou-

rageous. The king is a fortunate man to have such supporters."
He looked thoughtful. I turned to the lord on my left for a
few moments.

When I turned back, I found Dard patiently waiting for my
attention. "You've been looking for a secretary to help and
advise you, I hear," he said.

"Yes," I said eagerly. "Do you know of someone who
would be willing to accept the post?"

"As a matter of fact, being currently unemployed in the
occupation for which I was trained, I'd like to apply for the
position," he said, smiling a smile that sent a shiver through
my belly.

I nearly dropped my spoon. "You? But . . ."

"I was trained to be a king," he said lightly. "Who else
would be better equipped to tell a king the things she needs
to know?" Seeing my startled look, he added, "You're the
king's viceroy, aren't you? You stand in the king's place here
in the Forest Province? Therefore, to all intents, you are a
king."

"I think of myself more as an emergency repairman," I
said. "The King is the king, here as elsewhere."

He inclined his head graciously. "Long live the King. May
I hope to be accepted for employment?"

"Well," I said, thinking furiously, "the pay isn't very good."
There were ramifications to this proposal. It would give me
an excuse to keep him under my eye, effectively neutralizing
him as a threat. And he doubtless could (if he would) give
me exactly the kind of information and advice I needed. On
the other hand, given the devastating effect he had upon me,
could I stand to have him in constant proximity? To succumb
to the feelings he roused was unthinkable. To endure them
without succumbing would be hellish.

"As an added inducement," he said diffidently, "I'm an
accomplished wizard. I didn't know if you knew that. I can

protect you and your party against supernatural attack and spells by other wizards."

I desperately wanted to talk this novel proposal over with Hetwith. I no longer trusted my own objectivity, at least when Dard was so close to me "I'll think it over," I said. "Are you staying the night here at Woodsholme?"

"Yes."

"Then join me for lunch and I'll give you my decision, if you still want the job. There are a lot of implications that need to be carefully thought over."

"Prudent, along with all your other virtues. Very well."

Just then Hetwith rose and offered the toast that ended the supper. "Ladies and gentlemen, the King. May he reign in wisdom."

The guests and I rose and responded, "The King," and the party began to disperse to its separate quarters.

"Hetwith," I said. I drew him into the privacy of my bedroom and to the circle of chairs; the servants were clearing away in the dining room. He seemed ill at ease; I remembered the last time he had been in this room and the embarrassment he must have suffered. "Hetwith," I said. "That's all past. You should know me better than to think I'd hold a silly thing like that against you."

He looked confused. "What, ma'am?"

"Your little escapade in here—isn't that why you're twitching like a spider on a skillet?"

"Oh! That. No, ma'am. I knew you didn't care about that. Did you want to see me about something?"

I let it go. If he didn't want to tell me what the matter was, I wasn't going to insist. I told him about Dard's offer to act as my secretary, and outlined the advantages I had thought of.

"What do you think, Hetwith? Is it a golden opportunity or a clever trap? Or can we tame the Forest King into a useful secretary?"

Hetwith looked troubled. "He didn't strike me as exactly clever, ma'am, but I can't say I feel easy about recommending to you to keep him around you all the time. Of course, to refuse him might make an open enemy of him, and I don't know that we can afford that, but..." he trailed off uncertainly.

"Well?" I prompted.

"You were falling under his spell again, there at the supper table. And you've been sending me everywhere but where you are. I don't like to say it myself, but I think that if you're going to have him around you, you ought to have me too."

I laughed. "You'll just be confirming him in his notion that you're jealous."

"Does he think that?" Hetwith said grimly.

"So he says. Oh, come on, Hetwith, it's nothing to be angry about. He'll get over the idea when he knows us better."

"Maybe. But if you're going to hire him as your advisor, keep me by you, too. I don't trust him."

I had not often seen Hetwith so determined that his point of view must prevail. But from the set of his jaw, he felt strongly about this.

I sat back and considered. I had reason to trust his judgment, but I wasn't sure I wanted him around. He was too perceptive. He had noticed the sexual attraction between Dard and me immediately, even if he was too tactful to call it that. Was that why he was insisting on staying by me; to protect me from Dard, or myself? If so, his understanding had failed him for once. I was not likely to succumb to mere lasciviousness. How little he knew of the temptations put in the way of a rising young female officer! The temptation to further one's career by way of the general's bedroom, the constant presence of healthy, reckless, attractive young men under one's command who could be relied upon to obey orders unhesitatingly, even if they were "Take off your clothes and come here," the knowledge that one was more or less expected to live up to the reputation of amoral raffishness shared by the female members of the officer's corps—I had overcome all those temptations.

Why, Hetwith would be horrified if he knew how many times I had successfully mastered the urge to reach out and touch him, or even put my arms around him and hug him, when he was in one of his self-condemning moods. Those impulses were not sexual in origin, but could easily be misconstrued, and I never indulged myself in them. Oh, yes, I knew how to subdue physical urges!

Hetwith was waiting quietly while I thought, gazing moodily into the fire. He knew that I could make a lightning decision if I had to, but that I preferred to mull things over and consider their different aspects. So I was surprised when he spoke.

"Ma'am?"

"Eh? What?"

"Why have you been keeping me away from you?"

I hesitated. There was a shamed air about him. I realized that it was not being separated from me that was bothering him—why should it, after all? It was not knowing why, nor what I intended to do next. I never made a practice of letting my subordinates worry unnecessarily about their futures; it was too destructive of morale. "I thought it might be a good idea to let some of the embarrassment fade away, after I interrupted you and your girlfriend the other day."

"I'm sorry..."

"Hetwith," I interrupted, "you don't have to apologize to me. How you spend your recreational time is none of my business."

"But, ma'am, I want to explain..."

"Damn it, Hetwith, there's nothing to explain. Drop the subject; that's an order."

Incredibly, he persisted, even in the face of a direct order to cease. There was a stubborn set to his mouth that told me he was quite willing to collect a reprimand in his record if that's what it took to have his say. "This is personal, ma'am, not official business. I respectfully request that you withdraw that order."

I glared at him. I particularly loathed being caught out in a pomposity. On the other hand this whole matter was starting to feel like an old-wolf versus young-wolf power struggle. And here I was dressed up in my semi-indecent finery. If the young wolf is going to go for the old wolf's throat, he ought to have the courtesy to wait until she's dressed like a wolf. "Hetwith," I said, "if you insist, I'll withdraw the order. But I know of absolutely no reason why this matter needs to be discussed further. I don't care what you do or with whom, as long as I can get a bath when I want it." Oh, dear, I thought, that was a little brutal. Hetwith had flinched when I said it.

Again, he surprised me. He looked me directly and deliberately in the eye. "I'm sorry to hear that, ma'am, because I care what you do, and with whom."

He had neatly put me in the wrong. I had to admire his adroitness. In one sentence he had made me look like a coldhearted bitch, and at the same time given me the warmest compliment I had ever received. There was nothing I could do but retire from the battlefield in complete disorder. "Ah, Hetwith, I should know better than to argue with you, especially when I'm tired. You've made your point. Go to bed; that's what I'm going to do." I shooed him out the door.

If there is anyone in the world who is thoroughly unhappy it is a light cavalryman on foot. And a light cavalry colonel is the unhappiest of all. I slipped as quietly as I could through the intertwined branches. All around me troopers thrashed leaves and snapped twigs. On my right, a perspiring Hetwith stumbled over a root and mouthed a silent curse. To my left, Dard ghosted through the brushwood with neither a sound nor a misstep. Here in the depths of the forest we were on his home ground, and his advantage showed.

Dard had proved to be an enormous help. Our first order of business as a team had been the suppression of banditry; Dard provided the intelligence, I the strategy, and Hetwith the plans. But a time comes in every plan when you have to get out in the field and get all sweaty and bloody.

The bandit houses had been destroyed; they were too vulnerable to a fast-moving body of experienced troops. The greater threat, the Houseless outlaws who dwelt in the trackless forest, were growing too wary to be easily tricked into the open where our superior armaments and mobility could be used against them. It had come down to going in and shaking them out, and that was proving to be difficult and dangerous. I had already lost two good troopers to mantraps set by fleeing outlaws, and we had so far killed or captured exactly none of them.

Ahead of us the forest opened out onto a clearing. There was a smell of smoke in the air. I signaled and the advancing line stopped. I nodded to Dard and the two of us eased forward. Hetwith, left in command of the dismounted contingent of troopers, fretted so at being left out that I could almost feel the vibrations through the skin of my back.

Dard laid a hand on my arm, sending chills through the base of my belly. In three weeks I hadn't gotten over the overwhelming attraction I felt for him. "Gone," he whispered.

I nodded. "Less than an hour ago; the fire's still burning. Wait!" as he moved to advance into the clearing. "Could be a trap." I turned and waved Hetwith up, giving the signal for "extreme caution."

We were extremely careful, but there were no traps set, just a hastily abandoned camp. At least we had made the outlaws run without most of their loot. The troopers gathered it up and we started on the weary trek back to the trail, where the horse holders waited with our mounts and the second contingent was posted to cut off the hypothetical fleeing quarry.

"Somehow they're getting warning ahead of time," growled Hetwith, wiping the sweat off his brow. It was a hot and tattered midsummer now, the season of sudden violent thunderstorms and oppressive air. I could see that he was refraining from giving Dard a suspicious look; they were both a little in advance of me.

Dard looked around mildly. "There isn't far to go to find the explanation for that," he said. "Your troopers are fine horsemen and fierce warriors, but a child could hear them coming in the forest in plenty of time to stroll safely away." I stumbled and he reached out and steadied me solicitously. He took every opportunity to touch me; instead of becoming inured to his touch, I was finding it more and more stimulating. Even, gods save me for an old fool, out here in the middle of the fly-infested forest! I sternly called my racing imagination to order and drew away.

"We're going to have to cut trails, that's all," Hetwith said. "The advantages are all with the outlaws. They know the terrain. They always have advance notice of our moves. They can duck and dodge until winter. The only advantage we have is speed and mobility, and we throw that away when we get off our horses and plunge into the brush and trees."

"You could learn to move in the forest," suggested Dard. "It would help a lot if you'd wear forester's boots instead of those heavy riding boots. And don't move as if you're on parade. Ease along, surrendering to the embrace of the forest, instead of attacking it." His own movements were an eloquent example of his words. He moved with an easy fluid grace, drifting over the carpet of needles with little effort, his feet in their soft boots seeking their own stability on the littered forest floor.

"What's that?" I said, cocking my head to listen. A thin, eerie whistling was coming from somewhere before us.

Dard stopped and threw up his head to listen. Then he started violently. "Have your people lie down. Tell them to close their eyes and put their hands over their ears. On no account must they look at the creatures or listen to their music! They must not move! Soulsingers are coming!"

"Supernaturals?" I asked, throwing up my hand to stop the troopers.

"Yes. They'll leave anyone they seize upon a soulless, mindless, still-living body. I'll cast a glamour over us to convince them to move on, but you must obey my instructions! They are deadly!"

The melodic whistling was coming nearer. "Hetwith!" I snapped.

"Yes, ma'am!" He wheeled to the right flank to relay Dard's instructions to the troopers. I turned to the left.

By the time we had everyone lying still on the ground, eyes closed and ears covered, with orders not to move, the whistling was very near. Dard, who had been standing still and tall, muttering what sounded like harshly rhythmic poetry, raised his hands and seemed to cast their contents (though they were empty) over the huddled forms. To my amazement, their outlines shifted and blurred, seemed to melt into a rough and hummocky section of forest floor.

"Lie down, man!" Dard said urgently to Hetwith. "I'll protect the Colonel. Lie down!"

Hetwith sank to the ground; Dard cast some of the nothing in his hand over him, and he seemed to become a rough, half-rotted log. Then Dard turned to me. Before I could prevent him, he grabbed me and bore me to the soft forest floor, half-covering me with his body. "Lie absolutely still," he whispered harshly into my ear. "Don't look or speak or listen." With a convulsive effort he cast the last of whatever it was over our two bodies, gathered my head in close against his shoulder, buried his own face in the curve of my neck and froze.

The whistling seemed to be right in among us now, but I could hardly hear it for the pounding of my heart, and next to it, thudding in a massive and slightly slower rhythm, Dard's. His breath tickled my throat, my saber dug crookedly into my hip, and he clutched me so tightly I could hardly breathe. I couldn't doubt that he was genuinely afraid of the creatures which danced around and through and over us; his breathing was ragged, and, ever so faintly, he trembled. As for me, there was no room in my mind for fear. I was almost paralyzed by the storm of lust the intimate contact of his body against mine stirred within me. We may have lain there for ten minutes, or a quarter of an hour. In that time I fought the hardest battle I had ever engaged; the enemy was my own treacherous, lecherous flesh. It was a victory for which I should have been given a medal, for it was the cruelest I ever won, but win it I did. When at long last, Dard released me and rolled away to sit up, I was in full control of myself again.

He looked at me, and those changeable eyes darkened; he swayed toward me as though he himself had not emerged entirely unscathed from a similar battle. But when I withdrew a little, he glanced away. "It's safe now; the soulsingers are gone," he said, his voice husky. He reached over and touched Hetwith, who stirred and sat up, the illusion that cloaked him vanishing with the first movement.

"Gods, I've never felt such evil!" he said groggily.

"It's safe now," Dard repeated. He gave me a tiny, secret, knowing smile, as if to say, 'Well, at least we were too preoccupied to notice that.'

Hetwith glanced from one of us to the other and his lips tightened. I sighed. Hetwith was, I had thought, the one human being in the whole world I could have relied upon to wish me happy and to keep my secret if I had had a secret to keep. Evidently not. He obviously disapproved of any fraternization with the local populace, even if the populace happened to be a king. I felt a little betrayed and a lot saddened. I must have been harboring a tiny hope that somehow I would be able to arrange a little affair with Dard, for now I realized forlornly that it would be impossible. Even if I cared to risk alienating my second, if Hetwith chose to, he would devise a scheme that would prevent it—and in a battle of wits, Dard wouldn't stand a chance against him.

When we got back to Woodsholme, there was a welcome surprise. The second relief train from King's City had come. With it were two physicians from the University, a man and a woman who had made a study of epidemics. They were welcome, and I gave orders that Hetwith's plan to turn the guest quarters of Woodsholme into a hospital should be implemented. "In the meantime," I told them, "you'll have to travel from the site of one outbreak of disease to another, mostly taking your supplies on packhorses." I rarely saw them after that and when I did they were exhausted.

There was no Exorcist with the train, though, and I had especially requested one. They would know how to combat the supernatural dangers that I had discovered were very real in the Forest Province and that had such a devastating effect upon its economy. Dard and the other wizards knew how to protect against the supernaturals, but not how to exterminate them. The Order of Exorcists did, though, having been founded for that precise purpose and having succeeded so well that supernatural infestations were as close to extinct in the main part of the Kingdom as made no difference. This, I found, when I opened and read the King's letter, was one of the reasons I hadn't been able to get one to help me.

"There are no Exorcists available at this time," he wrote. "There is a move afoot in the Department of Internal Affairs to abolish the order, and the Treasurer supports it. Only Alwin, of the four living Exorcists, is young and hale enough to travel so far, and if I let him go, they'll abolish the Order while he's not there to defend it. There are a couple of promising novices, though, and I'll send you one as soon as he or she qualifies. I hope this isn't inconvenient.

"I'm pleased to read in your report that you've successfully solved the Eyvind problem. As for the measures you suggest for economic recovery and suppression of the bandits, you have my complete confidence. Act in my name and with my full backing.

"I am enclosing a year's extension on your tenure as Viceroy. There are several boxes from your dressmakers and jewelers in the supply wagons. I believe that you'll be obliged to remain in the Forest Province at least through the winter. I'm having the Paymaster credit your account with the pay due a royal governor, as well as your colonel's pay."

Sure enough, there was a document confirming me as Viceroy and Royal Governor. There were boxes and boxes of clothes and jewels (my maid went into ecstasies when she unpacked them) and a box of new uniforms (my striker was pleased at that). One box even contained a collection of lacy nightwear! I rummaged through that one, half amused, half outraged. What silly, useless things to send all the way from King's City! I held one up, a rose-pink silken gown trimmed with crocheted ecru lace, and let the flimsy thing cascade softly through my hands. Something evoked the memory of lying in the dust, pressed against Dard's body, listening to the beat of our two hearts, the warm, musky man-smell of him in my nostrils, and I shivered and let the gown fall back into the box in a crumpled heap. No, these feminine fripperies were not appropriate for a colonel of light cavalry, certainly not one who had reason to keep herself heart-whole.

chapter
7

I was having trouble sleeping. The softness of the silken nightgown against my naked skin had something to do with it; I usually slept in my linen undertunic and shorts. I could be fully dressed and accoutered in under five minutes with that much of a headstart. But I had found the nightgown laid out for me when I got out of my bath, and it had been too much of a temptation to find out what that soft, soft silk would feel like against my skin. It felt heavenly. It was easy enough to rationalize that no one would see me so inappropriately dressed.

The real cause of my restlessness was worry. What was I going to do about the supernaturals that infested my province without an Exorcist to destroy them or drive them away? How could I winkle those pesky bandits out of the forest? What was I going to do about the tormenting attraction I felt for Dard? What would be the best thing to do for Hetwith and his career? He had a brilliant future. A mind like his could take him to any height in the military hierarchy. I might be sitting around the retired colonel's home in twenty years bragging about how the distinguished Field Marshal Hetwith had once been under my command, but not if he were buried with me in this distant corner of the Kingdom, out of the way of notice and advancement. If I had known I was going to be wintering over in the Forest Province, I wouldn't have brought him with me.

I tossed uneasily. He had volunteered, of course, when I offered him the opportunity to do so, first out of all the officers I had available to me to choose from. But it was hard to tell how genuine such volunteering was. It was difficult to say no to a superior officer, and it had seemed at the time that preferment might come out of the mission.

I could send him back to King's City with the returning relief train and order another officer to take his place. But who? I couldn't think of any who could replace him. I would miss his able assistance desperately. Would another colonel understand him and use his brilliance fairly? Be sure to see that he got the credit he deserved? And how would I get along without him in this strange land, governing strangers? I groaned and fluffed up my hot pillow.

Dard, now, was a known quantity. It was a straightforward battle between us—his sexual charisma against my self-restraint. I felt confident of winning. There was no trickery in Dard. He made his assault direct and obvious. It was part of his charm. I could see through him as if he were a clear pane of glass, at least when he was at a safe distance of two doors down the hall. If I thought that he genuinely cared for me, I might have been at risk, but as it was, I could think of too many ways he would benefit from discrediting the viceroy, and pride and duty both forbade me to give him the means to do so.

Still, I liked Dard. He made me feel good—feminine and desirable and exciting. He was honest and straightforward; I felt that he and I could be friends if only this sexual tension didn't exist between us. Hetwith and I could never be friends; the barriers of rank were too high, and I had always to be on my guard against his tendency to presume on any familiarity. I could never be sure that I understood him; he was too much cleverer than I, and too devious. These were powerful weapons in my service, but heaven help me if ever he turned them against me—and from the expression on his face this afternoon he wouldn't hesitate to do so if I became involved with Dard. I shuddered at the thought of standing before a court-martial in King's City, listening to him tell the judges how I had neglected my duty by becoming involved in a sexual liaison with a suspected seditionist.

My sheets were becoming wrinkled and grainy; I heaved myself out of the oversoft mattress to straighten them. Something made me raise my head and glance around the darkened room. Beside my bed, a little smile on the dead face, head twisted crookedly, broken rope dangling, stood Eyvind.

My breath stopped. I shuddered all over with horror. Eyvind glowed a little; I could see plainly every detail of the dead, staring eyes, the horrible burn on his neck from the rope when he hit the end of it, the disarranged clothing from having been placed in his coffin and buried without the usual funeral ceremonies.

I thought about my saber, dangling from the bedstead, but what use would an earthly weapon be against a ghost? I thought about screaming, but I was wearing that foolish gown, and if the whole company came piling into my bedroom I'd be the laughingstock of the Light Cavalry. The same objection applied to slipping out of the other side of the bed and running.

"What do you want?" I whispered quaveringly. The thing didn't answer, but slowly began to drift toward me. Its thighs came up against the side of the bed, and into it, as if it were air and impeded its progress not at all. With grotesque jerks, head wobbling on the broken neck, it raised its hands and reached for me. I snatched my saber and swung it at the specter, scabbard and all. It passed through without harming it. I screamed "HETWITH!" so loudly I could feel my throat fray, and scrambled out of the far side of the bed.

The specter continued to advance, reaching for me with clawing fingers, and I dodged it and dashed for the door, only to find it there before me. I nearly ran into it, coming so close I could feel a waft of bone-freezing cold emanating from it before I paddled backward out of its reach. Still clinging irrationally to my saber, choking with terror and my lacerated throat, I backed away from its inexorable advance. I drew the saber and cast aside the scabbard, though I already knew that the weapon was ineffective.

Then the door burst open and Hetwith flew through it, saber at the ready. The specter ignored his sweeping slash and continued to advance as I continued to retreat. Hetwith dashed around the thing and threw himself before me. Eyvind's ghost advanced, reaching for me again with dead mindlessness. Hetwith pulled me out of its reach with his left arm about my waist.

Dard came bounding through the door. Glancing quickly at the specter, he put down the lamp he was carrying and made a quick gathering motion with his hands. Speaking a single ringing word, he gestured widely. The ghost dissolved, dispersing into a thin cloud of dancing motes of gray before it vanished altogether.

Clinging weakly to Hetwith, sobbing with relief, I thought, Damn it, I've been rescued. I loathe having to be rescued!

Dard turned to me. "Did it touch either of you?" he asked.

I could only shake my head; Hetwith said, "No."

"It wasn't a real ghost," Dard said. "It was a construct out of the overmind. Some wizard made it out of the stuff of the collective unconscious and sent it to attack you."

There was a clamor at the door, and I saw Jenny's curious face peering in. Hetwith called, "Everyone back to bed; the excitement's over. Jenny, send them away." Her face disappeared and I could hear her shooing away the excited troopers as she closed the door.

I was still shuddering with the aftermath of terror. "Take her saber," Hetwith ordered. Dard stepped forward and removed the weapon from my icy fingers. Hetwith gave him his saber too, and supported me over to the circle of chairs before the fireplace. I sank down on the sofa. Hetwith sat down as I did, still holding me around the waist. I found his warm bulk immensely reassuring; I struggled to bring my breathing under control. I longed to hide my face against his shoulder, but of course that would have been grossly improper.

Then I realized that Hetwith was wearing only his undertunic and shorts and that Dard had on a dog's-wool robe with (from the look of his bare chest) very little beneath it. I was clad in that lacy rose-colored nightgown, which was a lot worse in its translucency than nothing at all. I blushed. I could feel the hot blood creep up my throat and suffuse my face. What an absurd picture I must have presented, flourishing a saber, wearing that silly nightgown!

Dard, bringing the lamp over to put it on the mantel, must have seen my distress. He fetched the spare blanket from the foot of the bed and wrapped it around me. He sat down in the facing chair. "We'll stay with you for a while," he said quietly, "to assure ourselves that it isn't coming back." I nodded, grateful both that they were staying and that Dard had made it seem that they were staying for their benefit and not mine.

We sat there quietly for a time, and I tried to get myself to stop trembling, but couldn't.

"Someone sent the construct," Dard said. "I'm afraid I know who."

"Your sister?" asked Hetwith.

Dard nodded. "It's possible. She hates Tevra enough to find a wizard who would do it."

"How dangerous was it?" Hetwith asked.

"Physically, not very," answered Dard readily. "But the overmind is tricky. A specter like that can drag its victim's consciousness into the overmind with it so far that it can never escape. I was ready to pull you back if it had touched you."

Hetwith craned his neck to peer anxiously into my face. "Colonel, are you all right?" he asked.

"I'm as well as I ought to be," I croaked. "Thanks to both of you."

"Line of duty, colonel," said Hetwith prosaically.

They sat with me for an hour, chatting about this and that, until at last my shaking stopped and I drooped sleepily. Then Hetwith rose and drew me to my feet. The blanket slipped aside. I had almost forgotten the garment I was wearing, and apparently so had Hetwith. He looked at me. Startled, he looked again. And then, so help me, he blushed. Dard, standing by, grinned. Hetwith flushed redder and redder. But he kept his self-possession long enough to lift me into bed as if I were a helpless grandmother and tuck the covers around me.

He swept Dard along with him out the door by the force of his glare, turning to say, "I'll leave my door open and keep an ear pricked." Then he strode offendedly out.

I giggled. It had never occurred to Hetwith that the colonel might wear such an improper garment, I dare say. If he had been asked, he doubtless would have thought I slept at attention in full uniform.

Not many days later, half the company dashed at a hard gallop through the forest, my good war mare Spider twisting and turning among the trees. She never put a foot wrong on the littered forest floor, but from the crashes and curses around me, not all the troop horses were so sure-footed. Ahead of us fled a band of outlaws; somewhere, two or three miles to the south, Hetwith and the other half of the company rode north at a less precipitous pace. We would drive the blown and panicked outlaws right into his arms, if the plan worked. A resinous pine bough slapped me stingingly in the face as Spider sailed over a log.

Ahead of me down the shadowed aisles of the forest I saw a leather-clad figure disappear into a stand of saplings. There was another, and another! The outlaws, at last! I raised a "View Halloo!" and was answered on either side. Corra's fleet chestnut crashed out of the brush, rider bent over its neck. I threw myself low alongside Spider's neck to avoid a heavy branch that would have swept me out of the saddle, and Spider, her blood up, took advantage of my momentary release of control to accelerate into a run.

The ground before us began to descend. I began to worry that we would overrun the outlaws before we came to Hetwith's slowly advancing line. I bellowed, "Trot your horses," to very little avail. My own mount shook her head in irritation as I fought to check her speed. Spider was the best war mare I had ever seen, tough, quick as a cat, bold as a lion in battle; but she was hardmouthed and hot. She wanted to run. Somehow she knew I was trying to catch those running men and women ahead and she meant to do it.

An arrow snicked through the pine boughs not a foot from my head. The outlaws were firing at us! Best to press them harder, then, so that they had no chance to lay in wait and aim. "Come on, Ninety-third!" I yelled, and set my heels into Spider's sides. Glancing over my shoulder, I saw Corra falling back, her chestnut winded and failing. I hoped the silly chit didn't get separated and lost. Her gelding was fast, but lacked bottom, and stamina was what was needed in this sort of hard going. My Spider was hardly sweated yet.

Far ahead of me, down an aisle of pines, I saw one of the leather-clad outlaws turn and draw his bow. I yelled again, and Spider flattened her ears and galloped even harder. I drew my saber and held it low. The man's arrow went astray, and in dodging the sweep of my weapon, he stumbled into Spider's shoulder and was sent tumbling. I left him for the troopers to finish and galloped on. There! Off to the left! Another of the vermin! Filled with the joy of the chase and the speed,

I reined Spider one-handed; she went charging down upon this new foe. She dodged behind a fallen log, which Spider had no choice but to leap over, landing in a tangle of fallen small trees that nearly brought us down. But Spider carried me through them in a jolting series of in-and-out jumps.

I pulled the mare up and looked back. My quarry looked at me with huge eyes. She was clearly terrified and hardly more than a girl. That long pale hair looked familiar. The girl scrambled under the log and ran into the forest. Spider would have followed, but I checked her. I had recognized the girl as Hetwith's bed partner, Ilena. What on earth was she doing out here? Come to think of it, I hadn't seen her at Woodsholme since the incident in my bedroom. She was pelting across the slope, along one of the long, open aisles, now, and I thought that she would have done better, if she feared pursuit, to take to the thickest of the brush where a horse couldn't follow. She stopped and peered back, and then ran on.

Spider was blowing, her nostrils fluttering and red-lined. It had been quite a run, the best I had had since arriving in the Forest Province. I put my saber away, patted her sweaty neck, and looked around for the company. It was certainly very quiet; fifty or so galloping horses should be making more of a stir in these woods than this. A bird twittered; a squirrel scolded me roundly. The giant pines sighed in the breeze. Oh, my. I had done it again: outrun my command. "Tevra," a knowing old captain had once said to me, "you're supposed to lead your troops, but not by so far they can't keep up with you. Your problem is that you like to ride. No cavalryman should like to ride." It was beginning to make sense to me. Colonels should definitely not wander off by themselves in enemy territory.

I rode back the way I had come. The trail left by Spider's galloping hooves was clear and black where the dry brown needles had been thrust aside. Surely I would intersect the detachment or at least its trail. I certainly hoped so. Getting lost would be embarrassing and possibly dangerous. This forest was infested with supernaturals, not to mention the bandits I had been so merrily chasing.

I pushed aside some low-growing boughs as Spider pressed through a stand of young pines. Had I come though this tangle at a gallop? Evidently, for there were the tracks, plain to see. How I had avoided being brushed out of my saddle was not so obvious. And this lichen-splotched boulder—had Spider jumped down from the top of it? I was lucky I hadn't broken both of our necks. There was no going up the way I came down; the thing was at least ten feet high. I'd have to turn to the left and skirt the rock to pick up the back trail on the other side.

I rode peacefully right into the ambush.

Spider shied as we came around the boulder. Standing quietly in my path, arms crossed, watching my approach with interest, was a tall, lean young man with sandy brown hair, dressed in a woodsman's leather tunic and breeches. He was smiling.

I reached for the hilt of my saber. "Don't," warned a voice on my right. I looked. I was staring at the point of an arrow resting in a drawn bow. It wasn't the only one. My gaze traveled over half a dozen archers, all with drawn bows and all looking completely competent. I looked to my left. More archers and a couple of swordsmen. There was a rustle behind me.

If they all loosed their arrows, I would resemble a porcupine. I removed my hand from the hilt of my saber.

"Will you dismount and visit with us for a while?" invited the young man courteously.

"Slowly and carefully," added the voice on the right.

Hoping that I wasn't pale, I eased off my horse. One of the swordsmen took the reins and led her away. It was awful, being afoot and helpless among my enemies. As I had before many a battle, I composed my mind in preparation for death, but in battle there was always a chance of survival and victory. It would take a major miracle to get out of this.

"Would you be so kind as to lend me your saber?" inquired the young man, with ironic civility. "No need to hand it to me, I'll help myself." He unbuckled my weapons belt, removing both the saber and my clip-sheathed dagger. "Please accept my apologies for the discomfort, but would you turn around and put your hands behind your back?"

Bracketed with those remorseless arrows, there was nothing else I could do. He bound my hands firmly with soft cord. At least he seemed to be taking some care not to cut off the circulation, but there would be no wriggling out of these bonds. I had always imagined that I would dislike being bound and helpless; the reality was far worse than I had ever imagined. Keep your head, I told myself silently. They may make a mistake and it would be a pity to die because you were too panicky to take advantage of it. But terror was growing within my mind, nevertheless, threatening to turn me into a meek victim. There was something utterly demoralizing about being at the mercy of those you knew wouldn't hesitate to harm you for their own purposes or even at their whim.

The young man who was evidently the chief of my captors came around and studied me. Then he half-turned and spoke to someone hiding behind the rock. "Is this the viceroy?"

Ilena came out of hiding, still panting from her run. "Yes. That's Colonel Tevra."

The young man turned back to me. "Your Excellency, allow me to introduce myself. My name is Hilmar. I'm Ernin Eaven's son. We won't hurt you unless you force us to, but we intend to talk to you and we don't intend to be hunted down by your outland cavalry."

"Under the circumstances," I said calmly, "I'm more than

happy to talk to you. I can't do much about the cavalry. They have their orders."

"Will they search for you?"

"Of course. We'd search for any missing soldier."

"I'll untie you if you'll give me your word you won't try to escape."

"I won't give you my word on that, but I will give you my word to call off the hunt if you'll let me go."

"Perhaps we'll accept that offer later. First, though, we must talk to you, and we can't do that here. The forest is full of soldiers. Pardon me, please," Hilmar said, and stepped behind me. My sight vanished as a scarf was wrapped over my eyes and secured. Hands took me by either arm and I found myself being rushed along at a much faster pace than I would have chosen, being unable to see. The hands supported me when I stumbled.

I felt a little better, knowing who my captor was. His words had been somewhat encouraging, too. Ernin Eaven's son! No wonder the lord of Spruceholme hadn't wished to talk about outlaws.

We hurried through the forest forever, or at least two hours—bound and blindfolded, the one seemed much the same as the other. When we stopped and I was released, I sank limply to my knees. I should have liked to have kept my dignity, but my legs wouldn't cooperate. "Soft," someone said good-humoredly. "Comes from riding horses everywhere."

"Soft?" said another voice. "You'd think so if you saw her bearing down on you like an avalanche, with that damn saber cocked to cut you in half and a grin of pure joy on her face. You'd die of fright, that's what you'd do."

"Likely enough. I nearly did anyway, hiding in that bush with hooves flying all around my head. Here, Your Excellency, I'll bet you'd like a drink of water."

What felt like a canteen was pressed against my lips and

I drank the cool water gratefully. "Thank you," I said, when the water was removed.

"You're welcome. There'll be a bite to eat shortly. Here, you can lean against this tree." Big hands readjusted me so that I was supported against rough bark.

I waited. The air grew cool, presumably as the sun went down. I shivered. My arms, twisted behind my back, cramped painfully. A horse snorted somewhere not too far off. I made a mental note of the location, just in case the information should be useful.

It grew cold, and I began to shiver in earnest. Footsteps approached, and I nearly jumped out of my mail shirt when something soft landed on me. "Sorry," said the First Voice. "Didn't mean to startle you. It's just a blanket. You looked cold."

"Thank you, I am cold. May I know your name? I can't go on thinking of you as the First Voice."

He chuckled. "First Voice, eh? That's fine, you can call me that. I'd just as soon you didn't know my name, if you don't mind. You're known to be a little hasty about hanging people."

"I never hang people who bring me a drink of water and a blanket."

"I call that a reasonable attitude." There was a pause and the sound of movements.

"First Voice? Are you still there?" I asked.

"Right here."

"Could I please have my eyes uncovered?"

There was silence. Then he said suspiciously, "Why?"

"Because I'm frightened and it scares me worse not to be able to see," I said.

There was a longer silence. "I'll ask Hilmar," he said at last. His steps receded.

He was back shortly, and removed the scarf around my eyes. "He says I can untie you, too, but I'd better explain something to you. I'm going to untie your hands, but I'll hobble your feet with rawhide and dampen the knot. It'll have to be cut to get it off. But even if you do get it off, it wouldn't be a good idea to run off into the forest. You'd never live until morning. There are lopers around, and sometimes death's candles. Ever seen anyone the death's candles have gotten at?" As he talked, he was working at the ropes behind my back.

"No."

"Well, you don't want to." My numbed hands came loose and he settled back on his haunches. Night had nearly fallen, but I could see in the last of the light that he was a middle-aged man with a grizzled beard. "Take my advice and stay close."

"I will. Thank you, First Voice."

It was only a few minutes until Hilmar came to where I sat wrapped in the blanket, rubbing my chafed wrists. "Your Excellency," he said formally, "will you do me the honor of allowing me to escort you to dinner?"

"It will be my pleasure," I said graciously, and gave him my hand to be helped up. He offered his arm and we minced (because of the hobbles) to the outdoor banquet that had been spread upon the needles. There was roasted venison, fruit, a pile of boiled tubers I didn't recognize, and mead to drink. The outlaws either ate better than their law-abiding counterparts or had put on a spread for my benefit. Looking around at the leanness of the thirty or so leather-clad men and two or three women gathered around, and the eagerness with which they piled into the food, I decided that they had done their best to provide a feast.

I felt better for a good meal. The outlaws would hardly waste food on someone they intended to kill. Besides, the roast was succulent and the fruit still warm from the sun, though the tubers were almost tasteless. I managed to drink only a few sips of the sticky sweet mead.

The meal finished, I turned to Hilmar. "I believe there was something you wanted to discuss with me," I said.

"I wanted to ask you if you intended to confirm the writs of outlawry Eyvind issued."

I looked at his face, ruddy in the flickering firelight. "It depends on why the writs were issued," I said carefully. "I can't condone robbery and murder."

"Not all outlaws are bandits. We live Houseless in the forest, but we live from the forest, too. We don't prey upon the innocent."

"Someone has been."

"Yes. We've done what we could to stop them. Everyone here was outlawed for resisting Eyvind's unjust laws and cruel taxation or for trying to protect the poor people from the oppression of the lords."

I see, I thought. Steal from the rich and give to the poor. Every culture I'd ever heard of had such a legend, and every bandit immediately laid claim to it. "The law is the law," I said. "Eyvind didn't make the laws. He paid for breaking them, and so will any criminal."

"Do you mean to hang every outlaw in the Forest Province, then?" Hilmar said dangerously.

"Of course not. The punishments prescribed by law are appropriate in severity to the crimes they penalize. I do intend to put a stop to robbery and murder."

Suddenly Hilmar drew his dagger and thrust its point under my chin. "I could kill you right now," he said.

"It wouldn't help. I can be easily replaced from King's City," I said calmly.

Hilmar glared at me. Then he put the dagger away. "The lords hate you," he said.

"I don't hate them."

He ignored that. "They hate you because they can't bully you and they can't buy you, and they know that you'll enforce the law without regard for rank. Do you know what the common people are saying about you?"

"No," I said.

"They're saying that you intend to marry Dard and make yourself queen. They're saying you've bewitched him."

"Well, they're wrong."

"They say that wouldn't a bad thing. They wouldn't have to pay taxes to King's City and they think you'll look out for their interests, being a commoner yourself."

"They get value for the taxes they pay, whether they think so or not."

Hilmar bowed his head for a moment, as if thinking. Then he looked at me shrewdly. "Will you review the writs of outlawry?"

"If you or any of your folk wish to present yourself at Woodsholme and request a review of your case, I will," I said. "If I find any that were issued by Eyvind because someone resisted an illegal act, I'll rescind them."

"How are we to know you won't just hang us?"

"The law doesn't allow me to 'just hang' anybody without a trial. I would answer to the King if I did."

"Will you issue a pardon for illegal acts forced upon us by circumstances of having been outlawed?"

"Not for murder."

Hilmar regarded me with a tinge of exasperation. "You don't seem to realize that you're in a very unpleasant predicament here. You're in the hands of desperate men. We could do anything we want with you and not be any worse off than we are now."

I smiled at him. "Thank you for pointing that out. We were talking so much like reasoning human beings trying to come to an acceptable agreement that I forgot to be terrified."

"If you won't guarantee our safety, I don't know how we can come to an agreement. We'll just have to keep you hostage. Have you ever wintered in camp?"

"Yes," I said, "and I didn't like it." I paused thoughtfully. "I know of a way that I can pardon you and your folk in good conscience."

He looked at me with sudden hope. "What is it?"

"By the laws of the Kingdom, crimes that are less than capital may be pardoned upon completion of an honorable term of service in the navy. The length of the term is specified by the judge who hears the case, and depends upon the severity and nature of the crime."

"The navy! What do any of us know about the sea? None of us has ever even seen it!"

"I realize that. But I think it's within my power as Viceroy to establish a foot auxiliary to the Light Cavalry. It could be called, say, the Light Cavalry Rangers. It would be an ideal organization for flushing bandits out of the deep woods, the more so because they needn't even know of its existence. It would have to be completely voluntary, mind. Those who chose to join would have to realize that they would be submitting to military discipline. Of course, they would be receiving military pay, too."

"What about officers?"

"I can commission officers." True, but risky; if His Majesty thought that I was stepping beyond what he intended when he made me Viceroy . . . "Of course, ultimate command would be my responsibility."

Hilmar paused, gazing thoughtfully into the flames of the campfire. "We'll talk it over," he said at last. "The Forest Folk have never taken well to military discipline, and we Houseless ones less than most."

I nodded. "If you decide to take me up, present yourselves at Woodsholme to be enrolled."

"That wouldn't do much good, would it? Since you aren't in Woodsholme, but here with us?"

"You wouldn't want to keep me here, of course, since kidnaping a viceroy is a capital offense and you wouldn't be eligible for pardon on account of service," I said, meeting his eye coolly.

Chapter

8

The reception I got at Woodsholme when I rode in early the next day was gratifying. I was headed for the door into the great hall, my mind on a nice hot bath, when Hetwith came pelting out and nearly ran me down.

"Colonel!" he said. "You're alive!"

"Why, so I am," I said.

"Are you all right, ma'am?"

"Well, I could use a bath, but aside from that, I'm fine. I'll need to talk to you as soon as I've changed."

"Yes, ma'am. May I say that I'm very glad you're back?"

"Thank you, Hetwith. I'm glad to be home."

Dard came bursting through the door, flinging both leaves wide. He brushed past Hetwith, who was standing to embarrassed semi-attention, and snatched me into a such a hug that I thought my ribs were creaking. "Tevra! I was so afraid you were dead or hurt. Did you spend the night in the forest? Were you lost? Are you hungry? Where have you been?" He hugged me again, so tightly that I couldn't have answered him even if I had been able to sort the questions out. Besides, it felt so good to be hugged, and I wanted so much just to stay where I was, that I didn't even formulate an answer. But I caught a glimpse of Hetwith's scandalized glare, and saw the avid curiosity of the Woodsholme folk, and remembered what Hilmar had said about Dard and me.

"Dard!" I protested. "Quit it! Colonels don't stand around on porches embracing secretaries."

"Perhaps not," he said without releasing me, "but princes sometimes do viceroys, if they've been lost all night and the princes were afraid they were hurt and needed help and certain officious captains have refused to send out search parties."

It was amazing how well my head fit on his shoulder and how completely right I felt to be held against his chest. "Hetwith was correct. That's Light Cavalry doctrine; anyone who gets separated from the detachment in enemy territory is on his or her own. Too many traps have been baited with captured or dead troopers. Let go, Dard; people are staring." But I didn't say it very forcefully.

"Dard," said Hetwith, so coolly that anyone who didn't know him well wouldn't have heard the menace in his voice, "the Colonel asked you to let go."

I pushed myself hastily away; it wouldn't do to have blood all over the porch, especially the hereditary king's. Dard looked steadily at Hetwith for a moment, and received a cool level stare in return. "Gentlemen," I said. They both looked at me. "My office, half an hour."

Dard nodded. "Yes, ma'am," said Hetwith, more smartly than he would have if Dard hadn't been there.

I came out of my bedroom, damp and clean, to hear them arguing—with the greatest civility, which was alarming. When Hetwith spoke with that clipped courtesy, he was a dangerous young man. "Permit me to explain to you that Colonel Tevra is not to be mauled about in public," he was saying.

"Any woman needs a hug now and then," said Dard mildly.

"Tevra is a colonel. Even if she did need a hug, which I take leave to doubt, it isn't your place to give it to her."

"Whose, then? As you say, she's a colonel and viceroy. I'm her only equal in rank in all of the Forest Province. You aren't suggesting that it's part of your duties to provide her with affection, are you?"

Dard probably came closer to death that instant than he ever would until he actually made the crossing. I could see part of Hetwith's back, and he jerked like a hooked salmon. "No," he said very quietly, "I'm not saying that."

"Then why begrudge her a simple hug? If that bothers you, Hetwith, you'd better get used to worse. I want her and I intend to have her."

"You won't get her. She's got more sense than to go tumbling into bed with you just because you want her."

"Perhaps. But what if she wants me? She does, you know. She needs to be loved—I don't suppose you have a doctrine in your cavalry for that."

"She isn't the fool you think she is."

"She isn't the coldblooded soldier you think she is."

It was definitely time to put a stop to that argument, but if I interrupted, Hetwith would be embarrassed. I backed down the hall to the door of my bedroom and slammed it vigorously. "Well, gentlemen," I said briskly, as if eavesdropping would never occur to me, "I have some interesting developments to discuss with you."

I told them about the newly formed Light Cavalry Rangers and the role it would be playing in the suppression of the outlaws. "And if you wouldn't mind, Dard, step down to Jevan's office and see if he's found those writs of outlawry. Make me a list, as much as you remember, of the circumstances under which each was issued."

"Of course," Dard said amiably. As he left the room, he detoured far enough to rest a hand lightly on my shoulder for an instant. I sighed. It was a shame that I had Hetwith's high opinion of me to live up to.

"Hetwith," I said when Dard was well out of earshot, "I found Ilena living among the outlaws. Did you quarrel?"

"Quarrel? No. After . . . after you found us together, I told her that I really didn't want her . . ."

"Hetwith! I've never known you to be cruel before," I interrupted, a little shocked.

"Cruel? I wasn't . . . their customs are different," he said lamely. "She didn't really want me, either, once her curiosity had been satisfied."

"Are you claiming that she was the aggressor?"

"As a matter of fact, yes, ma'am. Oh, I'm not saying I put up a valiant battle to protect my virtue, but that was the only time we were together. She wasn't really pleased with my performance. In fact, she said I was as clumsy as a turtle and about as exciting. Afterwards she said she wanted to go live with her House brother."

"I see. Well, it isn't really any of my business." The stupid little tart! What a thing to say to a sensitive lad like Hetwith. Of course, I had no direct evidence to base my surmise on, but I'd bet that given a responsive partner, he was as skilled a lover as any half-savage backwoods roundheels was ever likely to have. "I beg your pardon for prying. I just thought you might like to know where she was."

"Ma'am, I appreciate the opportunity to explain. I've been trying to ever since it happened. I know you thought I was involved in an affair with her and I just wanted you to know that I wasn't."

"Hetwith, I've never demanded of you or any of my young officers that they live celibate."

"You do."

"When I'm on duty or in the field, yes. It's been quite a while since I've met a man equal in rank in whom I had a sexual interest, and the regulations are crystal clear about the penalties for a senior officer who sexually abuses her subordinates."

I had managed to surprise Hetwith. "Sexually abuses?"

"Exactly. Any senior officer who uses his or her rank to

enforce sexual compliance from a junior is guilty of sexual abuse and deserves to be cashiered, at the very least."

"But . . . but what if the junior wants the senior to . . . er . . ."

I was really rather enjoying this. I found it hard to remember the last time I had shocked Hetwith. "Under the regulations, the senior officer is always assumed to be the aggressor," I said severely. "Quite rightly, too. Can you imagine a junior officer or trooper making indecent advances to a senior in rank? But you know all this, Hetwith. You know the regulations as well as I do."

"Yes, ma'am," he said. "But I never really thought the term 'sexual abuse' was meant to apply to the kind of healthy recreation I was talking about. If someone's being abused, someone's being hurt and humiliated. Otherwise, it's just fun. Unless the two participants are really serious about each other, and then it would be 'sexual abuse' not to show each other a little physical affection."

I might have known that I wouldn't keep Hetwith off-balance for long. "Perhaps, but wouldn't even the very worst sort of sadistic monsters immediately claim that it was all done in deepest affection, if the regulations allowed it to be an excuse? Then what protection would the lower ranks have?"

"I see that the regulations couldn't very well be changed," he said interestedly. "But we know that it's a regulation more often broken than honored."

"So it is, to the shame of the officers' corps. You can't expect me to condone the wanton breaking of a regulation just because almost everybody does it."

"No, ma'am, but I can expect you to take individual circumstances into consideration, especially since you never have been a stickler for regulation at the expense of the regiment. Just how did it happen that the entire regiment is mounted on half-breds destined for the King's Guard?"

"Oh, well," I said weakly. "There weren't any major regulations broken. Just evaded, a little. The cases aren't similar."

"Then, ma'am, let me suggest a similar case. What if Corra, for example, were to fall in love with one of her troopers, say that fresh-faced lad from Eastend. I don't mean just feel attracted to him, I mean really love him. And what if he loves her back, and being that he can very well see that she's a shy thing, he takes the initiative and they become sexually involved with each other and perfectly content to go on for the rest of their lives. Would you cashier Corra? Hang the trooper for assaulting an officer? Would you enforce the regulation?"

I thought about it. It was an extremely difficult question to answer. If I said that I wouldn't enforce the regulation, would Hetwith take it as permission to start treating the female troopers under his command as his own personal harem? On the other hand, I wouldn't cashier Corra or hang the trooper, and I'd just look ridiculous if I said I would. "Given that the circumstances were exactly as you say," I said carefully, "I'd call Corra in privately and give her the dressing-down of her life. Then I'd point out that she and her lover had some choices to make: if they couldn't live without each other, she had better resign. And if, after all of that, they were still adamant, I'd remove the trooper from her direct command and pretend I thought that had solved the problem. This is not intended to be interpreted," I said meaningfully, "as permission to disobey this or any other regulation, so if there's a junior lieutenant or one of the troopers you fancy, let me warn you right now that I will have your hide unless you can convince me that you really are permanently in love with her and she with you and that you intend to remain faithful to each other the rest of your lives. And I intend to be mighty hard to convince."

"Me?" said Hetwith, with a look of injured innocence. "I thought we were talking about you."

I laughed; I couldn't help myself. He'd neatly turned the tables on me again! One of these days I'd learn not to chop logic with him. "I can assure you that I obey the regulations," I chuckled. "Lieutenants and troopers and you are all safe from my evil intentions."

"Colonel," said Dard, coming into my office in some haste, "you'd better come and have a look at this. Your reinforcements have arrived."

I looked at him blankly. "Reinforcements? I didn't send for any more troops. Hetwith, did you?"

"Without your knowledge, ma'am? Certainly not."

The reinforcements were strewn untidily about the main courtyard—a bobtail company of some last-chance infantry regiment. It took only one appalled glance to assure me that a colonel had taken the opportunity to rid his regiment of every criminal, loafer, insubordinate, drunk, and incompetent he had when the orders had come to send troops to the far north. The captain in command was too old for his rank, with a dirty uniform and a bitter mouth. He slouched up to me, offered a sloppy salute, and drawled, "Gornan, Captain, Seventy-third Infantry, reporting, ma'am." His tone was just barely short of insolent. He handed me a packet of stained papers.

I looked him up and down, letting him see that I was unimpressed with his appearance. Then I turned and looked over his command. They were all men, as many infantry outfits were. They were filthy, and unshaven, and leering, and several were in advanced stages of intoxication. Seeing me looking in their direction, a lieutenant began to yap hysterical orders at them. They dawdled to their feet and began to form slovenly lines.

"Captain Gornan," I said icily, "I can see that you've had a difficult journey from King's City. If you will march your command down that road for about half a mile, you will find a stream deep enough to bathe in. Garabed!"

"Yes, Your Excellency?"

"Have some towels and razors and a large supply of soap brought out to these men. Obviously they've suffered some calamity and lost all of theirs. Gornan, how long will it take you and your command to make yourselves presentable?"

He shrugged indifferently.

"You will address me properly," I snapped.

"I don't know, ma'am," he grudged.

"Can you be ready by lunchtime?"

He started to shrug again, thought better of it, and said, "I guess so, ma'am."

"When you and your men are fit to be seen, report to the hall for a welcome banquet."

Garabed's crew arrived with the articles I had sent them for. I had him distribute them to the infantrymen and watched Gornan get his grumbling command into an approximation of marching order.

"Hetwith," I said, "get your company under arms. I want them to be ready for fights, disorderly conduct, thievery and possibly rape and murder. Dard, get all the personable wom-enfolk of Woodsholme out of sight, away from the hall. Garabed, as soon as you've given orders for the meal, see to it that every small article of value is locked up."

The orders Gornan had given me, which I took to my office to read, were just as I feared. Stripped of their pompous language, they told me that by order of the King, the Seventy-third was sending me a contingent, detached indefinitely to my command. Included were records and disciplinary files of each soldier.

Appalling as the disciplinary records were, I was more horrified to discover that Gornan had more than fifteen years in his current rank, placing him clearly senior to Hetwith, who had been in his for less than three. Gornan couldn't be expected to take orders from a junior captain, and he would with all tradition behind him expect to be made my second-in-command. There were other implications, too. Nobody, absolutely nobody, stayed a captain for fifteen years unless they were at once incorrigibly vicious, and clever enough to skirt a court-martial without being cashiered. Military custom was that incompetence would simply be transferred about until it found a place where it could do as little harm as possible, and that ordinary viciousness would find a home in one of the siege regiments.

"Ladies and gentlemen," I said to my assembled officers and staff, "we've just been presented with a serious problem. I'm sure His Majesty meant well when he sent us this rogue's company, but they're more of a threat to the Forest Folk than the bandits. I need a plan, ladies and gentlemen, and I need it before lunch. Well?"

We all waited for Hetwith, but he said nothing. He was staring abstractedly at the table before him. At last Ordent, the most senior lieutenant, said hesitantly. "Perhaps we could send them back and say we don't need them."

Patiently I said, "Thank you, Ordent. If we send them back to King's City, we'll have the greatest difficulty convincing the planning office that we do need reinforcements if we ever should. Any other ideas?"

"We could billet them at one of the abandoned log houses, as far away from any civilians as we could get them," offered Corra shyly.

"That plan has some merit, but it has its disadvantages, too. There are already too many bandits and outlaws in the Forest Province. If we just left them there without anything to do, it wouldn't take them long to turn outlaw as well. Then we would have nearly our own number of trained, battle-hardened troops to fight in addition to the problems we already have. Anyone else?"

"I could cast a spell on them that would attract attacks from the supernatural," said Dard, but not as if he thought his offer would be accepted.

I gave him a cool look. "Getting them eaten might solve

the problem of what to do with them, but it might be a little difficult to explain at an inquiry. Besides, just imagine what havoc nearly a hundred supernaturals with bellyaches might cause."

There was a long silence. Ordent coughed. The lieutenant next to him shuffled his feet. Hetwith continued to study the table surface. I was surprised that he hadn't yet come up with any suggestion; it was unlike him. "Think about it, ladies and gentlemen," I said. "We must make good use of them, and we must think of a way to protect the Forest Folk from them. It will have to be detached duty, because I absolutely will not replace Hetwith as my second with Gornan."

Hetwith glanced up at me, his expression unreadable. Dard said, "Is there a question of his replacing Hetwith? Even to my civilian eyes he's clearly incapable."

"Yes, but he's senior. However, there is no question of it; I will not tolerate it. This job is hard enough as it is. I can't be expected to do it without Hetwith." I was surprised myself at the emphasis with which I spoke. Most of the officers were staring at me with frank astonishment. Hetwith had looked away again, no doubt embarrassed. Dard was gazing at me intently, a little smile on his lips.

"Dard," I said, "is there really a spell that attracts supernaturals?" The faintest glimmering of an idea was beginning to form at the back of my mind.

"Why, yes, there are several," he answered. "But I wasn't serious."

"But you do know them?"

"Yes."

"H'mm. Thank you." I glanced at Hetwith. He had resumed his study of the tabletop. I sighed. "Everyone be thinking about this problem. See me after lunch if you come up with anything. Is there anything else we need to talk about?"

"Excuse me, Your Excellency," said Dard. "A courier arrived from Long Meadows House while I was downstairs.

He carried an invitation from Anlon Carmi for a ball next week."

"Blast. I suppose we have to go. To whom was it addressed?"

"To the viceroy and her officers. I received one separately."

"Very well. Send a polite acceptance, if you please. Will you attend?"

He looked apologetic. "It would be less than tactful of me to refuse."

"As prince?" I watched his eyes carefully. If any of the Forest Lords would willingly involve himself in schemes to crown the Forest King, Anlon Carmi would, and I still was not certain where Dard's loyalties lay.

Dard smiled ruefully. "I fear his invitation was addressed to 'His Majesty the Forest King.' But I'll sign my acceptance 'Prince Dard, Secretary to the Viceroy,' if you like."

"I think it would be wise," I said gently. "The Forest Province has enough problems without civil war. I'm sure you realize that the courage of the Forest Folk couldn't begin to prevail against the might of the King in King's City, but I'm not sure Anlon Carmi realizes it. His Majesty could put an army of a quarter million in the field if he had to, and still leave the southern borders defended."

Dard's eyes widened. "I'll see to it that Anlon Carmi hears of it," he said, after a pause. "There's one other thing you ought to know. Anlon Carmi's wife died about two years ago from the plague."

"I'm sorry to hear it. Why ought I to know it?"

"Well," Dard said reluctantly, "As well as governor, Eyvind was Lord of Woodsholme. In the old days, lordship of a Great House often passed by force of arms. There has been some talk among the more conservative Lords that by overcoming and executing Eyvind, you've made yourself Lord of Woodsholme."

"I'm just here for the duration of the emergency," I said. "I make no claims on Woodsholme."

"You needn't. The lords will decide whether you are or aren't. But if they decide that you are heir of Woodsholme, lordship will pass to your husband. Anlon Carmi would like to be lord of Woodsholme."

"He can certainly save himself the effort of proposing to me," I snorted.

I thought Dard might have something to add, but Garabed entered just then. "Your Excellency, the new soldiers are back and lunch is ready to be served," he said.

"Are they presentable?" I asked.

"There is considerable improvement," he said stiffly.

"Very well. What suggestions do you have for quartering them temporarily?"

His ready answer demonstrated some careful thought. "The third wing is devoted mostly to quarters for visiting Lords, but the Houses of three of the apartments there are extinct. If I were to remove the remaining three into the fifth wing and the second wing, the whole third wing could be made into barracks. It is somewhat secluded from the rest of Woodsholme. There's only one way back into the central wing and that could easily be guarded."

"Excellent. Put your staff to work on it immediately."

Garabed's analysis was correct. The new troops were presentable—barely. They were washed and shaven and their uniforms were clean, if wrinkled and shabby. Their attitude had improved not one iota. Gornan, seated on my right at the luncheon, shoveled food into his mouth without a civil word. The rest of his command, taking their cue from his behavior, bordered on insolence. I mentally sighed with relief when the meal ended with no obvious insubordination. Once the infantrymen were marched away to be installed in their new barracks, I led Hetwith, Dard, and Gornan to my office. As we filed up the stairs, I whispered to Dard.

Gornan eyed Hetwith, who had been introduced to him as my second-in-command. "Where's the second's quarters, buck?" he asked. "I'll move in now. Get your stuff out."

"That won't be necessary," I said coldly. "You'll have an independent command. Hetwith stays as second."

He looked at me, and then at Hetwith, and leered suggestively. "Second's quarters are right near yours, I take it? You hear stories about the female officers of the Light Cavalry, but I never believed them before."

"Captain Gornan, if you ever again fail to address me with less than full military courtesy and the respect one officer owes another, I'll have you arrested, tried, and hanged for mutiny so fast your feet will be dancing on air before you've had time to remember each of your unsavory sins." I said it coolly, but I meant it. I almost hoped he would continue his insolence. There was no doubt in my mind that his sorry command would be better off without him, and hanging him would certainly prove a salutary lesson to the rest.

Gornan, however, had some elementary sense of self-preservation. "Yes, ma'am," he said, almost smartly. But his expression was disbelieving.

"Perhaps the captain isn't aware," said Hetwith softly, "That the colonel is viceroy, acting governor, and king's justiciar."

Clearly Gornan hadn't known it or hadn't considered the implications. Understanding dawned on his brutish face, and with it, a tinge of fear. I could hang him if I wanted, and if there was ever an inquiry, my subordinates would back me. Fear was as close to respect as a man like that ever came; it would have to do for now.

"Captain Gornan," I said, putting aside the incident, "the Forest Province has several serious problems. Some of them are curing themselves with time, and some we have gone a long way toward solving. There's one problem, however, that we have been able to do nothing about so far. That's the one I intend you to take full responsiblity for."

"What's that, ma'am?" he said.

"The Forest Province is heavily infested with supernaturals. I want you to destroy them."

"Supernaturals? Ghosts and goblins? Things that howl at night?"

"Things that kill and eat healthy active troopers, or drink the breath of children, or consume the minds and souls of their victims. There are dozens of kinds."

"How do you expect me to find these things?" He stopped, then remembered. "Ma'am."

"Ah," I said. "That's the best part. I'm going to arrange for them to find you. Prince Dard here is a wizard. He knows spells that can draw the supernaturals to you, where you can trap them and destroy them."

"A wizard?" His look at Dard was disbelieving.

Dard made a gathering motion, then gestured at the tabletop in front of Gornan, who was sitting at my conference table across from me. Snakes began to drop out of the air and crawl across the table toward him, hissing in their eagerness to be at him. He leaped up and backed away with a startled oath. The snakes plopped heavily to the hardwood floor and slithered after him.

"I see," he gulped, kicking at a reptile that was trying to bite his boot.

Dard gave another elegant gesture and the snakes began to crawl away. He picked one up and dropped it negligently out the window. The rest disappeared into snakeholes in the floor and walls that certainly had not been there five minutes ago.

I made an effort to look as if I were quite used to this sort of thing. Out of the corner of my eye I saw Hetwith composedly sorting out the maps and papers at his place. "Colonel, here's the map showing the most recent supernatural attacks," he said. As he handed me the map, his back was to Gornan for an instant, and he gave me a tiny mischievous grin; my heart lightened a bit to have Hetwith back in good spirits.

"The region where the most attacks have been taking place in the last few weeks seems to be centered here, west of Aspenhall," I said. Gornan sat cautiously back down in his chair, after a surreptitious glance under the table, and I shoved the map across to him. "Hetwith, have you got that map of deserted log houses I was making the other day?" I'd always liked maps; lacking Hetwith's intuitive brilliance, I found seeing things in their proper spatial relationships helped me to explore the implications of the data I collected. All my officers brought me all kinds of information from all of their missions.

I had been trying to see if there was any geographical correlation to the decline of population the Forest Province was suffering, thinking that perhaps some areas were less healthy than others, but so far I had found none. Now the map I had made showing deserted and declining dwellings would prove unexpectedly useful. When Hetwith found the map on my desk, we compared the two and I picked out an abandoned house fairly near the most heavily infested area.

"You can set up headquarters here. This will keep the civilian population out of harm's way. As soon as you've cleaned this area out, you can move to the next most infested area, and so on." Gornan bent over the maps and nodded. His surly attitude was improving a little, and I guessed him to be the sort of soldier who needs to have an immediate objective. "Dard, I won't be able to spare you from your duties. Do you know of a wizard for hire that knows the spells?" I gave him a long hard look, hoping that he would interpret it to mean, one we can trust not to conspire with Gornan's company of scoundrels.

"I think I know just the man," he said. "He's made a speciality of the spells you'll need, although he usually uses them for drawing supernaturals away from inhabited areas."

"Good," I said. "Gornan, you and your men can rest up tomorrow, while Dard arranges for this man to join you. At the same time, he can instruct you and your officers on the species of supernaturals you're likely to encounter and the best ways to kill or destroy them. The next day you can take up your station. I'll have Garabed make up some packs of fresh food. We haven't much; we're just beginning to recover from a famine, but you'll want to give your men a change from marching rations. Do you have any questions?"

"No, ma'am," he answered, almost briskly.

"Very well. Then you'll want to inspect your company's accommodations. You'll be billeted with them, of course; I can see that keeping them under discipline is a difficult responsibility." I looked him straight in the eye as I said this; I wanted him to know just whom I was holding responsible for the behavior of the thugs he commanded.

He took my point. "Yes, ma'am," he said. "My boys are a little rowdy at times, but they know better than to cause a rumpus in the viceroy's palace."

Or they soon would, anyway, I thought. "I'm delighted to hear it," I said. "Dismiss."

Gornan safely gone, I dropped onto the sofa with a whoosh of relief. I would rather have had one of Hetwith's schemes to depend upon, but it seemed as if my own modest effort might work, with the additional advantage of doing something about the death and destruction caused by the various supernatural predators and parasites.

"Dard," I said, "are they going to be able to do any good?"

"Well," he said cautiously, "it depends upon what kind of supernaturals they come up against. Many kinds can be fought by force of arms. Others can be combated only by wizardry. And a few are just too strong for either. Fortunately, the spells would have to be terrifically powerful to attract those, and the man I have in mind is pretty feeble. As long as they only come up against nightstalkers, lopers, breathdrinkers, and such they ought to be able to do a lot of good. Some of them are going to get killed."

"I can live with a few casualties if the results are worth it. I don't like to send men out to get killed for nothing, though."

"It always surprises me, Tevra, when you talk like a cold-blooded soldier, because I know you for a kind and warm-hearted woman. You constantly consider the best interests of the Forest Folk, who aren't even your people. And still you can send your own men and women out to die without a second thought."

"Never without a second thought," I said.

"We're soldiers," said Hetwith. "It's our job to risk our lives, as Tevra has, many times. And officers, especially senior officers like Tevra, have to come to terms with the idea of sending others to their deaths. She does everything she can to minimize the risk."

"In the Forest, we don't subject our women to having to learn such terrible lessons. Women should be protected and cared for."

"In the old days, we in the Kingdom thought the same," I said. "Women stayed at home and the men went to war. But we found that women paid too high a price for the privilege of being protected. Too many of the men never came back, or came back with foreign brides, dooming the women they would have protected to useless lives. We found it was better to forgo the privilege and take the rights and responsibilities."

"If all the women of the Kingdom feel as you do, I find it wonderful that there are so many citizens. Who raises the families?"

I laughed. "By no means all of us choose a military career. Most of us are wives and mothers. Some of us become merchants, traders, or manufacturers. Many go into the civil service. But the point is that there is no woman in the Kingdom for whom there is no place. There was a time not so long ago that a woman in my position could only choose between prostitution or suicide."

"Your position?" asked Dard, and even Hetwith looked up at me.

"Yes. I was one of the Unchosen." I gulped, my inward eye turning back to that long-ago terrible hurt. "In the province where I was born, it's the custom for the girls of marriageable age to go at dawn on Midsummer Day to the Choosing Ground, where they wait all day for their future husband to claim them. In olden times, it was the first time a girl ever saw her husband, and the men had to choose their wives on the basis of a scant few minutes' acquaintance and the display of bridal goods each girl spread around her. Nowadays, girls go to the Choosing Ground having made their arrangements ahead of time, and it's largely a formality. But now, as then, a girl gets only one chance on the Choosing Ground, and if she is still unclaimed when the sun goes down, her parents gather up her bridal goods and take them home, where they mourn her as dead." I stopped. The luxurious palace was gone from around me, and I saw once again the westering sun in its haze of dust, heard the merrymaking of the weddings back in the town, and felt again the bitter desolation as I realized that he was not coming—not for me.

"You made an arrangement with someone who never came," said Dard softly. I hardly heard him.

"I had an arrangement, I thought, with Allian. He was handsome and merry and all the girls loved him. And he chose me, the plain, the shy, the girl who at eighteen had never had a boyfriend. We had thought he would choose Berita, the prettiest girl in town, because they were always together. But that spring he walked with me, and talked of our future, and asked me if I would be on the Choosing Ground come Midsummer. And when I told him I would, he kissed me. He made me no promises, you see. He just let me fool myself." I stopped again, and in my mind's eye I saw him walk with his long evening shadow across the Choosing Ground, past me without even looking, to Berita's side, where he took her hand. I saw her looking at me as they walked past me, laden with her bridal goods. Her smile was full of malicious triumph, and the smile he bent upon her was one of tender possessive pride.

I remembered suddenly that all this had happened many years ago, and that time should certainly have dulled the hurt by now. My vision cleared and I saw Dard and Hetwith looking at me. Dard's face was full of sympathetic sorrow. Hetwith wore a brooding, distant expression, and I realized that I had never spoken of my past before I had joined the army. I shook myself out of my mood of self-pity. "But he chose Berita instead," I said briskly, "and really it all worked out very well. I've made a far better officer than I ever would have made a wife. Can you imagine me, a housewife?" I asked, and tried to laugh lightly.

"But why?" asked Dard. "Why did this..."

"Bastard," supplied Hetwith savagely.

"Bastard," agreed Dard, glancing at Hetwith. "Why did he let you think you had an arrangement and then betray your trust?"

"I never knew," I said. "My parents came and took the bridal goods away—I had a sister for whom they would be useful—and never spoke to me again. I left the town that night. I've never been back. I think perhaps Berita put him up to it. He was very much under her influence. She hated me because I was by far the better horseman, and because she had always come second to me in school. She was very spoiled on account of being so pretty and couldn't bear to be second-best at anything, although she was too busy with her flirts to attend to her studies and too lazy to practice her riding for the Games. I had beat her badly that winter in the horse-taming event, and the mare I rode then was the same I brought with me to the Light Cavalry. The Unchosen aren't supposed to take anything with them from the Choosing Ground, but when I left I found my mare saddled and tied by the path I had to take to leave, and in the saddlebags were my best clothes and a sum of money my parents couldn't afford to part with."

The sultry darkness had hidden the hot tears of humiliation and fear that I wept into the mane of my gallant little mare Needle. With her help the morning sun had found me far away from Willow Crossing, and with her help and the money I had been able to enter the army as an officer cadet, instead of a common trooper. Officer cadets had to supply their own mounts and equip themselves, besides passing a written examination. Years later, when at last I could, I had sent twice the amount to my parents.

"What vicious customs your folk have," said Dard angrily.

"The point is, that had we followed your gentler customs, there would have been nowhere for me to go. My useful life would have been ended."

"Nothing like that would have been permitted to happen to you. No man or woman goes homeless."

"Yet you trade women back and forth among the houses like sheep," said Hetwith.

"Nubile girls can't remain in their ancestral houses forever. There is the danger of inbreeding. The men must stay because it's they who do most of the hunting, and they must know their hunting grounds. No girl is forced to go; they're always eager enough, and are welcomed warmly enough. Certainly no one would ever be cast out to make their own way in the world."

"I've done well enough for myself," I said.

"So you have. Are all the Unchosen as courageous as you are, and as lucky?"

I was silenced. Most of the Unchosen were so shattered that they simply gave up and drifted into thievery or worse. I had been lucky. I had had Needle, and the money, and a good education. "No," I said quietly. "There's something to be said for either side of the argument. Whatever the fate of the women no one wants in either society, I'll still maintain that it's better to have the choice, and you'll still maintain that the price is too high if some fail to make the right choice."

"Forgive me," Dard said gravely. "I can hardly bear to think of the pain you must have felt, and be unable to make it right. It makes me angry. It's so cruelly unfair."

"I believe that Tevra narrowly escaped a terrible fate," said Hetwith. "She's no common drudge, to be keeping a house and washing some man's shirts and breeching his brats. You've never seen her in the exaltation of battle, as I have, or handling a thousand half-mutinous soldiers. You haven't watched her planning some strategy that a lesser mind couldn't even have grasped if it had been explained to him, and planning it so cleverly that only half the troopers and equipment and supplies were lost that any other commander would have thought well-spent for half the gains. It would have been a terrible waste if what's-his-name had chosen her, like keeping a tiger to catch mice."

I turned to Hetwith, surprised at his passion and greatly complimented. I had never known he thought so well of me as a soldier and an officer. Dard, too, was looking at him with amazement. "I hadn't suspected you of such eloquence, Hetwith," he said. "But I don't understand how you can justify risking the life of such a woman in battle. If it were a waste for her to be keeping a man's house, how much more of a waste would it be for her to be lying dead in some border skirmish? And there would have been sons and daughters to carry on her courage and compassion."

"I don't choose to risk her life in battle. If I had my choice, she'd stay safely away from any danger. But if Tevra chooses to do so, who are you to deny her the right?"

I think they had completely forgotten that the subject of their argument was standing by them, squared off at each other as they were. I marveled at Hetwith's dark intensity, at Dard's blazing golden sincerity. "Do you dare to claim that you care only for Tevra's freedom?" Dard said. "If you were honest, wouldn't you be glad if she chose to relinquish her freedom? Or would you rather see her dead than happy?"

Hetwith lowered his head, shaking it like a goaded bull. "Tevra would never be happy tamed and controlled."

"You mean you'd never be happy if it were some other than you doing the controlling. You'd tame your tiger to catch your mice, if you dared."

Hetwith's eyes blazed with rage and his saber leaped half out of his scabbard. Dard stood before him, proud, tight-lipped, defying him to strike. I drew my breath to shout an order, really frightened that Hetwith in his anger would neither hear nor obey. But evidently he realized that Dard was unarmed, for he slammed the weapon home again and turned away.

"Gentlemen," I said softly, but with the voice of authority, "kindly quit squabbling at once. Dard, I'm sure you don't realize just how deadly an insult you've offered Hetwith. You've implied that he would behave improperly toward a superior officer, for which there could be only one reason—that he hoped to gain preferment in exchange for sexual favors. If you had really understood what you were saying, he would have killed you. Since you were also implying that I would give preferment in exchange for sexual favors, I might hold his coat while he did it. Hetwith, when I need you to defend me I'll let you know. Now let's get to work."

We did so, but my mind was not entirely upon the plans we discussed and the decisions we made. It disturbed me that these two, both valuable to me, were daily becoming more and more antagonistic. I didn't quite understand what I had done to spark animosity between them, but I would have to find a way to reconcile Dard and Hetwith to each other.

chapter

9

The great hall at Long Meadows House was nearly as large as that at Woodsholme, and crowded with most of the Forest Lords and their families and retinues, the principal folk of Long Meadow's subsidiary houses, and all the folk of Long Meadow House. Poised on Hetwith's arm, ready to make my entrance and dance the opening dance with Anlon Carmi, I took a deep breath as if about to plunge into an icy sea. I was dressed in amber and old gold this evening, my most modest ball gown. Hetwith in his uniform was the very model of military dignity, and I glanced at him, enjoying the picture he presented. He was not as spectacularly handsome as Dard, nor did he project Dard's overwhelming sexual charisma, but he was every inch a soldier. I was proud to be walking into the room on his arm.

Anlon Carmi held me too tightly as we danced the opening dance, and his compliments were just short of insults. I was glad when it was over. Dard claimed me for the second dance. He held me tightly too, but I found his familiarity comfortable rather than offensive. As we whirled about the floor, I looked up into his eyes, remembering our first dance together. He was remembering too; his eyes were as dark as a stormy sky, and as shot with lightnings. I gasped at the impact of his glance, and closed my eyes, yielding myself to his guidance, half-ecstatic with his almond-scented nearness and the music.

When the music stopped and I opened my eyes, I found that I had been steered to a secluded corner of the hall. The honey-dark woods of walls, ceiling, and floor, the earthtoned blankets that draped the hand-hewn furniture, all drank up the light of the few oil lamps that had been placed about for illumination, and the whole hall was dim. Even though there were fewer conversation rooms than at Woodsholme, the darkness, the resin-scented air, and the shadowed niches formed by the supporting structure of huge boles, gave the place a feeling of intimacy, and I felt dreamily safe in leaning against Dard for a moment. He felt my pliancy and drew me gently closer.

"I wish we were home," I said, content in the unguardedness of the moment.

"So do I," said Dard, his voice low and husky, and he caressed me gently, stooping to nuzzle at my neck. I sighed. I really must get back to the dance floor, I thought distractedly. Dard's hand was at my waist, and I shivered deliciously as he gently drew his fingertips up my bodice to softly trace the curve of my breast.

"Colonel," snapped Hetwith, "allow me to escort you to your next partner." I jumped guiltily away from Dard, to find Hetwith offering his arm. I glanced at his profile as he marched me back to the center of the huge room. It was set and cold. His mouth was a grim line and his jaw muscles were bunched. Oh, dear, I thought, I've disappointed Hetwith. Not that he wasn't completely right. Colonels have no business kissing and petting in dark corners as if they were giggly adolescents. I wasn't here, after all, to enjoy myself, and if I had been, that was an extremely improper enjoyment to indulge in. Consider the political repercussions if Dard and I had been observed by anyone other than Hetwith!

Consider, furthermore, the problems that little moment of

self-indulgence was going to cost me. Dard would probably think that I was his for the taking. Who could blame him, after the intimacies I had invited? Now I would have to think of a way to disentangle myself without offending him, a task that would be made doubly difficult by the fact that, no matter how convinced of the necessity my mind was, my body was of a different opinion.

Hetwith was disgusted with me; I could hope that I hadn't entirely forfeited his respect, but it would be no more than I deserved if I had. He was as aware as I was of the difficult political situation we faced in the Forest Province. The opinion of the common people was but tentatively favorable; a scandal could turn them against us. The lords were inclined to oppose us; they held the real power, and the help and support of their hereditary ruler was proving invaluable in reconciling them to our programs. To jeopardize our whole mission for the sake of a few seconds' physical gratification was the act of an irresponsible fool.

By the time Hetwith handed me over to my next dance partner, I was as grim as he was. It was a real effort to smile and be courteous to the lord with whom I danced.

Hetwith was waiting for me when the dance was over, and I took his arm meekly. "Hetwith," I said as we promenaded slowly around the hall, "the political situation here is very delicate."

"Yes, ma'am?" He was looking straight ahead.

"Yes. I can't afford to offend anyone unnecessarily. There aren't enough of us to hold this province together by force."

"No, ma'am."

"We're among enemies here tonight. We need to remain constantly alert, and at the same time give an impression of carefree enjoyment," I persisted.

"Yes, ma'am," he said unforgivingly.

"Damn it, Hetwith, try to look like you're enjoying yourself. I loathe these balls more than you do, and I'm managing to be cheerful about it."

"You looked to me as if you were enjoying yourself, ma'am."

I turned sharply into one of the alcoves, and Hetwith came with me perforce. I smiled sweetly at him, and snarled through my smile, "How dare you! Let me show one little instant of human weakness and you feel free to condemn me. I'm getting very tired of living up to your standards for my behavior, Hetwith. I notice you hold no such standards for yourself." I stopped and gulped. I was angrier at myself for the prickle of tears behind my eyelids and the tightness in my throat than at him for his presumption. "Do you find that my weaknesses disgust you?" I went on, keeping my voice from quavering with an effort of will. "Then I'll sign your request for transfer tomorrow and dispatch you to King's City to deliver it yourself."

Hetwith was taken aback, I could see. "Disgust me, ma'am? Certainly your weaknesses don't disgust me. I've never noticed that you have any, except for liking those miserable ration biscuits. There's been many a time I wished you had a few vices, so you'd know how we lesser mortals feel. And I've got no intention of requesting a transfer, ma'am, unless you ask me to. And then it won't be a request for transfer, but a resignation from the service I'll ask you to approve."

Impulsively I laid a hand on his sleeve and looked squarely into his eyes. "How could I get along without you? Having you here has been the only thing that has made this wretched mission possible." I had a personal rule against touching a junior officer; usually they're particular about the fit of their uniforms. Besides, it would hardly be appropriate to a senior officer's dignity to be patting and pawing at her subordinates. But Hetwith, though surprised by my gesture, was clearly pleased by it.

"I don't know, ma'am," he said, and smiled ruefully at me. "No better than I could get along without you, I hope."

I smiled back, tucking my arm through his and letting him draw me back into the promenade. "Try to understand," I said softly into the ear he bent attentively toward me, "that I can't be perfect all the time. I won't disgrace the Ninety-third, I promise." It was as close to an apology for my interlude with Dard as I could make to a junior officer who really had no business even noticing his superior's lapses.

"No, ma'am," he said.

By the time supper was served, after the ball, I was half asleep. I had danced with a dozen strangers, and walked with Dard, though there had been no more private moments, and danced one of the romping folk dances with Hetwith. Most of the time I spent making conversation and wishing I was somewhere else.

At supper, I found myself seated at Anlon Carmi's right, while on my right Dard was placed. I wondered a little at this; as I understood Forest etiquette, he should have been at the hostess's right, being the highest ranking male guest. He wondered at it too; I saw him quirk an eyebrow as he was escorted to the place. For myself, I was glad enough to have him by me; it meant that I would have one congenial companion for the meal.

"What a delicious supper," I said graciously to Anlon Carmi. It was, too; quails broiled with pine nuts, venison stewed in berry wine, heavy chestnut-bread, and half a dozen light confections of various combinations of maple sugar, honey, and fruits.

"Thank you, Your Excellency. Everything here is native to the Forest Province. I find local products to be infinitely superior to imports, don't you?"

I didn't like the way he said that, with a provocative sneer, but there was nothing in his words to give offense. "There are indeed many delicious foods to be gathered from the forest," I answered coolly.

"I've heard it said that Your Excellency finds other products of our province to your taste also," he said, and looked directly and insinuatingly at Dard. A shocked titter ran down the table. I became suddenly as conscious of Dard's presence by my side as if he had begun radiating a stove's heat.

It was worth a try to ward off whatever mischief Anlon Carmi was plotting. "Yours is a beautiful province," I said. "I think it can be rivaled only by the Black Mountains at the eastern border of the Kingdom for scenic grandeur. Tell me, Dard," I said, turning my shoulder on Anlon Carmi, "do you prefer forest or mountains for beauty?"

Judicially he said, "There's much to be said for the secret depths of the forest, perhaps a green glade walled around with graceful trees and crossed by a sparkling brook. I hear, though, that the mountains are wild and grand and spectacular. And Hetwith was telling me the other day about the southern deserts, which he says have a stark beauty different from either. I should like to see them, I think."

"Yes, they are beautiful. The colors have a whole different range there, and the land is filled by the sun. But it isn't easy to adapt to life in the desert, and for all its harshness it's fragile and easily damaged. I believe the forest is better to live in, though I haven't seen a winter here in the north." This inane conversation, I thought, wasn't deflecting Anlon Carmi's purpose one bit. He hadn't turned to the lady on his left, but listened scornfully to us babble about scenery.

Simple courtesy was forcing me to include my host in the conversation. "Have you traveled, my lord?" I asked.

"Not so widely as you, Your Excellency," said Anlon Carmi. "Nor are my ... experiences ... so varied and extensive." There was no mistaking or ignoring the leer on his face or the way he looked from me to Dard and then to Hetwith, halfway down and across the table from me. Hetwith laid his spoon down carefully, leaving his frothy sweet unfinished. Anlon Carmi's voice was loud enough to carry even to the foot of the table, and the guests made an appreciative audience for his innuendoes. Hetwith and I were the only two outlanders who had been bid to the supper; the rest of the guests were of Anlon Carmi's party, and they waited with glee for what was coming next.

"To what experiences do you refer, my lord?" I let the cold disdain I felt for the man color my tones.

Anlon Carmi grinned crookedly. "Why, your—er, combat experiences, of course. Will you share with us the details of your more interesting—er, passages at arms?"

"War stories make poor hearing at table, my lord."

"Oh, I agree. All that blood and dust. No, I had hoped you might favor us with an opinion of the skills of the men of the Forest as compared to your own imported variety."

"Make yourself clearer, my lord, and I will indeed give you my opinion." Hetwith had pushed his chair a little away from the table and I heard a subdued clatter as he disentangled his dress saber from the furniture. I wasn't armed with anything more deadly than my fork.

"I shall be clear, Your Excellency." Anlon Carmi glanced triumphantly around the room, making sure that all his followers were savoring his victory. "We were wondering who, of the men of Spruceholme, the outlaws in the forest, our own prince, or your soldier, was the best at assuaging the hot cleft of an outland slut."

In one motion I rose to my feet and slapped him so hard he fell out of his chair. "My opinion, my lord, is that you are the nastiest-minded little heap of filth it has ever been my misfortune to have to smell. Of courtesy to guests, courage, or honor, you obviously have no conception, so I shall not point out where, in each of these areas, you have fallen below the standards expected of a common pig in a sty."

Anlon Carmi scrambled to his feet, the imprint of my open

hand branded across his face in fiery red. "If you were a man," he blustered, "I'd challenge you for that. Is there any man who would stand your champion?"

"I need no champion. I accept your challenge."

Dard spoke hastily beside me. "Her Excellency accepts your challenge. Let the day be the day after tomorrow, the place the field before Woodsholme, the weapons to be at the choice of the combatants. Her Excellency's champion will stand forth then."

Anlon Carmi nodded. There was an expression of malicious triumph on his face. I don't think it had occurred to him that I would take action; he had meant to humiliate and outface me, thus effectively destroying any power I might be building among the lords. But he was willing to fight. "Let it be understood that the lordship of Woodsholme goes to the victor." He sneered again.

"As does the lordship of Long Meadows," said Dard. He took my arm and we walked with quiet dignity from the dining room, through the hall, and out into the night. Hetwith marched directly behind me, gathering up our party by eye as he went.

Dard had come separately. He rode only if he couldn't avoid it, having a true woodsman's aversion for any transport but his own feet, but it was several hours' ride home and I meant to use the time to confer. "Dard, ride with me," I ordered. I had ridden Pride, and that sturdy fellow could easily take a double burden. Hetwith appeared out of the darkness and boosted him to the horse's crupper.

He put his arms nervously around me. I was still dressed in the amber evening gown, not having wished to tarry to change. Even in the tension of the moment I was aware of a shock of desire emanating from the strong arms that encircled me.

As we rode out of the environs of Long Meadow House into the darkness of the midnight forest, I could hear Dard murmuring a spell to protect us from the predatory creatures of the night. I wished again for my saber, packed somewhere among my gear, along with the garrison uniform I had worn for the ride from Woodsholme. I shivered. Summer was fading into fall, and the nights were cool. Dard, more warmly dressed than I in his fur and bleached fawnskin, evidently felt me shiver, for he pulled himself closer and wrapped his arms more tightly around me. I was grateful for the warmth, even if I found his nearness distracting.

Hetwith reined his horse in beside Pride in spite of the narrowness of the trail, no doubt so as to participate in an impromptu strategy session. "Tell us about the customs of the Forest Lords when one challenges another, Dard," I said.

"It's not a good situation," Dard said unhappily. "Win or lose, you'll lose, I'm afraid. The custom requires that a man fight his own battles, and if a woman is involved in a challenge, that her lord stand as her champion."

"I see. That means that if I send a champion in my place, I'm acknowledging him my House Lord?"

"Worse than that. You'll have to swear personal fealty to him. That means that he owns you, body and soul, and has the bestowal of your favors. Your children will all be assumed to be his, and he'll have all rights over them. That's if he wins. If Anlon Carmi wins, he'll have all those rights over you. He may give you to any of his henchmen or take you himself."

"If he wins, you can expect to see that custom violated! Are these battles to the death?"

"Not unless there's an accident. One combatant usually yields to the other."

"What weapons and armor are allowable?"

"Any weapon that can be held in the hand. Bows are considered unsporting. Armor can be whatever a combatant chooses, though stamina and quickness of foot are supposed to be an important factor, and most go unarmored."

"Are horses allowed?"

"There's no precedent either way. The last of these combats happened before there were many horses here."

"Then the politically wise thing to do would be to fight on foot."

"Yes. You'll choose one of your officers for your champion, I suppose. Would it do any good to offer myself?"

"Thank you, but no. Your hereditary rank still carries a lot of weight with the common folk."

"Colonel, I'd be proud to be your champion," said Hetwith tightly. Even in the autumn moonlight, his eyes glittered feverishly.

"Thank you too, but I won't be needing a champion. I'll fight Anlon Carmi myself."

There was an immediate chorus of protest so vehement that Hetwith's horse shied.

I waited until the two of them had subsided. Then I said mildly, "There doesn't seem to me to be any other reasonable solution. I certainly can't swear fealty to one of my officers. I equally can't place myself under the lordship of any of the Forest Lords. And I have no qualms at all about my ability to best Anlon Carmi."

"Women don't fight challenges," stated Dard.

"Perhaps not, but colonels do."

"But what if you win? You'd be Lord of Long Meadow House. You'd have to take a lady and—no, it wouldn't work."

"What if you lose?" put in Hetwith. "You'd belong to Anlon Carmi—if he didn't kill you. Ma'am, let me fight for you. I give you my word that I'd release you from your oath immediately. Wouldn't that work, Dard?"

"Between the two of you, any arrangement you agreed to would work, but in the eyes of the Forest Folk you'd still be her lord. And what position the lord of a viceroy holds I haven't the least idea."

"I shall fight Anlon Carmi. It was *my* honor he insulted. If either of you wants to take a piece of him, you can have whatever's left. When I win, I'll simply find some worthy soul the common folk will follow and turn the lordship of Long Meadows over to him. Or I may even reinstate Anlon Carmi, if he apologizes handsomely enough. I'm sorry if I'm upsetting a lot of customs that are dear to your heart, Dard; and Hetwith, I want you to know that there isn't the least doubt in my mind that you could whip Anlon Carmi and six like him to a standstill, but I'm not going to listen to any more objections from either of you. That's the plan and all I want from you two is help in making it work."

There was a long silence. Then Dard asked plaintively, "Would it be so very bad, acknowledging a lord? Our women don't find it so impossible to contemplate."

"That's not the point, Dard. I'm here in the Forest Province on the king's business. I may not, I will not, do anything to lessen the chances of that mission's success. To acknowledge any lord over me would be to give away the power His Majesty put into my hands."

"I don't understand you. Surely you have a life apart from your duty to your king. Hetwith, do all the king's colonels devote themselves so single-mindedly to the king's interests?"

"Not all. But then not all would be made viceroy, either," answered Hetwith. "Maybe you don't understand how great an honor that is, what a great trust the king places in anyone when he gives away all that power. Tevra speaks with the king's voice, acts with his hand, answers to no one on earth except the king himself." He paused. "But I don't understand her either, Dard. Even His Majesty is allowed a little pleasure, a little foolishness."

"I'm not a king," I put in drowsily. I was leaning comfortably against Dard's chest. "Do I understand that you gentlemen are urging me to behave with impropriety?"

"No, of course not," said Hetwith. "But only tonight you were accusing me of being disgusted with your behavior. I felt no disgust, but you obviously thought I should. You've said to me a hundred times that you don't expect me to live celibate. Why would you think I would expect you to?"

"When was this?" asked Dard.

"When I found you two cuddling in a corner. I got quite a tongue-lashing for what you did, or maybe for what you didn't do."

"Were you disgusted by that?" asked Dard.

"No. But our Tevra hates parties of any sort, and she feels self-conscious in those dresses. If she was going to lurk in corners, I might have expected her to lurk with me; I know how to tease her out of her fits of shyness."

"I'm not shy and I wasn't lurking," I said, but was ignored.

"Your feelings were hurt, then," said Dard to Hetwith.

"I was angry at you. You were taking advantage of Tevra's perfectly natural disinclination for crowds to try to seduce her. It wasn't fair."

"Ah, well, fair," Dard said dismissively. "I thought we agreed that she deserved an occasional hug and a little solace."

"It isn't your place to solace her," said Hetwith, with some heat.

"So you keep telling me, but you never tell me whose place it is."

"Not yours. Why, right now you're taking advantage of riding double to hold her again."

"Horses scare me. It's so high off the ground."

Hetwith snorted. "If you were riding with me, you wouldn't be half so frightened. I'll bet you'd manage to hold onto the saddle."

Dard chuckled. "You're probably right, but I don't think I'd enjoy it half so much. What would you do if you were riding with her?"

"Take her off to the wilderness and tie her to a tree until this foolish combat is over."

"It's certainly an idea. Unfortunately, she's in charge of where this horse is going, not I."

"It isn't an idea," I said. "Hetwith, I'm surprised at you. You've seen me in battle. Do you honestly think Anlon Carmi can best me?"

"I've seen you in battle, ma'am. You're good. You're quick and clever and a professional soldier. But I could beat you, on foot, where you didn't have the advantage of your horsemanship and your perfectly trained warhorse. I'm sorry, ma'am, but I could take you down without hurting you and hold you until you had to give up."

"I suppose you could, with the advantage of knowing how I fight, though it might not be as easy as you seem to think. But fortunately for me, it isn't you I have to fight, and Anlon Carmi doesn't know me. If one thing's sure it's that he'll underestimate me."

Hetwith literally groaned. "Oh, ma'am, you don't fight clearheaded. You're a berserker. From the time your saber touches enemy steel, you're in a war trance. I've seen you. I've seen you go on fighting with your whole shoulder mangled and never know you were hit until I told you. Remember?"

"I remember. That was war, not single combat. And if I kill Anlon Carmi, it won't be any great loss."

"It will if he kills you. What weapons will you use? Your saber? On foot? He's got the reach of you, and he won't hesitate to hurt you. Please, ma'am, please let me fight him for you."

"Stop it, Hetwith. I can't let you fight my battles."

"Please let him," said Dard, soberly. "Or me. The political situation can be retrieved. Hetwith is right. Anlon Carmi is stronger than you are and twice as treacherous, and with the lordship of Woodsholme at stake he'll be pleased enough to kill you."

"And I say the same to you, Dard. You can't fight my battles. You aren't even a soldier. And don't either one of you decide to interfere without my permission; I won't tolerate it."

I won't say I wasn't frightened when I stood in the meadow before Woodsholme, watching the preparations at the edge of the forest where Anlon Carmi's people were readying him for combat. I also felt extremely short; I had never before gone into battle on foot, and it was a strange and lonely feeling. But a horse simply would not do; it would give the people the idea that I was taking an unfair advantage over my opponent. Besides, in single combat a warrior afoot has a considerable advantage over his mounted enemy, if he knows how to use it.

I was wearing a simple campaign uniform with mail shirt. I was armed with my familiar old saber, battered and plain as it was; years of use had accustomed my hand to its weight and balance. It was really too long for me when I was on the ground, but there simply hadn't been time to accustom myself to the slender point weapon favored by the Forest Lords. My heavy dagger hung in its clip-sheath at my belt. A quick yank with the left hand and it would come away, sheath and all, its weighted handle an efficient bludgeon, or it could be shaken free with a flick of the wrist and inserted between ribs at close quarters. These two were my only weapons.

Anlon Carmi, across the field, kept peering at the group who surrounded me. He was trying, no doubt, to figure out who he would be fighting, for only the three of us, Dard, Hetwith, and myself, knew that I would take the field in my own behalf.

One of Anlon Carmi's House sons came forward and addressed us in archaic words of ceremony.

"The Lord Anlon Carmi has come to prove his righteousness upon the body of the champion of the outland whore who calls herself viceroy and governor. The lordship of Long Meadows House does he offer freely as proof of his claim. Let the Right prevail!"

Hetwith stepped forward (having been well coached by Dard). "Her Excellency Tevra, Viceroy of the King, awaits here to prove her righteousness upon the body of the false craven who calls himself Lord of Long Meadows. The lordship of Woodsholme does she offer freely as proof of her claim. Let the Right prevail!"

There was a stir and a muttering among the onlookers. Hetwith should have mentioned the name of the champion before uttering the final phrase. They did not yet understand that I would fight.

Anlon Carmi came up behind his herald. He was simply dressed, his clothes chosen for freedom of movement. He carried a harpoon in one hand, the coil of line attached to the loose head tucked into his belt. It was a weapon used to hunt the larger game animals of the forest. He also carried the unedged point sword Dard had expected. "Who is to be the woman's champion?" he inquired harshly.

I stepped forward, eyeing the harpoon with some misgivings. What in thunder did he want with the thing? "I accept your challenge in my own behalf," I said proudly.

Was there a flicker of triumph in his eyes? He was certainly not as taken aback as I had expected. "Is it that none of your men folk would stand champion for you?" he sneered. "What a pack of cowards you call friends."

"On the contrary, I have had the greatest difficulty in dissuading everyone who knew about the challenge from begging for your filthy blood, Anlon Carmi," I said. "I needed a bit of exercise to work up an appetite for supper."

He tossed his head. "So be it. Let the Right prevail!"

"Let the Right prevail!" I agreed. We fell back a few paces. The noncombatants cleared the area.

We moved cautiously toward each other. He was holding the harpoon ready to throw, and I had my saber at the ready. If he threw the harpoon at me, I meant to deflect it and hopefully sever the shaft; the saber is basically an edge weapon, though it does have something of a point, and mine was sharper than any razor and pounced with the fine powder from the far south that keeps the blade from sticking in the wound.

With his harpoon, even if he didn't throw it, he had the reach of me. The opening moves would have to be his. In my favor was only the fact that he would underestimate the speed with which I could maneuver the seemingly clumsy weapon. I moved forward, my eyes slightly unfocused the better to see his movements.

He feinted at me, the line held loosely in his left hand. I evaded the thrust easily without bringing my saber into play. Quick as thought, he sidestepped and lunged. His intention was clearly to impale me and use the line to draw me close enough for a death blow. I evaded again by a hair's breadth, and a twist of my wrist sent my saber seeking for his flesh. I wasn't close enough to score, but he drew back as the blade whistled within inches of his body.

He withdrew to the far edge of lunging range, a mistake. If he had continued to press his attack I would have been hard put to it to keep eluding his thrusts. I followed up the advantage he had given me by dancing forward, saber weaving hypnotically through the air. A quick backhand slash should have severed the harpoon's wooden shaft and left the weapon useless. But he saw the blow coming and caught it on the metal point with a clang.

I was a bit off-balance; he saw his moment and thrust viciously at me. The harpoon grated over my mail shirt and skittered off. The force of the blow half spun me around, and I relaxed into the momentum of the swing, soaked it up and redirected it into a low sweep of my saber. The edge caught his thigh and opened the clothing. A thin red line burst into existence on the surface of the skin beneath. Had I been a bit closer, the fight would have ended there, and Anlon

Carmi would have walked on a wooden leg for the rest of his life, but at least I had drawn first blood.

I was rapidly losing the advantage I had had at the beginning when Anlon Carmi had underestimated me. I read a new respect in his face as he circled me, trying to jockey me so that the sun would be in my eyes. Grinning, I slipped past him, turning him into the sun.

I flicked a flurry of little chops at him, forcing him to give ground and parry with the harpoon. I intended to exploit the relative clumsiness of the weapon, but Anlon Carmi fooled me completely. Just as I thought I had bewildered him and tangled him in his own shaft and line, he cast the weapon aside and leaped at me barehanded. Of all the things I had expected, this was the last; he landed on me with all his weight and momentum, driving me to the earth and nearly knocking all the breath from my lungs. His left hand pinned my right hand and the saber to the ground; his right sought for and found my throat and the two pulsing arteries at either side. My vision began to swim as his fingers tightened.

Oh, dear, I thought. Hetwith and Dard were right. I ought not to have fought him. He's too much stronger than I. Then his grip loosened. "I must apologize," he said conversationally, "for my slurs upon your virtue. I knew they weren't true when I said them."

"If you would like to make that apology public," I husked, "we can stop this silly fight and get on with business."

He laughed. His face was so close to mine that my eyes were crossed. "Oh, no. We'll stop this fight when you're ready to kneel in front of me and beg me to be your lord. I am willing to guarantee you that you'll never be expected to warm anybody's bed but mine unless you want to."

I thought of the dagger at my left side. He was lying on my left shoulder but my arm was free, and the clip-sheath could—perhaps—be worked off my belt, although there wouldn't be a chance of drawing the dagger.

"But yours?" I said randomly, stretching my fingers toward the dagger. Keep him talking until he got careless and I had the dagger, that was the plan. "I'd rather warm your stable-boy's bed."

"I don't have a stableboy," he said. "I'll look into getting you one. I'm quite prepared to stay here all day, doing this every once in a while" he closed his fingers on my throat "until you see reason."

My fingers grasped the scabbard and began to tug on it even as my vision faded again and my ears rang with a strange tintinnabulation. The scabbard was stuck, of course. I hadn't breath to say anything when he eased the pressure. "Or," he said, "I might give you a taste of treats in store for you when you belong to me." He pressed his sneering mouth against mine. My first impulse was to bite him, but I thought I felt a little give in the catch of the scabbard, ignored his slobbery mouthings (except for keeping my mouth shut tight against the thrust of his tongue) and worked the scabbard free.

I flung the scabbard off and tucked the point of the dagger neatly under his rib cage, pricking the skin enough to draw blood. "If you don't get off me," I said quietly, "I'll take a lot of pleasure in ramming this dagger home." He grunted in surprise and pain and his grip loosed. I erupted from his hold, flinging him backward. As he wallowed helplessly on the ground, off-balance, I brought the saber across his throat and sliced through the skin with a nice precision, just enough to open the skin and not enough to cut his throat. I'll swear he thought I had for a moment, though. He was horrified when he brought his hand away from his neck all covered in blood.

He recovered quickly. Leaping sideways from a crouch, he whirled and snatched the loose line of the harpoon, jerking it to him, seizing it, and hurling it at me in one movement. I had just turned to renew my attack; the lily-iron head caught me in the left side, just where the mail shirt rode up with my sudden movement, penetrating the skin of my flank between ribs and hip. I could actually feel the barbed points setting themselves into my flesh. Anlon Carmi gave a hoarse shout of triumph and grabbed the line with both hands, playing me like a fish as he drew me toward him.

Gods, but the harpoon head in my side hurt! The force of the blow staggered me, and for an instant I thought he would drag me into his reach before I could overcome the numbing shock. When I tried to slash the line with my saber, he yanked on it savagely, causing the blow to grow astray and bringing an involuntary yelp of pain to my lips.

Then my wits returned to me and I used the momentum of his pull on the line to help my own leap into a body-to-body clinch, bringing the dagger in my left hand across to have it ready for use and driving my shoulder into his midriff. He grunted as the air was expelled from his lungs.

So close to him, my saber was an encumbrance and I let it fall. Reaching over my shoulder with my left arm and across with my right, I seized him by his left arm and flipped him over my shoulder with a wrestler's throw I had learned long ago as a cadet. I hurled him to the ground as hard as I could, hoping that he would be stunned or winded. He was at least considerably shaken when he hit the ground with a bone-jarring thud. Hastily I scooped up the saber and cut the harpoon line that still bound us together.

Anlon Carmi was dragging himself to his knees when I landed on his shoulders knees first, with all my weight and strength, driving him to the earth again and grinding his face into the trampled sod. I bestrode him like a horse, holding the saber poised over his backbone with both my hands. "You'd be well advised to yield, Anlon Carmi," I said.

He was hardly able to speak, what with my weight on his back and his mouth full of dirt. "Kill me, damn you," he gasped. "I'll never yield to a woman."

"Oh, I don't think severing the spine kills a man," I said.

"I think it just paralyzes him for life. I'm not sure, though."
I bore down upon the saber a little.

He groaned and scrabbled vainly with his fingers, but there
was nothing to help him within reach. "If it makes you feel
any better," I said kindly, "think of me as a colonel of Light
Cavalry and not as a woman." Knowing he couldn't see me,
I gritted my teeth with pain, hoping he would surrender before
I fainted. I could feel my strength leaking steadily out of the
wound in my side where the harpoon head was still embedded.
I bore down a little more upon the saber's hilt.

"You'd cripple a man and enjoy it?" he groaned.

I laughed in what I hoped was a suitably bloodthirsty manner to encourage him in this view. "Only those who call me
'slut' and 'whore'," I said. My vision was beginning to blur.

His body suddenly went lax. "All right," he said dully. "I
yield. Let me up that I may swear fealty to you."

"I'll have your word on it," I said, wondering if I would
have the strength to rise if he gave it.

"I give you my word," he whispered. "Let me up, please,
my lady. I can't breathe."

I managed to struggle to my feet, and he slowly dragged
himself into a kneeling position before me. "My Lady Tevra,"
he said, "I beg leave of you to declare myself your faithful
liege man. I surrender the lordship of Long Meadows House
into your hands, you having proved the righteousness of your
cause by the strength of your body."

"Your service is accepted," I managed to say, giving him
my bloody, grimy hand to kiss in token of submission. "I
accept from you the lordship of Long Meadows House. Rise
and go in peace, my liege man." I could feel a cold sweat
breaking out all over my body as the shock of the wound
gripped me. Where, oh where was Hetwith? I needed him
now!

As Anlon Carmi rose to his feet he looked into my face,
and I staggered and nearly fell from the force of the hatred

I saw in his eyes. I would have done better to have killed him. I certainly had an enemy now. Then he turned and walked away.

The universe expanded to include the ring of onlookers, and I looked around. "Hetwith!" I called weakly.

"You won, ma'am," he congratulated, materializing out of the crowd. "Here, you're hurt. You'd better come and see the healer."

"I think I'm going to throw up," I said inanely. My knees buckled. But I managed to walk back into the palace on my own, and Dard and Hetwith between them got me up the grand staircase before I collapsed.

chapter

10

I made good use of my convalescence, catching up on the paperwork I had let pile up. When I had begun to feel a little better, I summoned a meeting of the thirteen great lords to consult about the lordship of Long Meadows House. They were unwilling to choose a suitable lord, and I sensed considerable hostility. "You can't just give away a lordship," exclaimed one indignantly. "Once it's settled upon you it's a lifetime responsibility."

"Exactly," I said. "Even if I were not disqualified by my sex from becoming Lord of Long Meadows House, I shall be in the Forest Province only a few more months. I was sent by the king to help in the emergency, and the emergency is nearly over."

Ernin Eaven looked sadly at me. "I don't think you understand, Your Excellency. You can't leave. The responsibilities of lordship require your presence at Long Meadows House."

"How can she be a lord?" growled Ragnal Menwin, a crony of Anlon Carmi's and public leader now of my most implacable enemies. "Whoever heard of a female lord?"

"I have no wish to be Lord of Long Meadows House," I said. "I'm viceroy and justiciar and colonel of Light Cavalry, and those are enough for me."

"There are privileges as well as duties attached to lordship," said Ernin Eaven.

"Are there?" I snorted. "What are they? Sexual access to all the women of a House? No use to me. Good food? I have all I can eat. Fine clothes? I wear a uniform. Gentlemen, surely there's one among your House sons who's wise and strong and compassionate and conscientious, who would make a good lord for Long Meadows House. Name me the man and I'll turn the duties and the privileges over to him gladly."

"It might work," said a younger lord from the east whose demesnes I hadn't yet visited. "If Her Excellency would marry the man, lordship could pass in the female line. It's been done before."

"Only with an own daughter of the previous lord," objected an elderly man. "And what of the lordship of Woodsholme? Some of us have thought for some time that she was obligated to accept that responsibility." He glanced spitefully at Ragnal Menwin. He wasn't on my side; he was just against Anlon Carmi and Ragnal Menwin.

"Her husband could assume the lordship of one and she could take the other," answered the youngster.

"I'm not going to marry anyone!" I said. "I can't accept the duties of lord of either Great House. I hope you gentlemen can agree on a suitable candidate for Long Meadows House and for Woodsholme next spring, because if you can't, I'll appoint someone to suit my own taste." Hilmar, Ernin Eaven's son, would make a good lord for Long Meadows, I thought.

They left, grumbling and insisting that I had an obligation to accept a lordship, although they disagreed vehemently on which I should accept. Aristocracy, I decided ruefully, was an outmoded institution, and inefficient to boot. I should have evinced greedy eagerness to assume the lordships; they would have opposed the idea vigorously.

I sighed and moved stiffly to the sofa by the window. The red and gold glories of autumn were mostly gone by now, and there was a crackling fire in the fireplace. The sky hung low and sullen over the bleached meadow. Snow would begin to fall soon, and for most of the winter, travel would be disagreeable and dangerous. The winters in the forest belonged to the silence and the creatures of the supernatural— snow devils and the heat-feeding snufflers. The lopers grew bold and hungry, and creatures so alien they had no names roamed the winter-stark woods. Humankind huddled around its fires and practiced its arts to beguile the long night.

I had sent most of the horses south to the plains to winter where there were hay and grain to be had. One last supply train had come and gone, taking with it the two physicians the king had sent. Reports from my contingent of infantry detailed excellent kills of supernaturals, with heavy casualties among the men. Gornan had "respectfully submitted" that he and his men could winter over where they were. I had sent Hetwith to find out whether the position was tenable; he had been gone for several days already.

I was nearly healed from the wound Anlon Carmi had dealt me, and from the surgery necessary to remove the harpoon head. At any rate, I was healed enough to be restless at being mewed up in Woodsholme, eager to be out and about. There were things that needed seeing to. The successes of the summer and fall were endangered by the rebellious mood among the lords, who resented the ties that were being forged between the common folk of the Forest and the king in King's City. Princess Morir-Alsis-Alina was stirring up trouble, too, her hatred of me finding a ready ally in the deposed Anlon Carmi.

Another worry was the food supplies. There were enough for an ordinary winter, when everyone counted on losing weight anyway, but in spite of the relief supplies there was not enough food on hand for an unusually long or severe winter. And with the lowered resistance of semi-starvation would come the plagues.

Worse, when winter settled fully over the forest, there would be very little I could do about any of these problems. I could only prepare now as best I could and then set myself to endure.

There were my personal problems, too. My injury had saved me from having to deal with the effects of my folly in allowing Dard to caress me so intimately. He and Hetwith were squabbling as much as ever.

When Dard came in a few minutes later with a handful of papers, his usually cheerful face looked as gloomy as I felt. "Is there any word of Hetwith?" I asked over my shoulder.

"Not yet." He came and sat beside me, staring into the hypnotic flames in the fireplace.

"What's the matter? You look as if your best dog died."

"It's going to be a long winter. No one's called me 'Your Majesty' for nearly a month."

"Are you pining after your throne?"

"Not exactly. It's just that if I'm not a king, I'm nothing. I have no House, because the king is supposed to consider the welfare of all the forest, not just one House. I've got nothing important to do. I don't even have a way to make a living."

"You make an excellent secretary."

"Who but you in all the Forest Province needs a secretary? And you're leaving in the spring."

"It's this gloomy weather that's pulled your spirits down. I've felt it too."

"I've lived through a good many winters. Never before without hope, though."

"Without hope! Surely you're overstating the case."

"I think not. Before you came, it seemed that we were drifting farther and farther out of contact with the king in King's City, and that one day soon I might just quietly assume the title and duties of the Forest King and no one would care. And I was heart-whole in those days, too, taking my pleasure where my fancy inclined me. The Forest Kings had that privilege, and any lord or householder was proud to name a son or daughter of the Forest King among his House children. The King married, of course, for the begetting of an heir and for reasons of state, but he had no House of his own and was welcomed in all Houses."

"And you're afraid that as ties with King's City are strengthened, these privileges may be denied you?"

"I don't care if they are denied me. I don't want the freedom of the Houses anymore."

I would have had to be incredibly stupid not to sense where this conversation was leading. I was about to have to face the consequences of folly. "Dard," I said, "the king in King's City has no desire to rob you of your rank. He simply won't tolerate civil war or insurrection within the Kingdom, and there is no means by which you can take the throne except by war."

"I don't care about that either, except that I really would like to have a worthwhile job to do. I'd like to have a place to belong and a House family to call my own. And a real family as well."

I was suddenly struck with an idea. I sat up straighter. "What about Long Meadows House? I have the gifting of the lordship there. Why don't I make you Lord of Long Meadows?"

He glanced at me, smiling wryly. "How long are you prepared to stay to maintain me in the position by force of arms? Neither the folk of Long Meadows nor the other lords would accept me except with a sword at their throats."

He was right. The folk of Long Meadows were loyal to Anlon Carmi, and while they had been grudgingly ready to accept me in his stead, since I had won the position in a highly orthodox manner, they would never accept anyone I forced on them outside the strictures of custom unless the other lords accepted him. The lords, I was finding, were not the staunch monarchists I had assumed. The distant rule of the king in King's City had suited them well, leaving them pretty much to their own devices. The Forest King had been a check upon their powers, as they had upon his. I sighed.

Dard leaned toward me, his eyes darkening. He laid a hand gently on my upper arm and traced lightly with his fingertips down the curve of my elbow. I shivered under his touch. "Anyway, I'm no longer willing to seek my pleasure wherever it may be found," he said so softly I had to lean forward to hear him. "There is no pleasure for me but in your presence, Tevra." Easily, gently, he leaned forward and kissed my mouth.

Gods, how I wanted him! The sweet, sweet taste of his lips on mine, the faint scent of almonds, the feathery touches of his fingertips, the storm-darkness of his eyes swayed me as if I had been some pliant reed in the wind. Policy, good sense, duty, Hetwith's expectations jangled into disorder in my half-bespelled mind and spilled out like broken shards.

My body ached to press itself against him as tightly as our lips were pressed. When he slipped an arm behind me and gently pulled me toward him, I came willingly, raising my arms. I put one across his broad shoulder, fitting as neatly along his side as if I belonged there. With the other hand I traced the curve of his jaw, as softly as his free hand sought the fastenings of my tabard and the shirt beneath.

When at last his hand found the flesh beneath my shirt and cupped my naked breast, his breathing quickened and he broke the kiss, burying his face in the curve of my neck, kissing and nibbling while he fingered the erect nipple beneath his hand. I moaned in pleasure and stirred softly within his grasp, pressing my thigh against his hip. With my free hand I traced the perfect whorl of his ear, traveled down the great corded muscle of his neck, sought his chest and tangled my fingers in the soft golden hair.

"Tevra," he gasped, raising his face from my neck and nuzzling at my ear, "Tevra, let's go into the bedroom. Someone might come in suddenly, and, oh, Tevra, there's so much more we need to explore."

Gods! Someone might come in indeed! Hetwith might walk in any minute! I sat bolt upright and yanked my tabard into position, sliding away from him along the sofa, panting still from an excess of desire. Moving away from him didn't lessen the sexual power he held over me; if anything, it strengthened it, and the breast he had been so lovingly caressing throbbed with pleasure still where his fingers had lain. I longed to go with him into the enormous bed next door, to yield myself utterly to him, taking him into me for our mutual pleasure; but I dared not. Hetwith would find out, as sure as anything, and then he would leave. He would look at me with that disgusted expression and would ride away, transferred or resigned, his last memory of me that of an aging wanton. I couldn't bear that.

Dard looked at me in astonishment. "What is it, Tevra?" he asked anxiously. "Did I hurt you?"

"No, Dard, my dear. It was only that I realized that I was doing things I should not have permitted myself. I must apologize; that was inexcusable."

"Inexcusable? Oh, Tevra, come here. Let me hold you and love you and I'll soon help you to forget your fears."

To counteract the nearly overwhelming desire I felt to melt into his arms once more, I inched away from him. He watched me with hurt and bewilderment on his face. "I can't, Dard. If I've teased you, I'm sorry. The only excuse I can offer is that I'm so attracted to you that when you kiss and touch me I hardly know what I'm doing."

"I don't understand. You want me, and the Forest Gods know I want you. Are you apologizing for that?"

"No, I can't help that. I'm apologizing for letting you find out that I wanted you. We did very well as friends, but we can never be lovers, and it was stupid and cruel of me to let you believe otherwise."

He got up and moved over to the fireplace, where he leaned one hand against the mantel and stared down into the fire. I watched him; there was pain in his face, and a struggle with himself I only partly understood. I rose quietly. Either he would understand me and we could continue to be friends or he wouldn't and I would have made another enemy. There was nothing I could do about it now. I intended to soak away my agitation in my luxurious bath.

"Wait." His voice had a ring of command in it such as he had never used to me before. "Tevra, you owe me something—at least you owe me an explanation. And you'll do me the courtesy of hearing me out."

I stopped. "Very well," I said at last. "I don't blame you a bit for being angry. I'll admit that I've acted badly."

"I'm not angry. Don't apologize to me again. No man needs an apology for being desired by a woman he desires. Tell me why you think you have to deny us both the pleasure of loving one another."

I was abashed. There was no reason I could put into words. Could I tell him that I was afraid to stand before the king and admit that I had consorted with his enemy? Could I tell him that I feared my subordinate's unspoken censure? Could I tell him that I feared the intensity of my desire for him, and that he was just too handsome to trust? They sounded like balderdash even to me. He waited patiently, watching me intently. "There are reasons," I said at last. "Political reasons, practical reasons, reasons I can't find the words to explain. I can only ask you to accept them."

"I can't accept them if you don't explain them to me. I'm not as smart as you or Hetwith; I can only comprehend what I can feel. My feelings tell me that there is no real reason we can't become lovers. They say that if I were to kiss you and hold you once more, all your phantom reasons would melt away."

I straightened. "Honor is no phantom. Duty doesn't melt away, however much we might wish it to," I said evenly.

Dard looked inquiringly into my eyes, and I met his gaze with honest directness. He sighed. Moving slowly, giving me a chance to react if I chose, he put his hands on my shoulders and drew me into his embrace. He kissed me on the temple, a gentle, almost brotherly kiss. "Honor," he said sadly. "Duty. Those are very difficult motivations to argue with."

He drew me back to the sofa, and down upon it, and I went defeatedly with him. But he offered no overtly sexual caresses, seemingly content just to hold me, and I sighed and burrowed against his shoulder. I felt raw all over. For a long time, I was happy to remain where I was, deeply grateful that he didn't renew his sexual overtures, for I surely would have succumbed, and I knew that it would have been wrong to do so.

"I know why you're so frightened of loving me," he said at last. "Hetwith." I started guiltily. "You're afraid he'd be jealous, and you can't stand the thought of losing him."

"Of course he wouldn't be jealous," I said indignantly. "Why should he be? But he wouldn't approve. He knows as well as I do that a colonel on detached duty simply does not run her detachment into risk for mere pleasure's sake."

"What a lot of power you credit me with! How exactly does loving me put your whole detachment at risk? Are you afraid that I'll blast them into oblivion with some sorcerous spell to keep them from interrupting us?"

I couldn't answer him. Of course taking him into my bed wouldn't place the company in any danger as far as I knew. I turned my face farther into his neck. "Oh, Dard," I said sadly. "Don't torment me so."

"Do I torment you, my love? It's only fair. You've tormented me ever since I saw you standing in that glorious red dress at the ball. Another thing, my heart: I resent being referred to as 'mere pleasure.' I won't settle for mere pleasure from you. If I thought it was only a tumble in bed you wanted of me, I'd leave you alone gladly."

I thought guiltily that a tumble in bed was exactly what I wanted of him, but I was too cowardly to say so aloud. In any case, things had gone beyond the point of such simple solutions. If only I had obeyed my instincts in the first place, and invited him to spend the night with me after that first ball, the whole thing would have been over with by now and I could have gotten on with the business of governing. I would have had some happy memories to warm the long cold nights to come, too. I sighed again.

Suddenly I wanted desperately to talk the whole thing over with Hetwith. He would come up with some incredibly clever solution that would leave everyone happy and satisfied, I was sure of it. But how shocked the poor lad would be if I tried to confide in him! How improper it would be for him even to know I had ever had such lascivious yearnings! "You don't have any weaknesses," he had said to me at Anlon Carmi's dance, and it was important that he go on thinking so. No, it was impossible, and I was on my own.

"Tevra, what are you thinking about?" said Dard, his breath tickling my ear, and I blushed. He held me a little away from him and looked at me and grinned. "Aha," he said. "Were you thinking that if I came to you tonight after everyone was asleep, you wouldn't turn me away?"

"No," I said hastily. "I was wishing I had invited you to stay with me after the ball." Then I bit my lip. Under the circumstances that had been an exceptionally stupid thing to say.

He looked a little startled. "It's a mistake easily rectified," he said hopefully. Then his face grew pensive and I could almost see his brain laboring through the implications. "I don't wish you had," he said, his jaw set determinedly. "I told you, I want a lot more from you than a tumble in bed.

I'd never have known whether you wanted me or if the spell had worked too well."

Well! I wasn't the only one to say stupid things. I had him where I wanted him now! I had only to tear myself free, leap to my feet and wax indignant over his wizardly treachery, and the incident would be satisfactorily resolved. I could forgive him magnanimously, too, and leave him feeling grateful as well as guilty. I pulled away a little. "Spell?" I said, carefully.

It was his turn to flush. "Well, everyone thought it would be such a marvelous idea for me to overwhelm you with my wisdom and dignity, and I knew that a colonel from King's City, rich and beautiful and sophisticated, would never be impressed by a backwoodsman with nothing more than a few pitiful ancestral pretentions. So I used a spell."

I hadn't the heart for indignation and recriminations. "Oh, Dard. You mean all this is just a spell? Remove it immediately." I felt weary and disappointed.

He looked at me with surprise. "It didn't work. It was supposed to make you admire and respect me. I might as well have cast it on one of those pine trees."

"I did admire you. I thought you were the most magnificently handsome man I'd ever seen."

"You were supposed to admire my wisdom and courage."

"What a peculiar sort of spell!"

"Did you really think I was handsome?" he said wistfully.

"Of course I did. I still do. Doesn't everybody?"

"I'm afraid not. I expect I would have led a life of unrelieved virtue if it hadn't been for my rank. The women of the Forest prefer dark men with secret sorrows. Hetwith, for example, is much admired."

"Hetwith? How extraordinary. Fond as I am of him, I'd never have called him handsome."

"Thank you, ma'am," said Hetwith from behind me. "My face has never frightened any little children."

I sprang away from Dard as though he had suddenly turned into a poisonous snake, and even he recoiled a bit. Hetwith stood in the door from the head of the stairs, pinched and tired. He had his saddlebags draped over one arm.

"Hetwith, come to the fire. You look chilled to the bone," I said.

"It's cold out there. We're going to have to see about warmer cloaks for the troopers." He dropped his saddlebags over the arm of one of the chairs and sank in to it. Dard rose and began making a mug of mulled wine.

"What do you have to report of Gornan's situation? No, stay in your chair. Just give me an informal report for now." He had begun to rise in obedience to years of training to make his reports while standing at attention. He sank back gratefully.

"Yes, ma'am. Gornan's situation is secure. He's lost nine men, with seventeen injured." He paused. Dard handed him the hot spicy wine. "He's set up as a subsidiary house to Woodsholme, with himself as householder. There are women there, and children, and they spin dog-fur yarn and collect chestnuts. Some evenings they have a party and all get roaring drunk, and I'd say there were going to be more children in about nine months. All the women belong to all the men, and they've been hunting and have enough food stored away for the worst winter you could imagine. It's like something out of the old tales, with drinking and singing and wenching. I wouldn't have believed it if I hadn't seen it."

"Where did the women come from? Did they kidnap them?"

"I don't see how they could have. The women are just as rowdy as they are and look like they're enjoying the drinking and singing and wenching more than the men."

"They sound like real throwbacks to the days of settlement," said Dard. "Our ancestors were mercenaries and reivers; they came here when civilization began to return to the Kingdom. They held their women in common. Our modern dances and balls are just pale imitations of the orgies they used to hold."

"Well, I'd bet those old-timers were pale imitations of what's going on at Gornan's house. They're happy, though, and they're killing so many supernaturals they've had to dig huge pits to bury the carcasses in. Gornan estimates at least two hundred. The only thing they like better than partying is fighting supernaturals."

"What will the effect of all this be on the Forest Folk?" I asked Dard.

"I don't think they'll have room for all the women that want to join them, or men either."

"Really? I'd think the women would be afraid. I can see that men might like it."

Dard and Hetwith glanced at each other, passing some message incomprehensible to me between them. "Some women," explained Dard gently, "like having a variety of sexual partners, just as some men do not. There are some vestiges of the old custom even today; though most people are paired, when they do change partners, it's usually within the house where they live, and all the children, even though they know their fathers perfectly well, are house children of the householder and House children of the lord."

"They're certainly free of guilt or shame," commented Hetwith. "They're as free and open about their pleasures as animals. I think Gornan and his cutthroat company have found their true niche in life."

"It sounds pretty debauched to me," I said pensively. "I'd feel better if I knew the women weren't being forced into complaisance. I suppose I'll have to go inspect the situation myself."

"No!" chorused Dard and Hetwith. "You wouldn't like it, ma'am," said the latter. "They're rather unabashed about their recreations."

"And they'd probably expect you to take part," added Dard.

"There's no point putting yourself in a position where you're going to feel obliged to take official recognition of their less conventional activities. They're doing what you wanted done, and if any of the women were being forced, you'd have heard about it before now."

I had to laugh at the pair of them. "I assure you that I'm not easily shocked. I have a responsibility to those people."

"Yes, ma'am, you are easily shocked. And I've been to some of the sleaziest bordellos in the river cities and I was shocked," said Hetwith firmly.

"Have you really?" asked Dard interestedly. "I'd like to hear some of the stories you could tell." So would I have, but I wasn't about to admit it.

"Once we get that other little matter straight between us, I'll be glad to tell you some evening," offered Hetwith.

"Once that's settled," said Dard, with a grin, "you won't be speaking to me."

"Oh, I know how to be a magnanimous winner," said Hetwith, grinning back.

I looked from one to the other of them, and made a startling discovery. They liked each other! Then why were they so antagonistic? "Gentlemen," I said sharply, "it isn't considered polite to leave the colonel out of the conversation."

"No, ma'am," said Hetwith.

"What is this 'other little matter' you mentioned?"

"It's personal," said Dard. "I wouldn't discuss it with you, and I know you're too tactful to try to force Hetwith to."

"I wish you two got along together better. My two most valuable subordinates, and you fight like two cats in a sack except when you're ganging up on me."

"The problem will be settled soon," said Dard. Hetwith suddenly grew very still. He gave Dard a long level stare and Dard looked blandly back at him. Ha! I thought. That's it. They have a bet on about whether Dard can seduce me, or something of that nature. I remembered hearing Dard tell

Hetwith that he meant to have me, but I hadn't heard what went on just before—and Hetwith had accused Dard of using unfair tactics at Anlon Carmi's ball. For a moment red rage flashed at the back of my eyes. Then it ebbed, leaving me feeling a little sick and very alone. I had thought better of them, especially Hetwith.

"Well," I said wearily, "Hetwith, you'll want a hot bath and a change. Dard, we have work to do."

That night, as I lay in my little corner of the huge bed, wondering if Dard would come and what I would do if he did, footsteps in the hall brought me wide awake. I heard a sharp whisper.

"Where do you think you're going?"

"I thought I'd make certain Tevra didn't need anything."

"She doesn't need anything you have to offer."

"Shouldn't you let her decide that?"

"Probably I should, but I'm not going to. Be careful! This saber might slip and give you a nasty cut."

I arrived at the door of my bedroom and opened it. I had expected the corridor to be dark, but since both Dard and Hetwith held oil lamps, it was well illuminated. "What's going on out here?" I demanded, in my querulous never-wake-the-colonel voice.

"Ah, nothing, ma'am. I just heard a disturbance and came to investigate," said Hetwith.

"Go back to bed. Both of you," I grumped, and closed the door firmly. Then, following my own advice, I grinned as I snuggled beneath the blankets. Hetwith wasn't going to make it easy for Dard!

chapter
11

There were a lot of strangers about Woodsholme in the next few days. With winter threatening, anyone who had business away from their own houses made haste to take care of it. Most of the apartments kept by the various lords were in use, and I had to put three troopers to helping Jevan deal with the rush of business. The Rangers came in, those who dared to have their writs of outlawry reviewed, and I was busy revoking them. Hetwith collected information from Rangers and visitors, and Dard was kept busy with maps and records. Garabed found it necessary to set up the long tables in the great hall to feed all the people. It seemed to me to be politically wise to mingle with the Forest Folk at mealtimes, and Dard agreed.

Only Hetwith's quickness saved my life.

At lunchtime one day I was standing near one of the fireplaces—I gravitated to them now that the weather was colder—chatting inconsequentially with some younger folk from Aspenhall, when I noticed a nondescript man dressed in hunting buckskins looking fixedly at me. It was not a friendly stare, and I shifted uncomfortably, but I attached no importance to the smaller muffled figure next to his. I turned back to the visitors from Aspenhall. When the hunter raised both hands, curving them as if gathering something out of the air, muttering at the same time, I caught the movement out of the corner of my eye, and the gesture was so sudden, and his glare so malevolent, that I dropped my hand to the hilt of my saber.

His smaller companion had edged closer. Suddenly I felt trapped. I have had just such feelings when circumstances have forced me to lead my command through unknown enemy territory. I stepped away from my guests to give myself room to draw my saber, when the man flung the invisible substance he held right at me. A paralyzing coldness struck me, ripping the breath from my lungs, freezing my joints, and crushing me to the stone floor, my muscles uncontrollable. The smaller figure flung aside the cloak that had hidden it. Princess Morir-Alsis-Alina stood over me with death in her eyes and a distorted grin of pure malicious triumph on her soft pink mouth.

I struggled to move, but I could only stir as feebly as a babe. The power of movement had been taken from me, and sensation as well, so that I couldn't even tell if my fingers still rested upon my saber hilt or had fallen away. Horrified, I watched her raise the slender wavy-bladed knife she carried above my defenseless body, pausing to gather her strength before she thrust it into my flesh. I felt death reaching out bony arms to take me as the knife flashed toward my heart.

There was a singing whistle in the air. A bright cavalry saber flashed. The Princess's hand was struck from her wrist, still clutching the deadly knife, and she shrieked in rage as the bright blood fountained from the severed stump. Hetwith, extended impossibly far, cannoned into the side of the fireplace, caught himself, straddled my body protectively, and looked about for another foe.

People were standing shocked, and the princess screamed and screamed. Dard appeared out of the crowd, seized her wrist in his two hands, and squeezed with all his strength to stop the flow of his sister's bright blood. Someone else fluttered about with a scarf to use as a tourniquet. On the marble floor the hand twitched.

Feeling and control were beginning to seep back into my limbs. I managed to lever myself onto my elbow, and Hetwith reached down with his left hand, scooped me up and propped me against him in the curve of his arm. His right still held the bloody saber as he swung me toward the grand staircase that led to my office and quarters. Troopers were beginning to stream into the hall now. Hetwith backed me toward the staircase.

"I can walk on my own," I hissed. "But my fingers are too stiff to hold a saber."

"Stay behind me," he ordered curtly, releasing me. I swallowed my reaction at being given orders by a captain and did as I was told. In this emergency, unsure how badly I had been affected by the spell, at least one more assassin about, Hetwith was acting with complete correctness to assume command, and my best policy was to back his move in any way I could.

The nondescript man in the hunter's costume appeared out of the milling, gabbling crowd on our left. There was a humming sound like a distant hive of bees. A huge glob of the grayish stuff that had made up the "ghost" of Eyvind was clutched tenuously between his outstretched hands, which leaped and jerked as if containing some mighty force. He screamed something unintelligible and hurled the stuff at me. Hetwith, quick as a panther, leaped in front of me, shielding me with his own body.

My muscles were still half-paralyzed, chilled and slow, and I couldn't force them to move fast enough to help him. I watched in nightmarish horror as the gray stuff struck him in the chest and clung to him, spreading over his body. He staggered, clawing at it without being able to grasp it. His saber rattled away on the stone floor; he clutched at his face, gasping as the gas thickened there. He lurched and struggled and sank to the floor as I fought with my deadened limbs to go to him. Then troopers were there, surrounding us, lifting his limp body, supporting me, hustling us both up the stairs, grim-faced and alert.

They put me in a chair by the fireplace and wrapped me in blankets, for my body still radiated a deadly cold. Hetwith they carried away down the corridor, presumably to his quarters. Several of them placed themselves on guard at the doors and windows, while others bustled about. I sat in my chair and struggled to regain control of my physical machine. My whole body began to prickle with the kind of pins and needles that come from restored circulation, and the bitter cold soaked inward toward my core, making me shiver until the heavy chair I sat on rattled. I gritted my chattering teeth and opened and closed my fists to pump the icy blood faster, and begged my own troopers to tell me if Hetwith were alive.

"Yes, ma'am," they told me. "He's alive..." and they looked at me strangely.

"Send for the healer!" I ordered, but they already had.

"She'll come as soon as she can," a young trooper told me. "She's with the Princess now."

"Then I'll go to him," I said, and struggled to my feet. They would have liked to have stopped me, but none of them dared. They contented themselves with drawing their sabers and escorting me as I shambled down the hall, shedding blankets because my fingers were still too stiff to hold onto them.

Two troopers were holding Hetwith's unconscious body down, while he moaned and twitched and tried to thrash about. As I came up to his bedside, a great red welt formed across his face, though no blow was struck, and he cried out in pain and rage. Even as we watched, the welt puffed up and then shrank and faded, and a great bloody gash opened on his chest and then closed and healed again, and he whimpered in terrible despair while tears squeezed from his closed eyelids.

I sank down on the bed beside him, grasping his hands between my frozen hands. "Hetwith!" I called. "Hetwith! Come back! That's an order, captain."

"We tried calling him, ma'am," said the trooper I had displaced. "He can't hear you."

"Hetwith, please come back," I called, softly but with all the intensity I could force into my croaking voice. "Please, I need you, Hetwith."

"Cold, so cold," he moaned. But he quietened beneath my touch.

"I want Lieutenant Ordent here," I said crisply. "Trooper, you find out what's happening downstairs. You, over there, find out how the Princess is and how soon the healer can come."

There was a chorus of "Yes, ma'am's" as the designated troopers scattered. In a very few minutes I had the salient facts. The situation downstairs was under control; the folk were upset and frightened but there was no panic or signs of general insurrection. The healer was tying off arteries in the princess's stump; she was expected to live, although she was very weak from shock and loss of blood and had made herself even worse railing against me. Dard was with her.

The company was alert and ready for trouble, but the sorcerer who had helped the princess to attack me was not to be found. Ordent had very competently set up sentries at all the entrances to Woodsholme, as well as at the foot of both sets of stairs leading to our quarters.

Hetwith continued unconscious. He seemed to know whether I was near, for he immediately grew restless if I tried to leave, so I had some of the troopers draw up a comfortable armchair next to his bed where I established myself and my blankets. There was nothing I could do but watch helplessly as the strange stigmata appeared on Hetwith's body and then faded or healed with unnatural speed.

Ordent came and went, bringing me situation reports. I gave my orders from Hetwith's bedside and struggled with my own debility. Jenny appeared with a mug of hot soup and fed it to me. I got up to walk about the room, hoping to hasten the loosening of my muscles, and Hetwith cried out in wordless horror at something only he could see. When I stumbled stiffly back to his bedside and took his hand in my icy ones he quieted.

The Princess's hand came crawling on its fingers past oblivious troopers, but when I cried out and they came to take it away, it vanished in a flurry of gray. I was beginning to feel like a spooked colt—as though everything were dissolving into chaos and terror and I must run and scream. But Hetwith seemed to sense my panic out of the depths of his unconsciousness and muttered restlessly, so I quelled the feeling and made myself do the cavalry exercises in my head, both the individual and the company evolutions, as well as the clumsy regimental maneuvers. This old familiar routine was wonderfully calming, and once again Hetwith responded to my mood and seemed to rest.

It was nearly dark when the door closed and I looked up. Dard stood over us, his face gray and grim and his clothes spattered with darkened blood.

"How is your sister?" I asked, watching him warily. I knew she was alive and expected to live, but I didn't know whether Dard would blame Hetwith for maiming her—it must have been horrible for him to see his lovely young sister mutilated.

"She's resting. The healer is staying with her. I came to see about you and Hetwith."

"I'm starting to come back to life. But I'm worried about Hetwith. He hasn't regained consciousness and he seems to be having terrible nightmares. Welts and wounds appear on him and then fade—I've never seen anything like it."

Dard bent over him and lightly dragged his fingers over his forehead. "Hetwith!" he called sharply. There was no response. He laid his hand over our two clasped ones. "Does he seem to know whether you touch him or not?"

"He seems easier if I stay near and speak to him. When I get panicky, he seems frightened too."

"Let go for a moment. Ah, I see." When I released Hetwith's hand, he stirred and moaned.

Dard took my freed hand in his. "You're cold; the ice-spell hasn't worn off yet."

"What about Hetwith?"

"Wait. Come away a little." Dard helped me to my feet and drew me away from the bed. Hetwith thrashed, groping vainly for my hand. Then he began to gasp as if running a race, sweat breaking out on his brow, straining with desperation, as his limbs twitched. "All right," said Dard. "Go to him. Call him. Say, 'Come to me, Hetwith; you'll be safe here.'"

Puzzled, I obeyed, but when I would have taken Hetwith's hand again, Dard guided my two hands to either side of Hetwith's face and held them there, covered with his own. As I called the words he told me to say, he murmured some doggerel under his breath, and I felt as if some current of energy were being directed from him to Hetwith through me. Hetwith gasped, then clutched at me desperately, as if he were falling and I were his only support. But the treatment seemed at least to bring him out of his nightmare, if not to himself. "Tevra," he moaned, "Tevra. Don't leave me here."

"I won't, Hetwith, I'm right here. Come to me! Hetwith! Hetwith!"

Dard sank down on the foot of the bed. "It's no good. He can't get out by himself."

"Out of where?"

"Out of the overmind. The second spell that was flung at you, the one he blocked, was meant to send you into the overmind, where you were intended to go mad with fear and shock. Alina told me. She bragged about it."

"I don't understand. You're talking as if Hetwith were somewhere else."

"In a way he is. All wizardry and most sorcery depends upon the collective unconscious, the racial memory . . . I shouldn't tell you this."

"Dard, if I need to know it to help Hetwith you'd better tell me."

He looked broodingly at me. "I only hope Hetwith can be helped. Well, the substance of the collective unconscious is infinitely malleable by a wizard's will. A wizard made that ghost of Eyvind that attacked you out of the stuff of the overmind, and those snakes I provided for Gornan were made of it. In the real world, it's nearly nonexistent. But when a human consciousness enters into the overmind, it has no way to tell whether the sensations it receives are real or illusory. A wizard's will can set up a little universe there with any characteristics he wants it to have. From what you tell me, I'd say the one Hetwith's trapped in, the one that was intended for you, is a particularly nasty one."

"Well, then, get him out."

"I can't, not without going in after him. He's too far in and he doesn't trust me enough to come when I call. I imagine the place is set up so he'd have to do something pretty terrifying to come to me—that's how I'd set it up."

"You said a wizard's will could change conditions there."

"Yes, but it isn't easy to change another wizard's universe. It's likely to do more harm than good. If I were to destroy the universe he's in, he'd find himself floating in absolute nothing, with no sensation to orient him. It only takes a few seconds of that to destroy a man's mind beyond repair."

"Dard," I said evenly, "quit trying to frighten me and tell me what we can do to help him. I don't want to be told that we have to just leave him."

"I'll have to go in after him." His face was pinched with—I realized—fear. It was evidently no small thing to venture into the overmind to bring someone out.

"I'll go—after all, he's my officer and my responsibility."

"No! You aren't trained. You'd get lost too, and Alina's malicious little plot will have succeeded."

I looked at him consideringly. A good officer learns to gauge her troopers' courage as she does their strength and endurance, and not to put more strain on any of these than they can bear. "I won't order you to do it, Dard. You understand the risks better than I do. What alternatives are there?"

He shook his head. "None. He'll go mad and eventually die if I don't get him out. The danger is that the wizard who cast the spell may be stronger than I. If he is, I'll be caught in the overmind too."

"Don't you know?"

"No. Some wizards enjoy pitting their strength against others, but I never have. And anyway, I'm only a wizard by courtesy because the Forest King was expected to know all the spells."

"Are you willing to take such a risk for Hetwith, since you never got along? Do you hate him for crippling your sister?"

Dard looked away from me suddenly. "I respect Hetwith, even if I don't exactly like him. Alina wouldn't have gotten hurt if she hadn't been trying to kill you, and using unfair means, too. We're rivals, Hetwith and I, but I wouldn't leave him to go mad."

"Will you help him, then?"

"Yes," he said with sudden decision. "You'll have to help me find my way out."

"Tell me what to do."

He walked over and lay down beside Hetwith. "Give me a couple of hours. Then start calling us both." He held out his hand, and I moved to sit beside Hetwith, where I could hold his hand and also reach across his body to hold Dard's.

"Emotional appeals will reach us more strongly than orders or logical reasons. The collective unconscious is not a reasonable thing." He slipped easily into the same unconsciousness that held Hetwith.

What a very long time two hours can be! As soon as Dard entered the overmind, Hetwith became as still and cold as death, and I thought he had died until I saw the pulse fluttering in his throat. Dard, too, was as lifeless as a corpse. I feared that it meant that Hetwith, not realizing that Dard had come to help him, had fled farther into the mysterious realm that held him prisoner. Neither returned my grip upon their hands or gave any sign of knowing that I was there. But at least the stigmata no longer appeared on Hetwith's body.

I grew cramped and tired and even colder, but I dared not let go of their hands for fear of losing one or both of them forever. I found that I had to lie partly across Hetwith's body. My muscles would no longer support me above it, though I feared I was interfering with his breathing, which was extremely shallow even without my weight on his chest.

I studied Hetwith's face, relaxed now as if in sleep, wondering whether I had told the truth when I had said that he wasn't handsome. I could see that young women might find it attractive. It didn't match any ideal of masculine beauty. But it was a good face, strong without brutality, sad without bitterness, with an appealing sensitivity about the lips. Quite without deciding to, I leaned down a few inches and tenderly kissed those softly curving lips.

Then I drew back, aghast at myself. Gods, what a disgusting thing to do! To take advantage of Hetwith's unconsciousness, unconsciousness that he had suffered in defending me, to misuse him so! Hot shame washed over me, and in my guilt I groped for some excuse. I was tired and overwrought; no harm had been done; he would never know. But they only made it worse. There was nothing that could excuse my action. How thinly covered by civilized morality is the primitive depravity in each of us! And how mortifying it was to discover that I was no better than the overtly perverse officers I had always condemned!

While I struggled with my shame, the second hour dragged past, and at last I began to call to Hetwith and Dard. I begged them to come to me. I told them I needed them. Mindful of Dard's instructions, I told them both that I loved them and missed them, and all the while I poured all the feeling I could muster into the summons, sternly suppressing the guilt I felt, for it seemed to me that they would hardly want to come to me if they knew what had happened. It seemed forever before there was any response, but at last Dard groaned and opened his eyes, and Hetwith too stirred and I felt him clutch at my hand.

Dard sighed heavily and spoke. "It's all right; he came out with me. What a vicious place that wizard created!"

"Are you all right?"

"Yes. Look to Hetwith. He'll need comforting and reassuring. He didn't have the advantage of knowing that all those terrible things were creations of one twisted mind."

"Thank you, Dard. Thank you for saving him."

"Thank yourself. He never would have come with me if you hadn't kissed him."

I flinched and flushed scarlet. "You and he knew when I did that?" I asked faintly.

"It was the only touch of cleanness in a perverted world of corruption," Dard said. He sighed again. "I have to sleep now. Hold Hetwith. Reassure him over and over that he's safe and that you're really you and not some illusion. Touch him; he'll need to feel as well as see and hear you..." His voice trailed off and he began to breathe evenly—asleep before he could finish his thought.

"Hetwith!" I said. "Wake up!"

"I'm awake," he said weakly. "Where are you, colonel?"

"Right here on your chest. I'm holding your hand. It's all

right, Hetwith, you're safe. Open your eyes and you'll see me."

He felt for me with his free hand, touching my shoulder. When he had established contact, he cautiously opened his eyes. "Don't leave me, ma'am," he said, shutting them again.

"I won't, Hetwith. You're safe now. All that you thought you saw and heard and felt was just an illusion. Rest now. I'm here."

Hetwith seemed to relax. After a while he asked drowsily, "Why are you so cold?"

"Dard called it an ice spell. The wizard cast it on me just before the princess attacked me. You saved my life, Hetwith."

"I'm glad. You saved my sanity, so we're even."

"I'm glad too, Hetwith. Rest now."

"I will. Come closer, ma'am, and I'll warm you."

I look at him doubtfully, but there was nothing but peace and exhaustion on his face, and Dard had said to stay with him. I bent my stiff fingers around the blankets that had mostly slipped off and pulled them up to cover all three of us. Then I stretched out by Hetwith's side and burrowed gratefully against his warmth.

"Rest, Hetwith," I whispered. "You'll be safe with me here."

He didn't answer, but his lips curved in a tiny contented smile. Then his breathing steadied and he was asleep.

chapter

12

Winter settled over the forest. Blizzard after blizzard howled down from the north, piling up the snow in huge drifts, leaving an iron coat of ice over everything. Woodsholme, as beautiful and luxurious as it was in the summer, was poorly designed for the harshness of winter, and the reasons for the thick walls and tiny windows of the log houses became obvious. There seemed to be no place in Woodsholme without a draft when those mighty winds swept across it. The fires burned constantly, but the warmth dissipated within a few feet of the liveliest fire.

I suffered bitterly from the cold, never having really warmed up from the ice spell cast on me by Princess Morir-Alsis-Alina's strange accomplice. At the same time, while the life of the Forest Folk slowed around me to a lazy winter crawl, I felt restless and ill-at-ease. I had kept Spider when the other horses were sent south, along with several of the stoutest horses for courier duty, and I rode to the nearest houses every time the weather cleared.

The forest, I found, could be beautiful in the winter, too, but it was an eldritch beauty, more inimical to humanity than the searing deserts of the far south. I heard the crack! of tree trunks split by the terrible cold, a sound one could hear for miles in the incredible silence of the winter-bound woods. I saw the stately stags, their antlers dropped after the fall rutting season, reduced to a diet of twigs and bark, stare in astonishment at me as if wondering what foolish human could be abroad in this cruel season. I saw the diamond sparkle of the sun on the snow, more brilliant than the gentler colors of summer, so that the eyes itched and smarted after a few hours in its inhuman glow.

Dard sank into winter torpor along with the rest of the Forest Folk, and would have been content to sit in front of the fire, wrapped in blankets and swapping tales. Nevertheless, he conceived his duty to be to escort me wherever I chose to go, because the supernaturals of winter, he said, were far more dangerous than those which ranged the summer woods. He dragged himself out of his warm cocoon, strapped long polished wooden boards to his feet, and kept pace with Spider, who had to lunge and plow though snow up to her knees and sometimes her belly, while he glided smoothly over the top.

I felt guilty at routing him out of his comfort, and I was aware that I was taking unnecessary risks to ride abroad in the depths of winter, but since the attack by the princess, I had been tormented by the memory of the kiss I had placed upon Hetwith's unconscious lips and by a feeling that the Forest Province was uneasy in its quiescence. I found no evidence of unrest, but I could not make myself easy.

I had awakened before either Hetwith or Dard, the morning after the attack, and had slipped from the bed where we had all slept tumbled together like a basket of puppies. By the time they roused, I was bathed and dressed and immersed in my usual morning routine. Hetwith had never referred to the kiss, and I was too ashamed to ask him if he remembered it; after that, whenever we were alone together, I contrived to be very busy with reports and maps and plans.

Dard had made several tentative attempts to renew the intimacy of those few moments in the fall, but I expertly headed him off before the thought had more than crossed his mind, and long before he could commit himself to an attempt at seduction. As if the cold of the spell had struck inward to the core of my sexual being as well as my physical one, I no longer felt any desire for him or anyone. It was as if the gentle touches I had found so sexually stimulating in the summer were now armored with sandpaper and rasped unbearably. After seeing me flinch away from the lightest of caresses several times, Dard tactfully kept a little distance between us. I worried a little about this condition, for I had always been a healthy female, as easily aroused as any, even during those long periods when I chose to live celibate. I wondered dismally if the condition might not prove permanent, and I would be doomed to feel only cool aversion for the most attractive men. But there didn't seem to be much I could do about it if it were so.

After one short spell of relatively good weather, when I had ventured to Long Meadows House to make sure the people there had plenty of supplies for the rest of winter, an endless series of storms settled over the Forest Province. There was no question of getting out of doors.

I set myself to the task of reorganizing my files one day when the wind howled about the walls of Woodsholme, bringing with it the faint eerie cries of snufflers. These semi-material supernaturals swam upon the wind, feeding upon heat. Their thin wind-borne cries alerted other of their kind to a source of warmth, and they were naturally attracted to Woodsholme, which leaked heat at every window and door. They made venturing outside really hazardous, aside from the dangers of frostbite and becoming lost in the blizzard. I once saw a corpse brought in from which the body heat had been sucked by snufflers. It was literally as solid as if it were a carven statue, and when they laid it on the stone floor, it clattered.

I hated to hear the things fluttering and snuffling at the

window panes. I kept the curtains firmly drawn across the windows. Unfortunately, the only warm spot in my office was directly in front of the fireplace, between the two windows. I had carried a huge stack of files to the couch, where I had spread them about me and was busy sorting them, when Dard entered.

"We'll have to set up one of the empty bedrooms as a records room," I told him, putting a stack of papers on the save-and-store pile. "The cabinets are getting full."

"There's more paperwork to ruling a province than you'd expect, isn't there?" he said, moving a stack of papers to the floor and sitting.

I glanced at him. He was pensive and serious, almost grim. "What's the matter?" I asked.

"I've been thinking about next spring," he said.

"So have I. How do you think the folk in the outlying houses are doing?"

"We were more prepared for this winter than last, thanks to your relief supplies. I expect they're all right."

"We can't continue to count on relief supplies. We'll have to think of a way for the folk to earn the money to buy grain from the plains."

"The folk have always been independent of the rest of the Kingdom, relying on the products of the forest to live."

"There don't seem to be enough products from the forest for all the folk."

"I've been thinking about that." Dard looked at me speculatively for a moment. Evidently he decided to confide in me, for he continued, "One of the responsibilities of the Forest King was to keep the population of the folk within the limits that the forest could support. He limited the number of children born by delaying the exchange of women, sometimes for years, and he could refuse permission for subsidiary houses to be built. When there began to be a surplus, he was likely to stir up trouble on the borders, so that some of the extra people were killed. My grandfather, in fact, had just that sort of problem when he attacked the Kingdom and found that he'd stirred up more trouble than he could handle. Once the forest became a province of the Kingdom, there was no longer any control of population growth; the royal governors didn't understand the problem. They encouraged early exchange of women, and the building of new houses, and they put a stop to the old custom of female infanticide."

"Female infanticide! I should think so!"

"Oh, it was a cruel custom. No one liked exposing their newborn daughters, and my father told me many times that if the Forest King was doing his job it wasn't necessary. There's a legend that the snufflers are the hungry, vengeful spirits of the baby girls who died alone and abandoned in the snow." He paused and glanced toward the window where the creatures snuffled and cried about the edges of the frames. He shuddered, and I found it hard to imagine the gentle Dard condoning that terrible practice. "The mothers always had a spark of hope, you know, for sometimes when the men went to bury the little corpse, they found nothing, as if the baby had been rescued by some supernatural agency."

"The bodies were carried away by animals," I said angrily.

"No doubt, but if it were your baby, wouldn't you prefer to believe that it might have been adopted and raised by some unknown creature?"

"If it were my baby," I blazed, "and anyone came to take it away from me and leave it in the snow to die, the problem of surplus population would have been solved before the would-be murderers laid a hand upon it."

Dard smiled. "I can imagine, but most of our women are not so fierce or so well-armed as you are. Don't upset yourself; as I said, the custom has been suppressed, and I don't think that any old custom was ever surrendered more thankfully."

I relaxed and grinned ruefully. "I'm glad; suppressing it's

no doubt one of the first things I'd have done. You were saying that at the time the Forest Province was annexed into the Kingdom, the population was already too high to be comfortably supported by the forest and that the policies of the governors made the problem worse?"

"Yes, and I believe that that's why we have been afflicted with famine, disease, and supernatural predation in the last few years. Our population has grown beyond the ability of the land to support it and nature is restoring the balance."

"I see. It certainly sounds reasonable. We need a program to increase the productivity of the forest lands. I'll look into raising the minimum age for exchange of women, too."

"I'm afraid it's too late. Long before such programs could have had much effect, hundreds of people will have died."

"Then what do you suggest?"

He hesitated, a troubled look on his face. "Tevra," he said at last, "you're completely loyal to your king, I know, and I honor you for it."

"I won't permit an insurrection, if that's what you mean."

"I had in mind taking a few thousand of the folk and leaving the Kingdom altogether."

I stared at him. "Where would you go?"

"North. When I was young I was restless. I spent all of one year exploring the northlands. I found a place where the forest comes down to the sea. It was incredibly rich country. A large number of people could live there in luxury. The sea is full of fish and shellfish. The forest teems with game. Fruits and nuts that are rarities here, grow in huge brambles and groves."

"Dard, the winters are harsh enough here. What are they like farther north?"

"Along the coast, surprisingly mild. I wintered there in a cave by the sea, and there was never a heavy snowfall. Lots of rain, but seldom even ice on the ponds. The sea was warm enough to swim in even in midwinter. There's a strong current from the south, and occasionally I found coconuts and other tropical plants drifting into the shingle. It's a beautiful place, too, with a waterfall coming out of the mountains that rise up from the shore. I'm sure a group of people could survive and even flourish there."

Slowly I said, "I see no reason why the king would object to such a plan. I might insist that you and your people swear never to attack the Kingdom or aid its enemies, but no one has ever been stopped from leaving the Kingdom if they chose. Have you picked your followers?"

"No, but I know who I'd approach with the scheme."

"Then wait a bit. I'll write to the king in King's City and tell him about the plan. Perhaps in return for guarantees of alliance he would be willing to acknowledge your claim to be Forest King."

Dard looked troubled. "Tevra, working with you I've found that there's a lot to being a king. I don't know that I can do it by myself."

"Of course you can. You were trained to be a king, after all."

"Until now I've been content to drift, claiming the privileges of royal blood but evading the responsibilities. Your coming changed that."

"I'm glad if my presence here has been useful to you, Dard," I said gently.

He looked into the fire for a time, seeming to brood. "What will happen to you when you go back to King's City?" he asked at last.

"The king told me I could expect some reward for my service here; it's possible that he means to give me command of a brigade. If not, I'm qualified for a regiment as soon as one becomes available."

"And then?"

"Well, in time I'll reach retirement age. I'll find some quiet little village where I can buy a cottage with a little pasture for my horses and live out my years as a minor local curiosity."

"What about Hetwith?"

"He has a brilliant future. He's been waiting to apply for his majority until just the right opportunity comes along, but once he does, he may well become a general or even Commander of the King's Armies. He has the ability."

"I've known him for nearly a year now and I never would have suspected him of ambition."

I paused doubtfully. It was true that Hetwith sometimes seemed to lack the hunger for advancement a junior officer needed to rise so far. "If he chooses to leave the military, his family is rich and influential. He could go as far as a merchant or in politics."

"You won't keep him with you, then?"

"If I get a brigade, I would certainly approve his application for major, and if he chose to apply for a position on my staff, I'd accept gladly and make him my tactical planner. But you can keep your best and brightest young officers with you only so long, and then for the good of the service you have to boot them out on their own. Hetwith has too much potential to waste his life commanding a company or on staff duty. He'll soon be yearning for a command of his own."

"Yours is a strange attitude. You're fond of Hetwith, and yet you've no wish to hold him."

"Fond isn't exactly the word. Hetwith is the most brilliant young officer I've ever had under my command. I admire his courage and his warrior's skills and frequently I'm astonished by his mental powers. I'll do anything I can to help him get on in the service because I believe in him—maybe more than he does himself. It isn't that I don't want to keep him with me. I'd gladly keep him as my second forever. But I have to consider first what's best for him, and if I get a brigade I'll have risen as far as I ever will. Colonel in command of one of my regiments is as high as my sponsorship will ever take him, and he deserves better than that."

"I see. Does he agree with your analysis of the situation?"

"Why, I've never talked it over with him. It seemed obvious enough."

"I'm not sure that's true. I think perhaps other things may be more important to Hetwith than the good of the service. They would be to me."

"Oh, well, you're a civilian and can't be expected to understand."

"I don't suppose so. Anyway, I talked my plans for going north over with him."

"You did? Why?"

"I thought he had a right to know that I intend to ask you to go with me as my queen and co-ruler."

I stared at him. Then I laid the stack of files carefully aside.

"I can't do it alone, Tevra," he said honestly. "I don't have any of that brilliance you admire so much in Hetwith. I can handle people but I get all confused when I try to make plans. I wind up making decisions based on feelings. I need you to help me and support me, and I need your son to be my heir."

"Dard," I said gently, "I'm a colonel of Light Cavalry."

"Don't say no yet. Let me finish, please. There's one more thing I've got to say ... you aren't going to like it, but you have to face it."

"What's that?"

"You're halfway to being in love with me. Before Alina's attack you were almost there. A woman needs a man to love, one who loves her back. I love you, Tevra. I worked out this scheme of going north and founding a new kingdom so I'd have something to offer you. Come with me."

"Dard," I said, more gently still, "forgive me, but I wasn't in love with you. I wanted you. That's a very different thing. I like you and enjoy your company, and for a while I lusted for you. But I don't want to go north with you and be your queen. Even if I were in love with you I wouldn't want that. I swore an oath when I became an officer and I can't, and won't, surrender my allegiance to my king."

He looked at me for a moment. "I don't understand you!" he cried despairingly. "You can't want someone you don't love. You can't love someone you don't want."

"You don't love me either, Dard. You see me as a solution to your problems. You're neither king nor commoner, and you're using me as an excuse to resolve that ambiguity. You don't even really want me, I'd guess. I think before I arrived everyone talked you into believing that you had to seduce me, and being a basically decent man, you couldn't endure the thought of doing it coldbloodedly. So you convinced yourself that you loved me and wanted me."

He rose suddenly, a violent movement. "No! Don't tell me how I feel! I'm not as smart as you or Hetwith, but I know more about feelings than the two of you together could figure out in years. You think, and he thinks, and neither one of you knows the first thing about how the other one feels, or cares as long as you've got everything reasoned out to suit you."

"Hetwith hasn't got anything to do with this discussion."

"I suppose you don't think so," he sneered.

"Dard, please. Your feelings are hurt, that's all. I'll tell you what: come to bed with me now, if you think you really want me. Once the desire is spent you'll understand what I mean."

He looked at me, drawing himself up so that he looked like a king. "Will you give yourself to me like you'd give a sweet to a fussy baby, just to keep me quiet? I told you before that I wanted more than that from you."

"It's all I have to give you."

To my surprise, he came over and sat down beside me again. I had expected him to storm out of the room, full of offended dignity. He had more courage than I had given him credit for. Taking my face gently between his hands, he looked deeply into my eyes, and I returned his gaze. I had been completely honest with him; not many men could have taken that bluntness, and I hoped that he would realize that I admired him for it, and respected him for what he was.

He sighed and his hands dropped away. "You haven't even that to give now, have you? If I took you up on your offer, it might be a pleasure for me, but it would be nothing at all to you. What happened?"

I looked away. "I don't know. It isn't you; you're as attractive as ever. Perhaps I haven't thawed yet from that ice spell."

"You have, long since. It only froze your muscles." Suddenly he laughed. "I know what it is. Poor Tevra!" He pulled me into a brotherly embrace, and I let my cheek rest on his shoulder.

"Well, what is it?" I asked presently. If my sexual desire for him had vanished, the comfort I found in his embrace had not.

"Embarrassment. Nothing but embarrassment."

"What have I got to be embarrassed about?" I asked indignantly.

"Kissing Hetwith when you thought he was unconscious."

My breath tangled itself in my throat and I could feel myself flushing so hotly my ears buzzed. I must have stiffened, too, for Dard began to rub my back gently, soothing me as if I were a fractious horse. "It wasn't such a terrible thing to do," he said after a time.

"You don't understand. A good officer just doesn't take advantage of her subordinates that way. It's a matter of honor, and of ethics. The kiss itself wasn't so terrible; it was that he had no way to defend himself from it."

"Do you think he would have defended himself from it if he had been able?"

"Probably he would have defended himself very capably, but that's not the point. He didn't dishonor himself, I did."

"But Tevra, you saved his life, and probably mine too. The kiss was the one thing that gave him courage to walk through the fire to me. The instinct that prompted you to kiss him was the soundest one you've ever followed."

"Oh, Dard, I didn't kiss him because I thought it would save him."

"Why did you kiss him?"

"Because..."

Dard waited patiently.

"Because of the way his mouth is shaped. No, that doesn't make any sense. Because I thought I could get away with it and no one would ever know. Because deep down under the civilization I have the same evil streak that makes women beat their babies to death and men rape little girls. I don't know."

"When you apologized, did he refuse to forgive you?"

I flinched. "I haven't apologized. I can't. I'm not even sure he remembers it."

"He remembers."

"Think how embarrassed he'd be."

"You're thinking how embarrassed you'd be."

"Why do you want me to apologize to Hetwith?" I counterattacked.

"I don't want you to apologize to Hetwith. I want you to fling yourself into my arms crying with gratitude and beg me to take you with me to the north country." I giggled weakly. "However, you're not going to feel that your honor's been restored until you do apologize. You can ask me any time you need to have your feelings explained to you. Or mine. But not Hetwith's; he's on his own."

"I'm proud to have you for a friend, Dard," I said.

"Plenty of people have made good marriages on less a foundation than that," he said wistfully.

"I offered..."

"I know what you offered. Don't do it again. I'm not made of iron. I'd rather have you proud to claim me for a friend than ashamed to admit that I was your lover."

I sighed. I regretted bitterly not having succumbed to Dard in the fall. He was a good man, a kind, strong, dependable man, in every way a lovable man. Maybe if I had taken him into my bed he would have made a place for himself in my heart as well. It was too late now. I had convinced him completely that I didn't love him, before I was entirely sure of it myself.

That evening after supper, as Dard and Hetwith and I passed through the office on our way to our quarters, I stopped Hetwith. "I'd like to talk to you for a moment," I said. "Come over to the fire." Dard was right. As painful as this was going to be for both of us, I had to apologize to Hetwith.

Dard, bidding us good night, went on to his room, and I unbelted my dress saber and dropped it at the end of the couch. It promptly slipped sideways to fall with a muffled clatter on the floor between the farther armchair and the end of the couch. I settled into the nearer chair in front of the dying fire.

"Fetch us a glass of wine if you like, Hetwith," I suggested. "This is a personal matter, not an official one."

Silently he brought glasses and wine, poured and handed me one, and then took his to the other armchair. I gazed into the glass, the ruddy firelight darkening the ruby wine and setting up wavering reflections in its depths. "I wanted to talk to you, Hetwith," I said at last.

"Yes, ma'am," he said woodenly.

"I suppose you know what it's about."

"I think so, ma'am." The room was nearly dark, the only illumination coming from the last flickering flames in the fireplace, but I could see that he was hunched into his chair as if expecting a blow. He was taking the matter of the kiss a lot harder than I had feared he would. It wasn't as if he had never been kissed before! Then I checked myself. This whole thing wasn't his fault, it was mine, and if he were taking it more seriously than I had thought then it was even more my responsibility to make it as right as I could.

I took a deep breath. "I want you to know how sorry I am," I said evenly.

"You don't need to apologize to me," he muttered sullenly.

I was a little startled by his response. "If not you, then who?" I asked. "After all, you were the victim."

He looked in my direction for the first time. "I wouldn't have considered myself to be a victim," he said, a note of anger in his voice. "But you have to admit that it isn't exactly fair. You've never even given me a chance."

"Hetwith," I said carefully, "are we talking about the same thing?"

"We are if you're about to tell me that you're going with Dard to be his queen."

"Certainly not! I was trying to apologize to you for... for..." I choked on the words. They just wouldn't come out.

"You're not going with Dard?"

"Of course not! I'm a cavalry officer. I swore the same oath you did. You can't think I'd forswear myself and go off just on any little whim."

"Er... no, ma'am. I didn't think about the oath."

"Well, do," I said sharply, and then realized that I was getting off the point. I groped around my mind, trying to find the right words to reintroduce the matter of the apology.

Before I could formulate an intelligible sentence, Hetwith guessed, "Then you must be thinking again that I'm disgusted by your weaknesses. I'm not. Anything you decide to do is all right with me. If anyone has anything to say about your behavior, he can address himself to me and I'll convince him it's none of his business in about a minute." This speech would have been amusing and a little touching if it were not for the defeated tone in which he uttered it. The words said that it was all right with him, but the tone said that he was deeply hurt by it. Whatever he thought "it" was.

"Hetwith," I said quietly, "you're upset by something. I'm trying to apologize for the only wrong I've done to you that I know of. This isn't easy for me and you're not making it any easier."

"I'm sorry, ma'am. I don't know of any wrong you've done me. I thought you must be planning to do something. I'll shut up and listen, if you like."

"Yes, please. You might not even remember, but I have to apologize."

"There's nothing you ever could have done to me that you need to apologize for," said Hetwith.

"Shabby behavior always dishonors the doer more than the victim, but still I owe you an apology."

"Are you talking about the time when I tricked you into signing leave papers and you changed the destination on them at the last moment and sent me to Eastend with a camel caravan?" There was a note of bitterness in his voice.

"Of course not. You deserved that thoroughly. I don't know why you wanted to go to Rainbow Lake, nor why you thought I wouldn't catch you if you made out leave papers for me at the same time, but you had to learn you couldn't manipulate me that way."

"You were too smart for me—it was too bad for both of us. You'd have gotten a surprise at Rainbow Lake."

"I'll bet I would have. You'd have been laughing all the way back to the fort. That's not what I wanted to talk about."

Hetwith sighed. "You find it hard to trust me, don't you, ma'am?"

"Hetwith, I'd trust you with my life—and have, several times. I'd trust you with my best war-horse. I'd take your word against any man's or woman's in the world, not excepting the king's own. I'd trust you with every last cent I owned, and throw in the shirt on my back. But I wouldn't trust you not to make a fool of me for the sake of a joke."

"We're even then, because I'd trust you with anything at all, except to pass up a chance to laugh at me."

"Hetwith!" I exclaimed. "When have I ever laughed at you?"

"I wish I knew. I've worked twice as hard as any other officer and bitten my tongue when my heart was breaking to avoid giving you a chance to call me 'this fine young gentleman' in that scornful tone of voice. And when I think of how you had the whole mess laughing at your imitations of some poor officer who'd been more than usually pompous, my blood runs cold. Did you imitate me when I wasn't around?"

"Certainly not."

"Not even when I got drunk and you had to get me out of jail in that little town on the plains?"

"Of course not. I told you what I thought of your behavior at the time—you may remember." He winced and nodded. "I never mentioned it again until this moment."

He hesitated. "You saved my life then, you know." His voice was so low I had to lean forward to hear him.

"Well, I'm glad," I said, startled. "I didn't think the jail was that bad."

"Not then, the next night."

I remembered. Hetwith had always been moody, but that time his mood had been truly abysmal. He had been drinking steadily for a week before he was jailed, and the time it took me to placate, threaten, and pay off enough officials in the little town to get him out had given him time enough to sober up. He had not appeared for breakfast the next morning, nor reported for duty, nor for supper. I had assumed that he was nursing a hangover of awe-inspiring proportions, put him on the casualty roster as sick, and sent my striker to him with some headache powders.

That evening, on my way to my quarters, I had seen him

sitting in a shadow on the steps of the headquarters building, such a dejected slump in his shoulders that my heart was wrung. I know very well that a man in his condition just wants to be left alone to nurse his sorrows in peace, but he had looked so lonely. I had walked over and sat down on the other end of the step, not close enough to crowd him, but close enough to be with him if he wanted company. I had not spoken, nor had he; we just sat there for nearly two hours, but I couldn't bring myself to leave. Eventually, he stirred, and I stretched my stiffened limbs and rose. "Up you come," I'd said cheerfully, drawing him to his feet by an elbow. "Things will look brighter after a good night's sleep. I hope you'll be better in the morning; I need you to help me." I'd steered him to the officers' quarters and turned him over to his striker to be put to bed, and then gone off feeling foolish, as if I'd wasted two good hours of sleeping time, no minor loss in those days of constant alarms and skirmishes.

I'd never known why he was sitting there. He hadn't been drinking again, as I'd first assumed; there'd been no bottle or smell of the stuff on him. Neither one of us had ever mentioned the incident until now—in fact, I'd almost forgotten it. The wild young Hetwith of those days had steadied and sobered, and though he had always had his times of dark self-doubt, he'd never sunk so deep, nor had he ever drunk himself sick again (though he'd had a good few wild carouses, from what I'd heard).

"I remember the incident, but I don't remember doing anything to save anyone's life," I told him.

He smiled wryly. "I don't suppose you would. I was going to kill myself as soon as . . . as soon as everyone had gone to bed. Then you came and sat with me. You sat with me until the time when I could have done it passed, and then you told me you needed me and took me off to my room. The next day you treated me like nothing had happened. I thought you ought to know."

"Why?" I asked, alarmed.

He smiled suddenly. I could see the curve of his lips highlighted for an instant by the glow of the fire. It brought back the memory of the kiss, and I could feel my face growing hot with shame again. "Before you felt you had to apologize for something you aren't even sure I would remember, I thought you ought to know that you saved my life once without knowing it."

Absurdly, I felt like crying. "Thank you, Hetwith. It makes it easier. I have to tell you that when you were struck by the spell that was meant for me, while you were unconscious. . . ." My throat was closing up again on me. I stuttered to a halt.

Hetwith sat quietly, waiting. At last he said softly. "Whatever it is, I accept your apology. I'd be willing to bet it bothered you a lot more than it would have bothered me."

I waved aside his acceptance. "I thought you were unconscious," I whispered.

He rose and came closer to me, seating himself on the arm of the couch next to my chair, leaning down to hear the half-choked whisper that was all I could manage. I couldn't look up at him. I knew I was blushing again. "I had to hold both your hand and Dard's—he told me to. To do that I had to lean on your chest and reach across you. I don't know what I was thinking of—I hope you believe that I wouldn't have done it if I'd had my wits about me, but that isn't any excuse. Anyway, I . . . I bent down and kissed you. I'm truly sorry." The apology done, I would have gotten up and made a dash for my room, but he was too close to me to permit a dignified rising.

He didn't make a joke of it. He didn't laugh. He didn't get angry. He just took the cold, sweaty hand that lay on the chair arm nearest to him and held it gently.

"I won't do it again," I said inanely, to break the silence.

"Colonel, if at any time in the future you find me unconscious, please feel free to kiss me all you want. I gladly grant permission, retroactively to include the last time." I looked suspiciously up at him. He was smiling, but not mockingly; I never would have suspected Hetwith of gentleness.

"Thank you, Hetwith," I sighed, "but considering all the misery that one caused I believe I'll give up kissing altogether. Why don't you pour us another glass of wine?"

Neither one of us had drunk much out of the first glass, but he went and got the wine and poured a few more drops in each glass. Then he put another log on the fire and settled himself in his armchair again.

We sat together for a while, sipping the wine and gazing into the renewed flames while we reminisced of old times. The companionship, the memories, and the wine slowly reforged the old easy relationship between us, and I knew that in the morning Hetwith and I would once again be the same smooth team we had always been. The knowledge comforted my troubled mind; I had not realized how terrified I had been of losing Hetwith until matters were mended.

Finally I rose wearily. "I'm for my bunk, Hetwith," I said. "Apologizing is wearisome work. No, don't get up. You look comfortable there. Good night." As I passed his chair, I stooped to pick up my saber; he looked up at me, and without meaning to, I met his glance. I felt the same impulse that had caused me to kiss him before; I swayed before I brought it under control. Confused, I hesitated, staring into his face.

"Pretend that I'm unconscious," he whispered.

I broke away from the intensity of his eyes and left with all the dignity I could muster. But it was a retreat, and I knew it.

chapter

13

The ice-protected peace of winter was shattered the next day. I had slept poorly and was late rising, and had hardly managed to get my day's work under way when an exhausted, bloody, frostbitten infantryman was brought to me. He was one of Gornan's unsavory company, but seeing the state he was in, I hurried to his side and supported him to a chair. "Dard," I barked, "fetch the healer." The prince departed at speed, and Hetwith came to help me with the reeling man.

"Report, soldier," I ordered. "What are you doing here in such a state?"

"We've been attacked, ma'am. A force of about two hundred and fifty insurrectionists came down on us at dawn yesterday. It was a guerrilla action—hit and run. We'd had an extra heavy encounter with supernaturals the night before, including some kinds we'd never seen before. We were caught unprepared. We weren't expecting a human attack, you see, ma'am. Most of us were still in our bunks." He paused and gulped. I nodded encouragingly. "Casualties were heavy," he continued. "Seventy-seven officers and men killed or mortally wounded. Captain Gornan's dead. The only officer left capable of command is Lieutenant Colpersan. He sent me to ask for relief and instructions. I was the least badly injured man left."

I surveyed the appalling condition of the soldier before me. He had a dozen minor wounds closed over with frozen blood. "Did you walk all the way from your garrison, soldier?"

"Yes, ma'am."

"There'll be a commendation in this for you. But first you need medical attention, a hot meal and a warm bed. Hetwith!"

"Yes, ma'am!"

"Alert the company. We're moving out in an hour. Full winter kit. Get Garabed to serve out a hot meal—double rations, and have another ready at midnight. We'll make the round-trip today."

"Today, ma'am? On foot? In three feet of snow? It's fifteen miles to Gornan's station!"

"Why do you think they attacked there first, if not to pull us away from Woodsholme? No, we've got to get there and back before it even occurs to them that we could be ready to move. They aren't military; they don't know what light cavalry can do."

"But thirty miles in the snow! Human beings can't do it. Especially not in leaky riding boots."

"We have to help our people there and we dare not leave Woodsholme unprotected for two days. You're right about the riding boots, though. Issue orders for any trooper that has them to wear waterproof boots. Uniform regulations are suspended for warm coats or cloaks, too. H'mm..."

"What is it, ma'am? You've got an idea; I can see the gleam in your eye."

"It depends. Where's Dard?"

"Here I am. I've brought the healer for your soldier and a couple of litter-bearers." He waved them forward and they carried the exhausted man away, the healer hovering anxiously.

"Dard, those board things you strap to your feet when you're traveling with me in the snow. How hard are they to learn to use?"

"Easier than riding a horse, at least just for traveling on a road."

"How many pairs could you round up in the next few minutes?"

"Most of the Forest Folk own at least one pair. I'd say a hundred or so could be easily found in Woodsholme."

"Good. Get them. Hetwith, we'll travel on those snow boards . . . all right, out with it. What have you thought of?"

Hetwith had been thinking, too. There was a grin of pure mischief tickling the corners of his mouth. As Dard hastened out to search for the snow boards, he drew me over to the large map of the Forest Province I'd tacked up on the wall. "You think the attack on Gornan's house was a feint to draw us out of Woodsholme, right?"

"How could it be anything else? Whoever controls Woodsholme, effectively controls the government of the Forest Province. We took advantage of that fact ourselves when we arrived. Besides, if our forces can be cut off from Woodsholme, we'll be cut off from our supplies, our horses, our equipment—in fact we'd be in a pretty pickle, with nowhere to go and nothing to eat. We'd have little choice but to retreat to the south, and by the time we could regroup, resupply and return, it would be spring and the rebels would be firmly entrenched. It would mean war. We'd have to call up at least a full regiment from King's City to retake the Forest Province. Hetwith, we've got to hold on to Woodsholme."

"Yes, ma'am. But we also need to quash this rebellion before it gets out of hand. We may not have any other base to operate from, but the rebels no doubt have hundreds. We've got to hit them hard, and soon. What better place than here at Woodsholme?"

"I think I begin to get your drift," I said slowly. "They're all set to come marching in as soon as we dash off to the relief of Gornan's outfit."

"Right, ma'am. And we let them. They aren't soldiers; it

will take them a while to think of consolidating their position. Then, just when they're busy congratulating themselves on how clever they are—surprise!"

"Hetwith, I can't tell you how glad I am you're on my side. Work out the details and let me know. I'll get the snow boards organized. We'll send some troopers to Gornan's to help evacuate the casualties."

"One more thing, ma'am," Hetwith said diffidently.

"What is it?"

"You might not like my saying so, but if there's an insurrection, it will likely be aiming to put Dard on the throne. You might want to check just where his loyalties lie."

I paused. "I'll talk to him, but I'd bet that he'll stand by us."

"Is that the colonel speaking, ma'am, or the woman?"

"Captain," I snapped, "don't teach me my business." And then regretted the harsh words; I intensely disliked him reminding me of my duty, but he was right to do so. "I'll talk to him," I said in a more moderate tone.

Hetwith looked at me. His expression was uncomfortably intense, and I thought he might say something else, but he restrained himself and turned away.

"Dard," I said, when I found him in the great hall, showing a dubious group of troopers how to fasten the snow boards to their feet, "a word with you." I drew him aside. "Dard, where do your sentiments lie? These are your people, and I wouldn't like to bet that your sister and Anlon Carmi aren't mixed up in it. Shall I relieve you of duties and confine you to quarters so you won't have to fight your own people?"

His face was troubled. "I won't fight against Forest Folk," he said at last. "But I can't believe that this insurrection is backed by the majority of the people or that it's in their best interests. Besides, if my sister is involved in it, she's probably got the same wizard that attacked you before working for her. I haven't been able to find out who he is, but I know this much about him; he's powerful. You won't find another wizard that can stand against him. You need me, Terva. You and Hetwith may know about military matters, but you can't fight sorcery."

I studied his face for a moment. "Thank you, Dard. I'll ask you to defend against spells and attacks by supernaturals. I won't ask you to use spells or force of arms against your own people. And when this is over, if you want to enter any special pleas for mercy, I'll listen. Is that fair enough?" I held out my hand for him to shake.

He took it and pulled me close enough to kiss me on the cheek. "Fair enough," he said. "And when this is over, will you listen to a special plea in my own behalf?"

"I'll listen. I make no promises." I glared at the troopers, who were watching these events interestedly, and went to find out what Hetwith was planning.

I spent the better part of that day up a tree. We marched out of Woodsholme—or perhaps it would be more accurate to say we skidded out of Woodsholme on the unfamiliar snow boards—and pressed as hard as we could for a good five miles down the main trail leading to the infantry station. Then we doubled back through the forest, paralleling the trail, while fifteen of our hardiest troopers pressed on to Gornan's house, dragging several snow boards weighted with deadwood to make the tracks of fifteen look like seventy-nine. When we got to the edge of the meadow around Woodsholme, twenty-six of our smallest and lightest went under the snow crust and tunneled back to a small door, where one of the five troopers we'd left to "guard" Woodsholme let them in. Not even Garabed knew that they were there. Hetwith was with the tunneling group.

I wanted to stay out of sight and at the same time keep a close eye on happenings at Woodsholme. The best vantage point I could find was halfway up a huge old spruce tree. I could see well and not be seen, but gods! it was cold up there. Precarious, too. My muscles congealed, tired by the unaccustomed strain of gliding along on the snow boards, and I had to pry my fingers loose from the branches occasionally and flex them, or I knew I would be unable to grasp my saber when the time came.

A reliable messenger had been sent to summon the Rangers, but they couldn't arrive before evening of the next day, and I wasn't absolutely certain of their loyalty if ordered to fight their own cousins. The rest of my command discovered that it was possible to burrow a nest out of the snow and not be utterly wretched.

They had orders not to move or speak; I assumed that the insurrectionists would send in scouts before descending on Woodsholme, and it would only have taken one incautious movement to have given away the whole scheme. As it happened, I overrated the enemy's tactical ability.

They came marching up the road in the midafternoon, bold as you please, and in through the front door. They did leave a couple of resentful sentries outside. I was counting under my breath. Count to a thousand; they'll have secured the five guards, who had been instructed to offer no resistance. Another thousand; they'll have their coats off and be calling for wine to celebrate their victory. Another thousand; the inside troops will be in position. White-clad shapes erupted out of the snow by the door and the sentries disappeared soundlessly; I slid down the trunk of my lookout tree, picked myself up out of the snowdrift into which my unsteady legs had pitched me, and blew my whistle.

We were across the snow-covered meadow, each heading for his or her assigned door or window with the precision of a dance company. Even as I burst through the door, I heard a yell of surprise. Most of the invaders were milling uncertainly about the great hall. Some of them had even put off their weapons!

"In the name of the king!" I shouted, "lay down your weapons!"

"Fight them, boys!" someone yelled. "There can't be many of them here!" The building erupted into a hand-to-hand battle.

There were three times as many of them as there were of us; but they were disorganized, poorly armed, and scattered by several efficient dividing moves. It was not long before they were throwing down their weapons, all except for a desperate little band of them that had gained a foothold on the staircase. These, I assumed, would be the ringleaders, and in fact, I saw Anlon Carmi, cursing as he tried to rally them to attack. Princess Morir-Alsis-Alina, I was glad to see, was not among them. But an unremarkable figure clad as a hunter was.

"Anlon Carmi!" I yelled. He turned and saw me, and a flash of malicious hatred convulsed his features. He reached out and grabbed the wizard's arm, hauling him to face me and pointing. "Anlon Carmi, your rebellion has failed!" I shouted. "Your only hope is to lay down your arms. If you do so now, I can assure you of exile rather than hanging."

He didn't answer, but spoke urgently to the wizard. The wizard began to gather something between his hands, but this time it was visible, an evil, ugly, pulsing, greenish-black something. It seethed and crackled and tried to evade his grasp and attack those who were standing near, but he clung doggedly to it, compressing it. Sullen green lightnings began to shoot through it.

I didn't know what the substance was, but that it was utterly deadly I did know. I also knew that when it was formed to his requirements, he meant to throw it at me. I started forward, intending to kill the wizard before he could be ready with his evil magic. I hadn't even reached the foot of the steps when he screamed my name three times and released the stuff.

It drifted and bobbled and darted here and there, but always it came closer and closer to me. I dodged and slashed at it with my saber. A shock of terrible pain traveled up the blade to my hand; the blade rang as if it had been struck a mighty blow. As if it had been a soft blade of grass withered by frost, the tempered steel writhed, twisted, and shrank. I flung the poisonously dripping blade aside and unclipped my dagger, casting the sheath away with a flick of the wrist. The crackling green substance inexorably followed my every move.

I raised my eyes to the party on the stairs. The wizard was leaning intently forward, lips moving. Was he guiding the thing? As quick as thought I reversed the dagger, raised my arm and threw it. I had won prizes at the dagger casting in officers' training; the weapon flew straight for the wizard's throat.

He saw it coming. He raised his hand and spoke one contemptuous word. My dagger flared with a brilliant light, then tinkled to the floor in a thousand scattered pieces.

Unarmed, I dodged desperately again, and was almost impaled on a point weapon, wielded by a pimply youth. One of my troopers dashed the point aside with his saber.

I ducked and slipped past the pulsing thing, but it reversed itself and followed, faster now, as if it had my scent. I was beginning to gasp. I looked about desperately. How long could I keep dodging? Wasn't there anything that would stop the thing? It was humming now, and I couldn't help but hear a note of hungry eagerness in the sound.

Then, spoken quietly, but with such enormous force that the stone walls of Woodsholme vibrated like the inside of a drum, there was one word: "STOP!"

The pulsing green thing stopped. I stopped. Every man and woman in the hall stopped as if petrified in his or her tracks. The wizard on the staircase reeled as if he had been struck a terrible blow.

Dard stood near me, his furs still dripping. His head was thrown back and his eyes were as hard and pale as crystals.

He made a drawing motion with his two outspread arms, and the greenish globe began to whine in a higher note. It bobbled and began to drift toward him.

The wizard on the staircase drew himself upright. He was trembling spasmodically; it was as if the inches that his evil creation was drawn nearer to Dard were being pulled out of his own flesh. He gestured suddenly, a small movement, but one of great forcefulness. The poisonous globe wavered and sank. Its slow progress toward Dard halted.

Dard stretched even farther, vibrating with an intensity of effort. Again he spoke, and again his single word had that air-shivering power. "Come!" he said. The evil globe jerked and quivered like a fish on a line, but it began to drift toward him again, and the wizard on the staircase groaned and sagged against the banister.

Anlon Carmi had been watching these events tensely. Now he shrieked aloud with frustrated rage. The rest of us were frozen with fascination at the sorcerous struggle going on before us. Anlon Carmi shook himself free and dashed down the stairs, his point sword extended before him like a lance. The bemused people in the hall parted before his charge, opening an aisle between him and the spot where I stood, completely unarmed. I crouched, ready to dodge to the right or left as seemed best, but there was no real hope of evading that light and maneuverable weapon.

Then Hetwith was there, parrying Anlon Carmi's blade with a ringing screech of metal upon metal, catching the tremendous force of his charge upon his own powerful forearm, and flinging the taller ex-lord back staggering. Anlon Carmi raged, shrieking incoherent curses, and Hetwith coolly brought his saber around in a backhanded parry that bound the lighter blade and deflected its point, leaving Anlon Carmi open to the thrust of saber or left-handed dagger. Only falling backward saved his throat, and even so his cheek was laid open with a bleeding gash.

Suddenly aware of the danger Hetwith presented, he whipped his blade around, feinted high and to the left, and lunged for Hetwith's right side. If Hetwith had attempted to parry the high feint, the lighter point sword could have darted in and spitted him like a rabbit before he could have brought the more awkward saber into position to defend. As it was, he managed to catch the point sword upon the basket hilt of his saber, deflecting it enough so that he could twist out of its way.

The maneuver brought him facing me, and I could see the same cool devilish smile on his face I had so often seen in the heat of battle. In battle, Hetwith became a cold, emotionless, infinitely dangerous fighting machine, his brain his most effective weapon.

There was a gasp from the bloody audience of the wizard's duel going on beside us. I turned and looked. The greenish-black globe was right before Dard, bouncing sullenly up and down in midair. Dard's hands were extended to either side of the evil thing, and from them a glowing golden nimbus was slowly growing to enclose it. As I watched, the nimbus coalesced, solidified, and then imploded, extinguishing the horrible weapon as if it were a blown-out candle.

The tension was released so suddenly that Dard staggered and nearly fell. The wizard on the staircase sagged to his knees, bumping down several steps before he could grasp the carven posts that supported the banister.

A ringing clash of metal brought my attention back to the battle between Hetwith and Anlon Carmi. They were body to body, weapons crossed over their heads. Anlon Carmi was obviously trying to overpower Hetwith by his greater height, but Hetwith was much the stronger, and inch by inch, Anlon Carmi was being forced backward, his knees buckling. Hetwith's head was down, his jaw set, the tendons of his neck standing out like ropes. Recognizing his danger, Anlon Carmi broke away, spinning clear to turn and lunge again, point aimed for Hetwith's chest.

Hetwith had lurched forward under his own momentum when his opponent faltered so suddenly; I thought for an agonizing instant that he would be run through before he could regain his balance, but I had underestimated his agility. Twisting like a dancer, his saber still poised above his head, he wheeled lightly aside, evading the point once again. Then, as Anlon Carmi, who had been so sure that his blow would meet flesh that he had committed all his strength and weight into the lunge, came within his reach, he grasped the saber's hilt with both hands and brought it down upon Anlon Carmi's head. The brainpan split like a ripe fruit and Anlon Carmi dropped, dead before he started to fall.

Hetwith must have been aware of my location throughout that whole desperate fight. With one bound he was at my side, left arm encircling me. The bespattered saber wove a pattern in the air as he fairly dared any other of the insurrectionists to attack me. But the spirit was gone out of them; they backed away, avoiding his eye. Their weapons rattled on the floor as they cast them down.

The immediate threat to Hetwith resolved, I turned back to the wizards' battle. Dard had advanced to the bottom of the stairs; the other had pulled himself to his feet again, a few steps from the bottom. They were locked eye to eye, as motionless as two statues save for their great heaving breaths; but the air around them seethed and hissed with the energies being summoned and banished. I was reminded of nothing so much as two great stags of the forest, heads down and antlers locked, striving for dominance with mighty shoves against each other.

At last the strange wizard spoke from between clenched teeth. "Prince Dard!" he gasped. "You would have been the Forest King. Why do you protect the invader?"

"I care about the welfare of the Forest Land more than I

care about my own consequence," panted Dard. "And I find your methods repugnant."

"Any methods are valid to use against usurpers!" spat the wizard. "Do you think the greedy king in King's City will turn over your rightful kingdom to you because you ask nicely?"

"He might," I said boldly. "It wouldn't hurt to try. His Majesty is most concerned for the welfare of his people, and if he could be convinced that it was best for the Forest Folk to have their king, he might well acknowledge Dard, with treaties to safeguard the special relationship between the Kingdom and the Forest Province."

Neither of the combatants looked away from their unwavering eye contact, but the strange wizard had heard me. He sagged ever so slightly. "Don't believe her!" he snarled.

"What?" said Dard, mildly. "You ask me not to believe one who follows the law meticulously, who fights honorably and mercifully, whose first concern is her duty and the welfare of those over whom she has been placed in charge? On the other hand, I may put my trust in one whose methods include assassination, assaults through the overmind against one who is not trained to defend against them, murderous sneak attacks upon men exhausted by fighting the supernatural for the benefit of us all, and bloody civil war. Whom, in all reason, should I choose to believe?" As he spoke, he seemed to grow taller and more robust, as if he gathered power from some unseen fountainhead.

The wizard snarled wordlessly. He flinched away from Dard's piercing gaze. He crumpled down upon the steps, to lie huddled and moaning, twitching feebly. Dard stepped forward. Looking down upon his vanquished enemy, he said, "You've misused your magic, and so I'll take it from you." He bent down, and it seemed as if he thrust his hand within the wizard's chest, and drew out some squirming, thinly shrieking thing the size of a squirrel, but misty as to shape.

The wizard writhed, and screamed hoarsely, a hollow, bereft sound. Dard held up the thing he had abstracted, and clenched his fist, squeezing the writhing shape until it shivered and vanished, leaving no wrack behind.

Then it was over, and the troopers were rounding up the insurrectionists and stacking their weapons. The remaining leaders of the rebels, clustered near the top of the stairs, dejectedly gave up their weapons and were led away. I thought to myself that exile would be enough punishment for them. Without leadership none of them had the spirit or intelligence to be a danger.

The commoners in the group I released, after accepting each one's oath of allegiance on behalf of the king in King's City. Then I turned to Hetwith, who had stayed so close to me that I could feel his breath, with his saber drawn. "Casualty report, Captain?" I said, recalling him to his duties as second.

"I have the casualty report, ma'am," said Corra. I caught Hetwith giving her a grateful glance out of the corner of my eye. "We lost three troopers and one officer dead, Senior Lieutenant Ordent. Twelve troopers received wounds, but all are expected to recover. Of the insurrectionists, fourteen are dead and forty-two are wounded, two of whom are not expected to live."

"Excellent, lieutenant. What about Prince Dard?"

"I'm here," said Dard. He was leaning against the banister, looking faded and gray, as if he had spent every crumb of his energy and could only just manage to stand up.

I went to him, offering my shoulder for his support. "What is it?" I asked gently.

"Another reason I don't like sorcerous battles of will," he said, with a feeble smile, "is that they're so very tiring."

"Can you walk upstairs?" asked Hetwith, arriving on the other side of him and helping to support him.

"Yes, I think so, with a little help." Slowly, one step at a time, Hetwith on one side of him and me on the other, we got him up the stairs. Once the office door was shut behind him, though, his knees buckled, and we put him on the couch in front of the fire. He looked flattened and colorless, and his pulse was so weak when I checked it that I was alarmed for him.

"Dard," I said, "are you going to be all right? Is there anything we can do?"

"Here's some brandy," said Hetwith.

"I only need to rest," said Dard. "I've spent a large portion of my life force and it will take time to build it back up." He took the brandy and drank it, but his hand shook so that Hetwith had to steady it for him. He leaned back and closed his eyes.

The aftermath of battle is a soul-draining, sick lethargy, as if the spirit rebels at the cruel necessity that makes soldiers of us and sends us out to kill our fellow human beings. I've known few soldiers who were not afflicted by this melancholy, and the few are the mad killers who make the very worst kind of soldier. There is nothing to be done about it but wait for it to pass. It cannot be drowned by drink, though many try, and forced gaiety only makes it worse. There is no joy in victory for those who have to fight the wars. The celebrations are reserved for those for whom the battles are fought, and for the homecomings, weeks or months later.

I sank down upon the carpet beside Dard, and found that Hetwith, who had gone through many of these episodes with me, was there before me. I leaned my forehead against his arm, and felt him lay his cheek against my hair, and there the three of us rested.

chapter

14

"Tevra, may I talk to you?" asked Dard, coming slowly into my office from the hall that led to staff quarters.

"Well, I'm glad to see that you're with us once more," I said with a smile. Dard had slept for the better part of three days after the abortive rebellion and his epic battle with the wizard, rousing only to eat prodigious meals. This was the first time I had seen him up and dressed. He was still very weak and pale, I could see as I turned to look him over. "Of course you can talk to me. Come over and sit by the fire."

I led him to the fire and he sank down upon the couch, pulling me down beside him. "Where's Hetwith?" he asked.

"Visiting the wounded, I believe. I was with him this morning, but this weather has all our spirits low, so he thought another visitor this afternoon would cheer them up." I shuddered and glanced out of the window. Mist swirled against the panes and hard little clumps of falling snow—by no stretch of the imagination could the stinging pellets be called "flakes"—struck against the glass with audible pings. It was midafternoon, but as dusky as if night were setting in. If our ruse hadn't succeeded, we might have been trying to make our way south through this. I shuddered again.

"Good. I wanted to talk to you privately," he said. "Do

you remember that you promised me that I could make a plea in my own behalf?"

"Yes," I said. A little tingle of pleasurable excitement started somewhere in my middle and spread. I repressed it sternly. This situation was going to take careful handling, the more so since I half wanted him to convince me.

Dard smiled at me and paused, looking searchingly at my face. "When you offered to go to bed with me, I was a fool not to accept immediately," he said. "With patience, I could have melted the ice you felt. And you'd have learned that you loved me. You underestimate yourself, Tevra. You could never have made that offer to a man you didn't love, whether you realized it yourself or not."

Troubled, I started to reply, but he continued, "I can't take advantage of your offer now, even if it's still open," he said regretfully. "If I could, I'd make that my plea. Taking me into your bed would be all the commitment you needed to belong to me forever. But it'll be several weeks yet before my energies are strong enough to lie with a woman with any hope of pleasing her or myself. I'm sorry, because every moment that passes I feel that my chances are fading away." Gently, he touched my shoulder with his fingertips. "Any day now, my chief rival will realize his own worth, and do as he should have long ago, and then you'll belong to him. There's no treachery in you, Tevra; you'll never betray a man once you've accepted the responsibility for letting him love you."

He lapsed into silence. What were the thoughts behind those darkening eyes? What rival was he speaking of? Hetwith? Probably. He had always mistaken the nature of the relationship between Hetwith and myself. Like many men, he was unable to understand that sexuality need not enter into a partnership between a man and a woman.

He turned to me suddenly. "Hold me, Tevra," he said

simply. "Put your arms around me, please. I can't pleasure you now, but I need your comforting."

I took him into my arms. I could feel that his overwhelming sensuality was only a muted echo of its former strength. I stroked his golden hair. "If anyone knows that sexual gymnastics aren't all there is to a man, I do," I whispered tenderly. I kissed him on the forehead, not seductively, but affectionately, and he sighed.

"Tevra, tell me you'll think about me. That's my plea. Don't convince yourself that for political expediency, or your sense of duty, or because you're afraid, that you have to stifle your feelings for me. We'll find a way, if you decide to come to me, that you can do so in honor. I don't ask you to commit yourself, not now when I can't consummate the bond, but I beg you to think about it. I'll ask you again when I can."

"All right, Dard, I'll think about you," I said firmly.

There was a clatter at the door. I looked around. Hetwith stood there, his face as stern and cold as if he were going into battle. He stood and looked at us, and I half-expected him to turn and go away. Tact, apparently, was not on his mind. He disengaged his saber from the door frame where it had caught and came into the office. Reluctantly, Dard sat up.

"The wind is rising," Hetwith said, putting a stack of reports down on my desk. "There's going to be a terrific storm tonight."

"Yes, I expect there is," I said. I hadn't noticed it, but the windows were rattling in their frames as gusts dashed themselves against Woodsholme, as if trying to blow it off its little rise of ground.

"I think I'll go to my room and rest," said Dard. "Tevra, will you visit me later?"

I nodded, aware that Hetwith was watching us out of the corner of his eye. As Dard dragged himself past the desk, Hetwith grabbed his arm and hissed something to him, too low for me to hear the words. I certainly heard the anger in them, though. Dard stood passive within his grasp, and said something even more softly. Hetwith released him with a violent gesture and turned away. Dard actually reached out and touched him (I'd not have dared to touch him when he was that angry) and spoke again, glancing back at me. Whatever it was startled Hetwith, for he flung up his head and looked into Dard's face. Dard smiled wryly, shrugged, and moved on into the hall.

I'd have given a month's pay to know what they said to each other. Hetwith was silent and tense all the rest of the afternoon. I had my supper brought into Dard's room that night and ate with him. The storm was in full blast now, and even stone-built Woodsholme vibrated under its fury. It made conversation difficult, and I wanted nothing so much as to bury my head under my pillow and think about what Dard had said.

I was awakened in the middle watches of the night by a grip on my shoulder, the signal used to rouse a sleeper silently. I reached for my saber even as I pushed the blankets back. The saber was not where I always left it, hanging from the right-hand bedpost! I recognized Hetwith bending over me by the light of an oil lamp on the bedside table. "What is it?" I whispered, groping again for my weapons. He was wearing only his undertunic and drawers, and I thought it odd that he wouldn't have dressed. Where was that damn saber? It was only my dress saber, fancy but too dull to cut cheese; it was all I had since my good one had perished by sorcery.

"Nothing," he said. "I wanted to talk to you. Your saber's on that chair."

I goggled at him. "Talk to me? This hour of the night? Dressed like that? Hetwith, this had better be important, and you'd better be sober!"

"I'm sober. I'm not sure how important it is to you, but it's of vital interest to me."

"Well, what is it?" I snapped, when he showed no disposition to go on. He was still leaning over me so that I couldn't have risen without bumping into him. I let myself fall back against my crumpled pillow, reaching for the blankets. It was cold!

He moved like lightening. He had always been incredibly quick; now he moved in a veritable blur. Even if I had guessed what he was going to do, I couldn't have moved quickly enough to have stopped him. His right hand pinned my reaching left to the bed. He cast himself down almost on top of me, imprisoning my right arm beneath the weight of his body. One leg was thrown across my knees, effectively immobilizing me. I opened my mouth to utter a startled protest, but he spoke before I could speak. "You've threatened to hang me half a dozen times, Tevra. Here's your chance. I'm going to kiss you." He slipped his arm behind my head, holding my face up to his in the crook of his elbow.

"Hetwith!" was all the protest I managed before his lips descended upon mine. From the suddenness and violence of his movements, I would have expected a bruising, teeth-bumping sort of kiss. It was no such thing, but as sweet and gentle as summer rain. I was still too paralyzed with astonishment to respond but I drank it in as a thirsty flower drinks the dew. When finally he broke away, gasping, I lay for a moment, dazed, staring up into his eyes. Half-shamed defiance was there, and hunger, and an intensity of feeling I would never have suspected in my young wolf.

"Hetwith," I began.

"No," he said. "I'm going to talk. If you're going to hang me, I at least want the satisfaction of having, once in ten years, made you listen." Instead of continuing, though, he kissed me again, as gently and as lengthily as before, but with more longing.

"Hetwith..."

"Hush." He kissed me again. "I love you, Tevra," he said, softly but with great passion. "I've loved you for ten years. I've wanted you more than I want food or drink. Every woman I've taken has only been a poor substitute for you. Every promotion I've accepted or refused has only been so I could stay close to you. I thought that someday you'd look around and see me as a man, but you never have." He was in real distress, trembling with agitation and cold, but his iron grip on my hand never eased and he held my head motionless in the crook of his arm. With something like a sob, he kissed me again, lips, eyes, cheeks and chin.

"Hetwith, that's not..."

"Gods, I hated it when you went on leave," he groaned. "You'd come back and tell stories about the handsome merchants or whoever your lovers had been. I could have murdered them. And I hated it worse when I rented the finest cabin at Rainbow Lake and had it stocked with every luxury I'd ever heard you mention and arranged all the travel. I spent my nights dreaming of how pleased and surprised you'd be when you got there. I had every minute of our time together planned! Then you found out that I'd fiddled the leave papers and sent me off with a camel caravan!"

I squirmed, as much as I was able. Most of the stories I told were complete fictions. How could I come back from leave and admit that I had spent two weeks admiring sunsets and fishing in the river? And my heart ached for Hetwith's disappointment and hurt. I had thought he was up to some scheme and had congratulated myself on outwitting the schemer.

"Hetwith," I tried to say, intending to tell him, but he rushed on unheeding.

"I tried a thousand times to tell you how I felt, but you never even heard me. Do you know how it feels to pour your heart out and not even be noticed? That was why I'd been drinking, that time on the plains that I got thrown in jail. I was waiting on the headquarters steps to see you one last time before I killed myself."

I frowned, trying to remember any passionate avowals, but there had been nothing of the sort. I'd have remembered, I was sure. Oh, there'd been a few jokes; the younger officers were always teasing me, and I had developed a large repertoire of witty answers that sidetracked them without hurting their feelings.

"You don't remember, do you?" he said bitterly. "Well, try and ignore this!"

Quickly he slipped beneath the bedclothes, pulling them up to cover us both. He caught my left hand again. I could have escaped from his hold in that instant, I think, if I had moved fast enough and decisively enough, but I didn't. He pressed his body against me, and there was no doubt of his profound arousal. A surge of desire throbbed through me, somehow deeper-rooted than the simple, healthy lust I had felt when Dard had caressed me.

"Hetwith, let go," I said.

"No," he said. "Listen to me. You're not going to bed with Dard. I couldn't endure to know that you were loving him. If you can't love me, say so and put me under arrest; I won't make a fuss. But please don't love him. He doesn't love you half as much as I do; he couldn't wait a tenth as long as I have." He kissed me again, and his kisses tasted salty; it seemed unbelievable that Hetwith the cool, Hetwith of the caustic wit, Hetwith could actually weep over me. His kisses questioned, sought a response. He pressed himself against me again.

I gasped. "Hetwith! Let go of my hands!" He shook his head, nuzzling at my breasts, which were covered only by the thin silken material of my nightgown. Gods, I thought. All those years of choking off any thought of desire for him before the thought had truly been born! All those years of longing to put my arms around him to comfort him when he despaired! All those wasted years of reminding myself again and again, over and over, that he was my junior officer and therefore untouchable! And all those years of assuming that his tentative approaches were mere jokes and turning them aside with a jest of my own. I could have cried myself with the pity of it.

I twisted within his hold, arching my back. "Ah, Hetwith, let go. Please, love, please, let go of my hands so I can put my arms around you. I've wanted to for so long!"

He stopped his nuzzling and raised his head to look into my face, and I smiled at him. It was a frightened and wavery smile, but he slowly took his hand away from mine and eased his body aside so that I could extract my numb arm from under him. I slipped my hands under his tunic, running them up his ribs and across his powerful back, enjoying the silkiness of his skin under my palms. His breath caught and he moved to slip out of the tunic, baring his torso to my exploring touch.

Then I gasped again, delightedly, as his hands began some explorations of their own. Breasts, belly, thighs, buttocks, he lingered over each, stroking and caressing until I throbbed with desire. My own hands drifted down to his waist, and shyly, lower, for I wasn't sure he would like more intimate caresses. I needn't have doubted. With a muttered exclamation, he threw off his drawers and lay back. But when I lightly touched his erect manhood, he caught my hand. "Softly, dearest, softly," he said through clenched teeth, and I pulled my hand away.

"Oh, did I hurt you?" I asked. I really knew very little of pleasing a man, but I knew that male genitals were very delicate and easily hurt.

Hetwith laughed a little, a delighted sound. "Hurt me? Never! But you must go slowly or you'll spoil all our fun." He looked up at me. "Besides," he said, a glad light in his eyes that I had never seen, "you have the advantage of me. Take off your gown, Tevra, please?"

Suddenly and belatedly bashful, I dropped my gaze. I dreaded this moment, for my stocky, scarred old body was not a thing of beauty. But I had gone too far now to turn shy. Gritting my teeth, I started to pull the garment over my head, but again Hetwith, evidently sensing my distress, stopped me. "Let me," he said softly, and taking the hem of the gown, began to lift it slowly, trailing his fingers over my shivering flesh as he did so, until I quite forgot to be bashful in the ecstasy his gentle touch on my bare skin brought. He threw the gown somewhere toward the foot of the bed.

We slid down under the covers, shivering with cold and anxiety. Naked body pressed to naked body, we began again the delightful process of exploration. This time, when I tentatively touched him, he moaned softly and eased himself more strongly into my grip. Then I forgot what I was doing as his fingers slipped between my thighs, prying them gently apart, stroking and caressing. "Oh, Hetwith," I sighed. As he raised himself above me my knees opened easily and naturally for him, accepting him gladly.

Once he had gained possession, he lay still for a space, marveling, perhaps, as I marveled at the joy I felt. Not just pleasure, though there was plenty of that, but sheer triumphant joyousness surged through me. I thought in that moment that if this madness lasted only for tonight, as devastated as I would be when I lost him, it was worth it for the fierce, glad look in his face as he looked down into mine. Then he began to move, slowly at first, but building up to a crescendo that left me without thoughts, awash in a sea of purest joyous pleasure, and I hugged him to me and called his name. As the shivers of pleasure died away, he gave one last root-deep thrust, shuddering and crying out wordlessly, and I heard in his voice the same joy I had felt.

Wakening in the dim, stormy morning, I found myself

tightly held. I raised my head a little, and looked at Hetwith's bristly unshaven face, a smug little smile of purest contentment on his lips. He had held me so all night, much to the detriment of our night's rest; I was a restless sleeper and unused to a companion in my bed. I wondered if I could ease out of his hold without disturbing him. But when I tried, he woke instantly.

"No, you don't," he said fiercely, eyes snapping open. "You aren't getting away from me again." His clutch tightened. There was a shadow of real fear in his eyes.

"Hetwith," I said tenderly, "I'll never sneak away from you again. I give you my word of honor." Smoothing his tousled hair, I stretched up and kissed him. The assurance seemed to satisfy him; he grinned a little sheepishly and loosened his grip a bit.

"I'm sorry," he said. "I woke up in the middle of the night thinking that by morning you'd have thought through all the moral, legal, ethical, and genetic implications of what we've done, accepted the blame, and convinced yourself to send me away out of your scheming clutches for my own good. Well, I won't go." He glanced at me, judging the effect of this small defiance upon me. I smiled. Reassured, he asked, "Do you always twitch so much in your sleep?"

I chuckled. "I've never had any complaints." That was true enough. I'd never let any man spend the night in my bed before.

He grinned. "I intend to enjoy getting used to it."

I slipped my arms around him and hugged him. "I used to want to do that so much when you had one of your black moods. Now I can."

"Tevra, dearest, now you won't need to."

I turned my face into the curve of his neck, luxuriating in the softness of his skin and the bristliness of his cheek against my forehead. But his words had started a train of thought that couldn't be ignored. I found myself stirring restlessly—twitching.

Hetwith began rubbing the small of my back gently, in little circles. "What is it?" he said.

"Hetwith, what are we going to do? We've managed to put ourselves into a completely untenable position."

"I don't see how, my love. What we do is no one's business."

"Right at this minute we're in direct contravention of about four major regulations. Besides putting both our careers in jeopardy."

"I don't care a bean for my career, and I can promise you I won't do anything to endanger yours."

"Don't care a bean! Hetwith, you could have a distinguished career. There's no telling how far you might rise."

"No, dearest. I'll go high enough to stay with you and no higher. If you need a major for your staff, I'll apply for my majority. But that's the last promotion I'll seek."

"But Hetwith, you're the most brilliant young officer I've ever commanded. This brain shouldn't be wasted on staff work," I protested, stroking his temples.

"Why not? Staff work is what it's good at. I couldn't handle the responsibilities you do, Tevra. You see the implications of things. You understand how the repercussions of one small action can change the course of a whole campaign. For every scheme I've hatched and you used, there were a dozen half-planned, wild, reckless disasters that you stopped before they ever happened. I would have rushed on and tried them all. Oh, I could see the flaws, once you pointed them out, but I've always needed your guiding hand. I'm a tactician, Tevra, but you're a strategist. It's your career we're going to concern ourselves with. You're not going to retire as a piddling brigadier."

I laughed a little at his grandiosity, but there were a few

tears in my eyes. There was one last little fear, though. "But Hetwith," I whispered, "what if I get pregnant?"

"I think we'll call him Hetron," he replied promptly, with such enormous self-satisfaction that I had to laugh. Hetwith laughed too, and while we were still chuckling and snuggling, Jenny came in with a perfectly straight face and two cups of tea on her tray.

Hetwith behaved like a perfect subordinate that day, his military courtesy as crisp as ever, his demeanor respectful. But when I looked into his eyes, the gladness of the night still lurked there, and the wry twist was gone from his lips. I had developed a deplorable tendency to smile softly to myself, too. It was amazing, I marveled, what a difference could be made by such a simple thing, such an ordinary, logical, necessary action.

I worried about Dard. I had promised him only yesterday that I would consider his proposal. How could I tell him that I had committed myself to Hetwith that very evening? He would surely feel that he had been unfairly used. There was some question in my own mind whether I had acted with honor, too. But then, how could I have acted other than I had? Hetwith's need of reassurance had been very great. It had taken a lot of courage to do what he had done; I certainly could have hanged him if I had been that sort of officer. Dard was right; it was an enormous responsibility to allow someone to love you.

It proved to be unnecessary to tell him. He dressed and came in to work at midmorning. He hadn't been in the room ten minutes before he looked keenly at me, at Hetwith, back at me. I couldn't help blushing a little, and Hetwith positively smirked. Dard smiled ruefully. "I thought this would happen," he said. He held out a hand to Hetwith. "The better man won, I suppose, or at least the more deserving one. I had hoped that you'd keep on waiting for her to make the first move."

Hetwith's smirk turned into a real smile; he took Dard's hand and shook it. "She wanted you," he said, "but she loves me. She's loved me almost as long as I've loved her, if only she'd let herself realize it."

"I know," said Dard, "but I hoped you didn't." He came over to me and gave me a brotherly kiss on the cheek. "You'll be happy," he told me. He looked back at Hetwith. "I don't suppose it's occurred to you that you're spoiling her best chance to become a queen?"

"It's occurred to me," said Hetwith promptly. "Has it occurred to you that she'll make a better brigadier than she would a queen, and on her own merits, not because of whom she marries? With me to back her, she'll command one of the king's armies some day. Who knows, if there's a war, she could even become Field Marshal."

"Will you be let to stay together?" asked Dard. "I thought there were regulations against this sort of thing."

"There are regulations against senior officers abusing their juniors, and regulations against juniors assaulting their seniors. I don't think this situation fits either of those cases." I smiled across at Hetwith, reminiscently.

"Tevra's always been unique," said Hetwith. "No one will think twice about our relationship if we're reasonably discreet."

"Brigadiers," I said happily, "are entitled to choose their own staffs."

Dard sighed and shook his head. He was a little hurt, I judged, but he was generous enough to wish us well. "Dard," I said impulsively, "come to King's City with us in the spring. I think you have an essential kingliness that shouldn't be wasted. Perhaps a little fishing village on the shores of the northern sea might prove enough scope for you, but I doubt it. Well . . . I can't speak for the king in this, but the succession of the Kingdom is hereditary—by adoption. The king spends most of his reign searching for a worthy successor. I'd like him to meet you."

Dard smiled. "I hardly think that the backwoods descendant of half-savage wizard-kings is what he's looking for. But I'd like to see King's City, and meet the king. Yes, I'll come. Thank you, Tevra." He started to kiss me on the cheek, stopped himself, and glanced at Hetwith. Hetwith gestured to him to go ahead, glowing with a winner's magnanimity.

I didn't become pregnant that winter, though I certainly ought to have. Eventually I got used to being held tightly while I slept, and Hetwith got used to a twitching bedmate. I had thought that he might soon begin to chafe restlessly at the bonds between us, but I was wrong. I found that they made a deep and fundamental difference to him, and almost as much to me. And if I occasionally found that he demanded too much of my time and energy, I had only to remind myself that I had willingly and knowingly entered into the relationship, and that he would be far more deeply hurt than I would have thought possible before that night if I ended it for mere impatience. It was easy to adapt to his failings; he gave me so much that had always been missing from my life. And if I felt a touch of sadness at the loss of my imaginary young wolf, it was more than compensated for by the glad look in my love's eyes and his newly easy smile.

Headline books are available at your bookshop or newsagent, or can be ordered from the following address:

Headline Book Publishing PLC
Cash Sales Department
PO Box 11
Falmouth
Cornwall
TR10 9EN
England

UK customers please send cheque or postal order (no currency), allowing 60p for postage and packing for the first book, plus 25p for the second book and 15p for each additional book ordered up to a maximum charge of £1.90 in UK.

BFPO customers please allow 60p for postage and packing for the first book, plus 25p for the second book and 15p per copy for the next seven books, thereafter 9p per book.

Overseas and Eire customers please allow £1.25 for postage and packing for the first book, plus 75p for the second book and 28p for each subsequent book.

Ghostly Avenger!

I awoke suddenly in the night, and there, at the side of my bed, a little smile on the dead face, head twisted crookedly, broken rope dangling, was the man I had personally executed.

My breath stopped. I shuddered with horror. The ghostly figure glowed so that I could see every ghastly corpselike detail. "What do you want?" I whispered.

The thing didn't answer but slowly began to drift toward me, raising its clawlike hands to reach for my neck. I slashed at it with my saber, which went through the figure, causing no harm. And then it was upon me, choking me to death!